KESSLER

*By the same author*

Secret Army
Secret Army Dossier

# KESSLER

John Brason

From the BBC-TV serial devised by John Brason and Gerard Glaister and directed by Michael Briant and Tristan de Vere Cole

BRITISH BROADCASTING CORPORATION

FOR CLIFFORD

who will for ever remain, for me,
and for millions of viewers – *Ludwig Kessler.*

Published by the
British Broadcasting Corporation
35 Marylebone High Street
London W1M 4AA

ISBN 0 563 17969 4

First published 1981


Printed in England by
Love & Malcolmson,
Redhill, Surrey.

# Author's Note

*Kessler* is in effect the fourth part of the BBC television series *Secret Army*. It was not originally part of the concept of the series which properly terminated at the end of the Second World War. However, the character of SS Standartenführer Ludwig Kessler became so popular with viewers and, indeed, entered the mythology of World War II in such a way as to be possibly more real and memorable than the persons upon which he was based.

It will be remembered by viewers of *Secret Army* that Kessler's Belgian mistress, Madeleine Duclos, bribed a Sergeant in the Canadian-manned POW camp to obtain Kessler's release, and together they fled towards the ruins of Hitler's Germany.

This seemed to leave something unresolved – an attitude clearly felt by viewers – so that the necessity of creating a follow-up short series of 'What happened to Kessler?' became incumbent upon us.

We decided that – just as in *Secret Army* we endeavoured to base every happening upon reality wherever dramatically viable – we would continue that policy and investigate just what *did* happen to people like Kessler. This involved considerable research into Nazi Organisations, particularly in South America. Characters such as Dr Mengele, and Martin Bormann exist. We make no pretence and pretend they are who they are not. They are named. Others have been given pseudonyms for fear of libel. We know their true identity. We believe the situation contained in the series and these pages to be very near the truth, allowing always for dramatic licence.

We also believe the story's background is much nearer the truth than has hitherto ever been portrayed.

(The name of one of the characters, Richard Bauer, is, incidentally, not chosen by accident. 'Riccardo Bauer' was the favourite pseudonym, or alias, of Martin Bormann in South America. It is the author's quirkish sense of humour that uses it in its present context . . .it also helps to impress detractors who may think we have not done our homework).

J.B.

# Short Bibliography


BORMANN DOCUMENTS in the National Archives and Record Service, Washington DC; the Library of Congress, Washington DC; Berlin Document Centre, Berlin.

FRIEDMAN, Tuvia *The Hunter*, New York 1941

KERSTEN, Felix *The Kersten Memoirs*, New York 1957

RUDEL, Col, Hans Ulrich *Aus Krieg und Frieden*, Göttingen 1954

*Trotzdem: Kriegs und Nachriegszeit*, Göttingen 1970

FARAGO, Ladislas *Aftermath*, New York 1974

SCHELLENBERG, Walter *Memoirs*, New York 1962

TURKOW, Jonas *It Happened This Way*, Buenos Aires 1948

TAUBER, Kurt *Beyond Eagle and Swastika: German Nationalism since 1945*, Conn. 1967.

VERNANT, Jacques *The Refugee in the Post-War World*, Conn. 1953

STEVENSON, William *The Bormann Brotherhood, New York 1973*

*AXMANN, Arthur Meine Flucht Mit Bormann*, Stern 1965

# PART ONE

# The Eurocitizen

# ONE

Without pretending to have the architectural magnificence of the Grand'Place, the shining metallic Atomion is the object that first impresses itself upon travellers entering Brussels. A leftover from the Great Exhibition it is a landmark of considerable scale seen from the road, the railway, and from the air as one enters the outskirts of the metropolis.

It attracted the attention of two young Israeli girls as their train moved at a leisurely pace into Belgium's capital city.

It made Monique Duchamps realise that she had not been back to the city of her birth, of her young life, of her war, since that day in May 1945 when she left all she had known to start life afresh in England as the new wife of Captain Stephen Durnford. Her plane circled the city. Monique took her eyes from this great metal edifice to the older buildings, the streets and parks she knew. The soft voice of the cabin stewardess announced their arrival over Brussels and requested the fastening of seat-belts, the extinguishing of cigarettes. At the same time there was a muffled 'thunk' as the undercarriage dropped and locked.

Driving along Route 104 in his now elderly VW 'beetle' Richard Bauer, thirty-eight, had turned off the main road at Leuven to enter the city by the arterial road through Tervuren. He too glimpsed the top of the Atomion through the trees then had to forget about sightseeing as the traffic piled up and the streets of the city started to swallow the vehicles running through its entrails.

The two Israeli girls, Mical Rak and Ruth Liebermann, handed their gear out of the coach onto the station platform and laughingly made their way with the disgorged throng towards the barrier. Their jeans, shirts, rucksacks spoke of their generation, as did the fact of their being in Brussels in

Europe, two thousand miles away from their homes in the new land of Israel. Their suntanned skins implied they led a healthy outdoor life in a kibbutz rather than at a desk job in Tel Aviv. The implication was incorrect. Both worked in Tel Aviv, though Mical's home was a kibbutz. Ruth's family lived between the city and the coastal beaches. Mical had no family . . . none alive, that is.

Monique Duchamps passed through the customs check at the airport without being intercepted. She had little luggage with her. She was intending to stay overnight . . . possibly two . . . and was distinctly nervous about the whole business. The city opened out for her as the taxi sped from the airport towards the centre. Landmarks known made her smile . . . those new made her sad. She remembered her old city and wanted it to stay the same for ever. Her youth had been hard but exciting. Her war even harder, and the excitement based on fear and determination to thwart the Occupation forces of Hitler's Germany. That was years ago . . . thirty-five years ago to be precise. Monique was no longer a young woman, yet as she drove through suddenly familiar streets it was as if yesterday was indeed only hours away.

The dark interior of the Café Candide was suddenly brightened by a shaft of light as Albert Foiret unbolted the front door and opened one half. Outside, the Grand'Place was bathed in warm morning light. The traffic moving without too much noise, the tourists with considerably more. Smiles flashed as heads turned to the superb buildings surrounding the square, and cameras clicked.

Albert stepped outside, enjoyed a lungful of air while it was still reasonably fresh, checked the time against his pocketwatch and found the Hôtel de Ville inaccurate as ever, shook his head and turned back into the Candide. Visitors to Brussels were making their way to the Grand' Place from every direction, anxious to gaze at what is arguably the finest square of its kind in Europe. Ruth and Mical were on their way: so were Richard Bauer and the hustling young television journalist, Hugo van Eyck, whose investigative programmes for BRT had caught the public imagination. Hugo van Eyck had become what is loosely termed a television personality and his self-regard had, not unnaturally, grown with his ratings. He did not pay too much attention to where he left his large Mercedes. He would get away with it. He was Hugo van Eyck.

Ruth and Mical entered the square as tourists. They wanted to stand, and stare, and marvel. Richard Bauer was on his way to a meeting. So was Hugo van Eyck. They were both going to the same meeting. It was with Albert Foiret, one-time Leader of Lifeline and a much-decorated war hero, more responsible than anyone for the repatriation of so many Allied aircrew who had had the misfortune to bail out or crashland in enemy-held territory during the years 1940-1944.

Bauer, van Eyck, Mical Rak, Monique Duchamps had one thing in common. They were all in Brussels to examine aspects of one man. A German. His name was Ludwig Kessler. Albert Foiret remembered Kessler better than most. He should. He thwarted him throughout the war while serving him in his restaurant several times every week of the occupation.

By the time van Eyck arrived at the Candide, Albert had placed his outside tables in the sunshine and was sitting sipping black coffee. The exchanges were simple and matter-of-fact. They had met only the previous day. Van Eyck was pumping him . . . pumping for anything that would bolster his intended TV programme which he fondly hoped would shake Western Europe with its revelations of 'Nazism today'. They were, of course, soon talking of Kessler.

'You know, Monsieur Foiret, it is surprising how few people seem to remember him. Those that do say he was a monster . . . others say he was not, merely a Nazi doing what he believed to be his duty. More in the mould of Heydrich than, say, Eichmann. But they all agree he inspired terror.'

'Does it matter?' Albert was none too happy about reliving his past. 'It's more than thirty years ago. No one cares. He's dead and gone. The whole Nazi business is dead and gone.'

Van Eyck smiled. 'We'll see. That's what my programme is about. You may be surprised . . .'

A shadow fell across the table and the coffee cups. Both men turned to see the tall, lean figure of Bauer standing by them. Van Eyck grinned again

'So. You found us! Sit down. M'sieur Foiret – Herr Bauer, West German Intelligence.'

Albert shook hands with Bauer and indicated to his waiter that another cup of coffee was required immediately.

Bauer sought to excuse his tardiness by blaming the road system.

'Why don't you Belgians put up more route indications in Brussels? I've been lost at least three times trying to get here. If you can't find the centre – what can you find?'

Albert chuckled.

'It's all part of a civil conspiracy to spread the tourist trade . . . decentralise it. I object, of course.' He eyed Bauer through narrowed eyes. 'M'nheer van Eyck tells me that you are interested in Kessler. May I enquire why? Surely he wasn't all that important?'

'More than one imagines. He was one of the old-guard. An "*Alte Kämpfer*", loyal and trusted. He was no special villain, I agree, not during the war . . . or since . . . but it is the position he now occupies that bothers us.'

'Us?' Albert's expression was questioning – as if he doubted the plurality – which he did.

Bauer recognised the implication. 'Well . . . yes. All right. Me, then.'

Albert narrowed his eyes again. 'Why?'

Van Eyck interrupted. 'At this juncture no one is at liberty to say very much. You said you wanted to come along this afternoon and view the material with my guests.'

'It would help me. Allow me to get back to my desk tomorrow.'

'No problem. I'll leave word at Reception. Just come straight up.'

'Thank you. If you will both excuse me I have two calls to make and my car is not very well parked. I'll see you this afternoon. M'sieur Foiret.'

Albert nodded as Bauer moved away. Both he and van Eyck watched him cross the square before they resumed their conversation.

Less than fifty metres away two Israeli girls sat at another table and wondered how anyone could possibly enjoy the curious Brussels brew known as 'kriek', which tasted of flat beer flavoured with blackcurrant juice. Mical Rak had journeyed from Tel Aviv on her own modest resources for the express purpose of seeing a man called Hugo van Eyck who had written to her mother for personal recollections of some one called Ludwig Kessler. Mical had learnt of this one week before her mother died in the asylum to which she had been repeatedly committed in the last two decades. She also learned the identity of the man called Kessler, who had sent her mother to Dachau. In company with several other young and pretty Jewish girls she had been forced into a position of camp harlot, then, when her looks deteriorated through maltreatment and malnutrition, she had become one of the several victims of the visiting camp doctor who used 'captive patients' for experimentation. His name had been Josef Mengele, later to earn reputation as the 'Angel of Death' in Auschwitz. Mical's mother had lost her mind during this period. She survived the war, and the holocaust, and was taken to Israel after it became a new State, where, in moments of sanity, she became useful as a kitchen attendant in a kibbutz commissary. There she had conceived a child . . . by whom no one knew . . . and Mical was the result. Brought up by the kibbutz, with her mother committed once more, it came as a shock for Mical to learn so much of the horrific background to her mother's appalling life. But mother died, and Mical wanted to know more. Van Eyck's enquiry was couched in a way that implied he knew more . . . and that the man initially responsible was still alive. She wanted to know about the man called Kessler.

'The man said Kessler was still alive. He was an SS and Gestapo man in charge here during the war.'

'What do they intend to do? Prosecute?'

Ruth was cynical about it all. She knew that after the Eichmann affair even Israel had bowed to world opinion and given up their attempts to bring the war criminals to eventual, if tardy, justice.

A Statute of Limitations was now a world agreement. Only men like Hess, Bormann were excluded, or war criminals whose crimes were such as to cause a shudder of revulsion throughout civilisation . . . criminals such as Mengele. But, in effect, no one pursued it any longer. It was a thing of the past.

Mical looked at Ruth. 'I want to see it happen. I want to repay a debt to my mother.'

But Ruth shook her head slightly. 'You know something, Mical? Being one of the "children of the Holocaust" is something I can do without. I've had that stuff pumped into me since I was a baby. It makes me scream! So it was awful. So let's forget it quick. Why keep on with this sackcloth-and-ashes thing?'

'Don't you care about the people who died like that?'

'There is nothing I can DO about it! I just want to live.'

'All our parents wanted was to live.'

Ruth looked at Mical, then dropped her eyes. There was no answer.

It was just before two that Albert's taxi drew up outside BRT's building. He did not notice that another taxi already stood there with a lady paying her fare from a voluminous handbag. Albert gave a modest tip and turned towards the entrance almost bumping into the greying woman.

Albert raised his hat and mumbled an apology.

'Don't you know me, Albert?'

The gentle voice stole across his memory and broke down the barrier of forgetfulness. The veil dropped and he felt a sudden trembling in his stomach. Slowly he turned to look at her, narrowed eyes to assist the focus. The face was unchanged. Lined and loosened of course, but there was no mistaking her. The liquid eyes, the generous mouth, the utterly disarming smile. He felt himself respond.

'Monique!'

He took her hand in both of his and looked at her hungrily, before taking refuge in commonplace remarks.

'They . . . er . . . said they were hoping to get you to come. I didn't realise we might be together . . . but I hoped.'

Monique smiled gently at him. 'How are you, Albert?'

'Not so bad for an old man . . . eh?' He chuckled, the deep

laugh that she remembered so well. The laugh that had covered so much, and hurt so much. Then spontaneously they moved close and kissed each other's cheeks . . . so simply. Albert put his arm through hers, then changed the position for hers-through-his. It felt better – more natural – and together they walked to the television building entrance. Inside they were met by an assistant, taken to the lift, and thence along an interminable corridor towards what was described to them as a cutting-room. During the walk they exchanged pleasantries.

'D'you still have the Candide?'

'But of course! I expanded. I have six restaurants now but I kept the Candide. It's still my favourite.'

'Could I come and see it?'

'Of course! Can you stay a few days? I want us all to have dinner together. What do you say?'

'All of us? You mean Alain . . . Natalie . . .'

'Just the four of us. Pascal is dead, of course. But you knew that . . .'

They stopped talking as they entered the cutting-room. Inside van Eyck was waiting, hands outstretched, and beaming. He indicated two young men by the Stienbeck editing-table, one seated, one standing. For some moments neither noticed a tall, lean man seated in the background – unintroduced. Bauer wanted it that way. When Albert eventually noticed him, a curt nod of the head cut out any possibility of conversation. After van Eyck had introduced his assistant to the 'Lifeline' pair he continued.

'You two had more opportunity than almost anyone in Belgium of observing Kessler in the flesh. I want you to look at a piece of film . . . Okay?'

The small screen of the Stienbeck lit up with the picture of a large factory complex. The name 'Dorf Industries' was legible. Van Eyck instructed his assistant to move forward quickly then turned to his guests.

'I'm going to show you part of an interview I browbeat Herr Dorf into giving. Tell me what you think.'

The film ran on until it slowed showing a white-haired man talking to van Eyck.

'. . . and I think we can modestly claim that it is one of the largest and most important plants of its kind in the world. We export to most corners of the world.'

'But not to communist countries?'

'No. We have no trade behind the Iron Curtain.'

'Would there be a particular reason for that, sir?'

Dorf ignored the question and continued, 'I am expanding into the United Kingdom shortly.'

'And you already trade and manufacture in South America, do you not, Herr Dorf?'

'Indeed. We have excellent trade facilities in Latin America. Though I myself have no control over its management.'

The face of van Eyck took on a shrewd look.

'Herr Dorf, it has been said, sir, that your name is not Manfred Dorf but actually Ludwig Kessler, native of Berlin.'

If Kessler was in any way shaken by this statement he gave no sign.

'Quite untrue. My name is Manfred Dorf. I was born here in Krefeld. I know of no Ludwig Kessler.'

'Can you explain why there are no documents relating to Manfred Dorf before 1947? No birth certificate . . . no record of parents . . .'

'So many buildings were destroyed in the bombing; thousands of documents destroyed, burnt, or simply lost. There is no mystery.'

'Your late wife was Belgian, I think.'

'Yes.'

'Do you deny that you were in Belgium and the Low Countries during the Occupation?'

'Yes. I do. I served my country in industry . . .'

Van Eyck interrupted. 'Skip some of this, Jaap . . . try there.'

The fast-moving picture slowed to normal pace once more and the high-pitched gabble became speech.

'. . . and you deny being a member of the SS? Are you saying you were never a member of the Nazi party?'

'It was not possible to be an industrialist in pre-war Germany without being a member of the party. As to SS . . . that is patently nonsense . . .'

Van Eyck stopped the Stienbeck and indicated he wanted the lights switching on again. Then he turned to Albert and Monique, who were both pale and silent.

'Well? Do you recognise Dorf? Is he Ludwig Kessler?'

Albert wriggled in his seat and sucked his teeth.

'It is difficult to be sure. After all these years . . . The screen is so small. People change.'

Van Eyck insisted. 'In your opinion?'

'I can't say. Possibly.'

Van Eyck sighed quietly and turned to Monique, 'Mrs Durnford?'

Monique did not look at Albert, nor look up. She studied her hands as she replied calmly and quietly.

'Oh yes. That man is Kessler.'

Van Eyck clenched his teeth in a grin, 'Are you sure?'

'Yes. Quite sure. There are some things one never forgets. I would know him anywhere. The hairs on the back of my neck stood up the moment I heard his voice. I know it is him.'

In the background Richard Bauer sighed almost with relief. Van Eyck showed his pleasure with the outcome.

'Thank you very much. If you would care to go with Wim, here . . . We have a few drinks laid on next door, and some friends you might like to meet. I will join you in a moment.'

The assistant showed Monique and Albert from the room leaving van Eyck to turn to Bauer jubilantly.

'What did I tell you! That's two independent positive identifications.'

'Two-out-of-four. Not good odds, M'nheer. I need to be surer than that. But I am encouraged, I confess. You indicated that I could have a copy of your programme to take back to Bonn.'

'We've had some VHS copies made. Get one, Hubert, will you?'

In the room next door two people waited, sipping drinks and chatting while a steward plied them with canapés. The door opened to admit Albert and Monique. For a moment only the eyes met and mouths opened. Then smiles of joy appeared. Monique went quickly to Natalie and they hugged each other with emotional hunger, silent and tearful. Albert stood beaming as if he had stage-managed the whole thing while the old man in the wheelchair waited his turn anxiously and with trembling hands. Monique came to him and bent down to kiss the slightly stubbled cheek.

'Alain, I had no idea. Oh, it's so good to see you all!'

Alain grunted. 'I only agreed to come because they said you'd be here. Why haven't you been back to see us, girl? It's more than thirty years!' He smiled. 'You don't look much different.'

'Flattery, Alain! I'm an old woman. Why are you in a chair? Have you had an accident?'

'No. No. Just a farmer's complaint. Acute arthritis. Can't walk at all these days. Still . . . mustn't complain.'

The conversation turned upon trivialities, important to them, before Alain returned them to the purpose of their presence there.

'Did he show you that film, and that interview with Kessler? It was him, you know. No doubt about it.'

'That's what I said.' Monique took his gnarled hand. 'Albert wasn't sure.'

'Huh! Natalie said she wasn't. Didn't you say that?'

Van Eyck joined them some moments later and they fell into reminiscences of the wartime scene, their recollections of incidents, their impressions of Kessler. At length Albert asserted himself and his traditional position as head of the group by asking what the whole thing was in aid of.

Van Eyck responded, 'As you know I do a regular TV programme called *In our time*. It looks into contemporary questions and matters of public interest and concern. The programme going out next is one examining the whole question of War Criminals and the persistence of Nazism. It has come into focus again in more than one country.'

Natalie shuffled with slight irritation. 'Isn't it a bit late for such things? Isn't it better to try and forget the war, concentrate on problems such as the Communist threat to Europe?'

Before the argument could proceed Wim re-entered and whispered to van Eyck that there was a Miss Rak waiting to see him. Van Eyck excused himself to his guests and left for his office to find a very pretty young Israeli girl standing waiting for him with the languid impatience of contemporary youth.

After the introductions Mical explained her presence, and van Eyck sensed she was a possible catalyst.

'You think Kessler did not die, don't you?'

'I'm sure of it. That doesn't mean I can prove it. Why is that important to you?'

Mical explained how her mother had been sent to Dachau on Kessler's order, and how her grandparents met their deaths there.

'Your mother was the only one that survived?'

'I don't think she ever really left Dachau. She watched her baby brother's head being smashed to a pulp by a guard. She found one of the bodies that she was loading into a furnace was that of her father. She managed to stay alive because she was young and bartered her sex for existence. She died last March. I buried her in the war cemetery outside Tel Aviv. She spoke to me about your letter . . . and told me all that I have told you. Now I want you to help me . . . I want this man brought to justice. I have come here to see that done. I have some money . . . I will do this thing. Help me.'

Van Eyck looked at her, his mind ticking-over as to how he could make the most out of the situation. The most for van Eyck, that is.

# TWO

If you draw a straight line from Brussels to Berlin, it will probably go through the German township of Krefeld. Which is what Standartenführer Kessler, alias Major Spitzwerg, alias Robert laGroise, did in May 1945 after being spirited from the Canadian POW camp, thanks to a flagrant bribery by his mistress Madeleine Duclos – later his wife. Krefeld is about twenty-five miles from the Belgian border, part of the sprawling collection of townships that form the industrial area we know as the Ruhr. It seemed as good a place as any. The whole area was devastated by Allied bombing and the invading Allied troops; the parachute manufacturers were out of business and Krefeld is the centre of silk and clothing manufacture in Germany. The Rhineland is a perfectly good place to settle. It is attractive. It is prosperous. Even in the dark days of defeat it was assumed, correctly, that it would once again prosper. It did. Kessler became part of that new prosperity and changed his name accordingly. Herr and Frau Manfred Dorf, together with their newly-born baby girl soon became respected, hard-working citizens of the new Germany.

The large metallic-blue Mercedes turned off the N9 after crossing the railway bridge, down a road which immediately showed its elevated status by the sudden dramatic increase apparent in the sizes of garden and residences. A garden suburb, Dürnast is a very pleasant, affluent place to have a home for commuting into the larger townships of the Rhineland. The blue-painted iron gates opened upon the mere press of a button from inside the Mercedes. The gravel drive was quite short, and the car pulled up outside the main entrance. Kessler, alias Manfred Dorf, stepped down from his car and glanced across at the seven, equally ostentatious limousines already parked to one side. His manservant, Franz, hurried from the house to assist him, but Kessler brushed him aside. He disliked any form of assistance that reminded him that he was seventy-eight years of age. He didn't feel it, and didn't want to be reminded of it.

'Go in to my guests and apologise for my late appearance. I will join them in a moment.'

Franz scurried away. He didn't argue or remonstrate with his employer. Nobody argued or remonstrated with Herr Dorf. He was too tough, too important, and too powerful.

'Herr Direktor Dorf apologises for being detained, and will join you in a moment. *Danke sehr*,' was the way Franz actually made the announcement. The dozen or more people in the large opulent room, nibbling canapés and sipping from fine imported glass continued their small talk. The servants wove in and out of the guests silently, unobtrusively plying them with whatever was on their trays.

'Your father works too hard, Ingrid. He is not so young any more. It is time to enjoy old age.'

The attractive upright woman in her early thirties smiled at Herr Neumann, a Prussian aristocrat who resembled the grey, lean horses he bred so successfully.

'I shouldn't let him hear you say such things. He prides himself on his eternal youth.'

'Don't misunderstand me, my dear. I admire him enormously. You know, Ingrid, he and I both started with very little after the war. My family home was in ruins, our fortune gone. But we worked hard and helped to make Germany rise again. Look at us today. Strong, wealthy . . .' He chuckled. 'Prosperity begins and ends in Germany today. You should see the rest of Europe!'

'Father is due to go to some Trade Conference in London in a day or so. Has he told you he is building another factory? This time in England.'

The equally equine Frau Neumann muttered sullenly. 'If England had listened to the Führer in nineteen thirty-six there would have been no need for war between us.'

A second group, nearer the double-doors, suddenly erupted into laughter as the tall, still-handsome Colonel Rückert quipped suggestively to his three lady companions who adoringly hung upon every word.

'But surely you don't fly any more, Colonel?'

The handsome face dropped very slightly as he turned to his overblown, overpainted and overweight neighbour, and he held up a black-gloved stiff fist, which clearly was artificial.

'You mean because of this?'

Eyes flickered nervously to the war-replaced limb and pretended to find nothing untoward.

'My dear Frau Weber, I was flying JU 88s for two years after receiving this hand . . . and the rest.' His hard pale blue eyes glinted at her directly. 'I have more steel plate inside me than the *Bismarck*. I am all spare parts, Louisa . . . But there is enough of the essential man still operational.'

He leaned forward and touched her arm, chuckled with the handsome, gallant laugh that was famous throughout Germany. Colonel Hans Rückert was, after all, Germany's most decorated war hero.

'You embarrass my guests, Hans. I positively forbid it.'

All heads turned at the sound of the last voice. Kessler, alias Dorf, stood in the doorway beaming. Ingrid looked at her father to see if she could detect any reason for his unusual lateness. Normally punctual in everything, meticulous, and correct, he was the archetypal German. His platinum blond hair had only recently lost its touch of metal. He was now white-haired, and with the slightest suggestion of a stoop, more the 'widow's hump' than a bending of the back. The lines were few, and signs of age were more apparent in small movements, tiny hesitations, momentary forgetfulness than in any major effect. Her father was well-preserved. So was Hans Rückert, who couldn't be all that much younger . . . ten years possibly, no more. It was the selection, the discipline, the vigour of mind and purpose that kept them young. All the ex-Nazis she knew had remained youthful . . . comparatively, that is.

Kessler joined the groups and made light-hearted small talk with all his guests in turn. He had just approached Rückert's collection of ladies when he noticed Franz trying to catch his eye and excused himself. The whisper in his ear told him that Heinrich Leitgeber from the Bank was waiting to see him, and that it was urgent. He slipped out into the hall where the small, neat figure of Leitgeber stood, still wearing his raincoat.

Kessler ushered him into the study and poured a glass of Madeira for them both.

'What is it?'

'The Bank is of the opinion that someone has been investigating your accounts.'

Kessler remained silent for a second then looked keenly at the banker.

'Can you be sure about this?'

'Reasonably. Bankers are aware when one of their clients is being investigated. It seldom happens to someone of your status, Herr Direktor. Why should there be a search? . . . your creditworthiness is obvious to anyone. But it IS happening.'

'There is no means of checking the source? I have nothing to hide . . . but I resent that it should happen.'

'Indeed. Indeed. We were alerted to the possibility by Becker and Seeburg in London. British bankers are highly sensitive in such things. We consider that all eight accounts with us . . . both private and company accounts . . . also the Handelsbank in Amsterdam . . . have been investigated.'

Kessler was silent . . . his mind hastily computing the possibilities. He sipped his Madeira.

'I imagine that such an investigation could only happen through an official source.'

'In your case, sir . . . yes.'

Kessler turned away for a moment . . . glanced at the window, still quiet and pensive, before he swung back to face the banker.

'I am greatly obliged to you, Leitgeber, for taking the trouble to come and see me personally.'

'I felt that such a matter should not be left to the telephone.'

Both pairs of eyes met and the nod of gratitude was implicit. The banker put down his glass.

'It might be prudent to inform your colleagues . . . those of them whose business involvement might be affected. I leave it to your judgement, of course.'

Kessler pressed the desk-bell summoning Franz, who quickly and silently appeared to show out the banker.

'Thank you, Heinrich.'

Leitgeber nodded, and followed Franz from the room.

It was fifteen minutes later that Kessler rejoined his guests, and his eyes sought those of Rückert and brought him quickly to his side.

'Do we have a problem?'

Kessler pulled his lower lip, 'Possibly.'

'Does that mean you will still be going to the Trade Fair?'

'Yes. But this needs looking into. Stay behind after the others have gone. We must talk . . . and I think we may have to speak with Maurer.'

In a rather shabby office overlooking Whitehall two forty-year-old ex-Guards officers, now part of what is loosely termed 'intelligence' sat facing each other. The one with the moustache, Gidney by name, represented MI5. It was his office. The visitor was his opposite number in MI6. His name was Deakin. The latter spread himself on the hard chair and thrust out his long legs.

'Is this official . . . or social?'

Gidney looked at him with a slightly blank expression.

'Does it make that much difference?'

'No. But if it's social you can offer me a drink.'

Gidney made a sucking noise in between his teeth.

'Actually it's official, but not terribly so . . . if you follow me.'

'No. But don't keep me in suspense.'

Gidney thrust his right hand up his crossed trouser leg and scratched just below the knee, revealing sparse patches of black hair above his green socks.

'It's your area, Tom. We want your West German pals to do a bit of sniffing for us.'

'Oh aye.' It was in such laconic moments that the distant Scots background showed.

Gidney handed him a plastic VHS tape-cassette.

'Better have a look at that. It's some interview stuff for a Belgian TV programme. BRT sent it to the BBC for comment and for help on archive film . . . investigative journalism, that sort of thing. I've just had it slung at me by the JIC.'

'Anyone we know?'

'Well . . . yes and no. By which I mean we know the man, but didn't know he was a possible war criminal and a Nazi. Rather embarrassing.'

Deakin sighed volubly. 'I didn't think anybody cared.'

'Ah, well . . . you see, this one's a bit different. He's an industrial big-wig. Government does a lot of business with his organisation. Last year we gave permission for him to open a factory here in the UK. It's all a bit egg-on-face time.'

'What d'ye want me to do about it?'

Gidney became confidential. 'Well, I can't actually touch

it if you follow me . . . officially, I mean. Can you push the ball into your friend's court?'

'Ye mean ye want the Jerries to put their own house in order?'

'Something like that.' Gidney now felt the time propitious to fish into his desk drawer – the bottom deep one – and produce the Scotch, which he poured abstemiously into two none-too-clean glasses. 'Will you talk to your opposite number and get him organised while the water's still warm? They seem to be on the fringe as it is.'

Deakin condescended enough to glance at the black plastic cassette in his hand, 'I hope this fits my machine. I'll have a look at it and see what I can do.'

While MI5 and MI6 were sipping their Scotch amicably, the West German Intelligence bureau in Bonn was receiving another visitor.

The bulky, bullet-headed figure of Herr Deputy Direktor Maurer sat behind his desk hunched defensively against the barrage of accusation being hurled at him by an irate Kessler.

'I don't care what you say, Maurer. I am being investigated. I want to know if there is anything official about it, and why.'

'No. It isn't the Bureau. I would know, I assure you. Can you be sure that this is true . . that there has been an investigation?'

'I have been round long enough to know by instinct. But there have been questions asked . my bank is convinced. The real question is . . . Who?'

It was then that Rückert spoke his first words with the gentle harshness that gave a whole new dimension to the man.

'That question has to be followed by "Why?", and then "How much do they know already?" ' He glanced at Kessler. 'Has anyone got a reason?'

'Not in the sense that you mean. No. There is only one answer. You recollect I told you of that television interview I gave . . .' Rückert nodded. 'Fellow called van Eyck. Belgian. I didn't like him and mistrusted his motives . . . but I didn't want to arouse suspicion by refusing. He had discovered my identity and couldn't prove it.'

Maurer interrupted. 'How did he know?'

'How do I know? One or two tenuous leads and a lot of speculation. Not really enough to make a stir. But I sensed he wasn't going to leave the matter there. My guess is that he is in touch with someone in this Bureau . . . someone who has started enquiries.'

'We don't know that . . .'

'No, but check it out, Maurer.' Rückert's latent hardness was apparent in the tone of his orders. 'If it is one of your people – get him off our back . . . quickly.'

The Belgian television personality, Hugo van Eyck, was also involved with the same problem, and with interference. Mical Rak had come banging upon his door once again asking for information. She had managed to force her way into his office in the TV centre and openly requested his file upon the man they thought to be Ludwig Kessler.

'All I want to know is where he is living now.'

But van Eyck was not about to give away the labours of months of dubious and difficult research, especially when he had plans to make the most out of what he felt instinctively was a 'winner'. Hugo van Eyck was not a bad man, merely one with an eye to the main chance. A man who lived by his wits and having one more suoject titillating enough to keep his viewers from week to week. He had been highly successful. His blend of slickness, wit and highly professional investigative journalism appealed to a great viewing public BRT knew his worth and kept the programme running while van Eyck produced the goods. The whole business of Nazism and war crimes had raised its head again recently. In France with bomb outrages, in Holland with the revelation of a war criminal still at large and prospering, and in Germany itself in unlikely links with the Baader-Meinhof group. The latter marriage made no sense to anyone and was not taken seriously . . . but the subject was in the air. Time for Hugo van Eyck to cash in.

'Why not?'

Mical's question came from the gut. She was incensed. It

mattered to her, and she could not understand the journalist's reluctance.

'Because the moment the spotlight is on him he'll disappear into the woodwork! I found him . . . I'll decide when that moment comes. Not you, kid . . . not anyone. Just Hugo van Eyck!'

'Don't you care what this man did to my family and thousands of others?'

'I care about making the best possible TV programme out of the subject. Period! Personal crusades against a bunch of geriatric Nazis isn't my scene. Tell you what, I'll give you his address if you promise to inform me of anything that ties him in. If it really is Kessler. Okay?'

Mical nodded. She would do what she promised . . . after she had done what she wanted herself, even though at this moment in time she had no idea of what that was. Just a vague feeling of having to do something. Six months previously the thought of vengeance had not entered her head. But, then, she had not thought of Kessler as still being alive and at liberty.

# THREE

Another VHS copy of the van Eyck programme was being placed into the machine in Kessler's study. The cassette had been obtained by Rückert through his organisation, which was infinitely more widespread than any government in Europe remotely suspected. The cassette locked into place and Rückert pressed the run-up button. The set blinked into life with a storm of 'snow' and horizontal lines before it settled to clock and clapper-board. The counter at the base of the picture counted the footage before the picture steadied and Rückert turned up the sound.

Half-an-hour later Rückert stopped the machine playing,

and pressed the re-wind as he turned to Kessler. Both men were silent and unhappy. They had watched snippets of interviews with Nazis living in comparative security in various places in South America. Pathetic, frightened creatures who lived in the bars and shadows of towns and cities from Tierra del Fuego to Buenos Aires and Maracaibo – old faces of old comrades-in-arms. But they thought most of all of an interview between van Eyck and the man calling himself Manfred Dorf, head of the Dorf industrial empire, a respected international industrialist being accused of false identity . . . the truth being that he, Dorf, was none other than Standartenführer Ludwig Kessler, one time Head of SS and Gestapo in the Low Countries, the much-feared Höherer SS-und Polizeiführer from 1942 to 1944, a territorial leader with the corresponding significance of Gauleiter. The lack of birth papers, the absence from census, the startling likeness to the military records photographs, the coincidences, and possibly the supreme coincidence of the Belgian wife whose name just happened to be Madeleine.

At the end of the tape the silence was instructive. Rückert's expression contrasted with Kessler's. The cold, unfeeling stare of the cobra. Kessler's reaction was controlled emotion. He had enough sense of proportion not to feel indignation, but anger was uppermost. Ingrid, who had joined them, had mixed feelings. She was, of course, concerned for her father. She loved him. She was also astute enough to feel something of the cold, ruthless plotting of Hans Rückert. Ingrid was a fervent neo-nazi. She saw the vague possibility that disclosure might just provoke the still-powerful Kameradenwerk into positive action, might make it possible for her own colleagues to join forces with the 'old hands' who held so much power and possessed so much experience.

In Brussels, and throughout Belgium, the BRT transmission of Hugo van Eyck's programme was watched with bated breath, and more than casual interest. Those who remembered their Occupiers remembered Kessler and were incensed. They assumed there was no smoke without fire, and were prepared to accept the unproven as unlikely-to-be-wrong. The outcry was heard later. Among the viewers were two Israeli girls sitting in their hotel room with mixed emotions. In the upstairs drawing room, above the Café Candide, overlooking the Grand'Place, Albert Foiret and his three guests sat silent for some moments after Albert switched off his large console. He had provided a sumptuous supper for his old 'Lifeline' comrades. They had talked of the war, of old times, old friends, renewed their lapsed warmth for each other. They had lost years off their ages as their faces grew animated with the multiform joys of recollection-in-tranquillity, and sad with sudden remembered pain and loss. Two persons kept returning to them – Pascal Keldermans, and 'Yvette'. The old, dignified, tall doctor who had shared their experiences, risked his life, and given them all succour and comfort. The young girl who had started it all, and been their first, top-echelon casualty – killed, by accident, by the very men she was intent upon saving.

Now, before them, they had watched Hugo van Eyck introduce his victims, scratch the surface of the latent horror they knew to be Nazism, and above all see before them – alive, active, blatantly successful, totally unpunished – the man who had been their avowed enemy throughout those years of war and occupation. Standartenführer Ludwig Kessler was alive to them once more. The snippets they had seen in the BRT editing-room were out of context, and no more than snippets. Here, in relation to the overall programme, following so close upon their reunion and the collected memories of the period there was no doubt in anyone's mind.

Monique sat back in her chair. 'I just feel sick.'

'So he got away with it!' Natalie sighed. 'What does it matter any more?'

But Alain was more dogged, just as he had been throughout his life. 'If that was Kessler . . . and we all know it was . . . he ought to be made to pay for what he did.'

Natalie returned to the argument. 'I wonder. He was fighting for his country in his own way. I'm not sure we have the right to accuse him.'

Monique shook her head, 'He had hundreds of people killed.'

'So had every general in the war . . . ours and theirs. What's the difference?'

Alain rounded on Natalie. 'You're saying Nuremberg and all that was a farce . . . not legal? What were we supposed to do?'

Albert, as ever, tried to be diplomatic and calm things.

'Now don't let's quarrel about things lost and past. It was probably not Kessler at all.'

Monique's face hardened. 'Don't equivocate, Albert. It was him. We all know it.'

'In any case it's too late. The time to punish is after the event . . . but not a quarter-of-a-century after!'

'You just want to forget it?' Alain's anger was mounting as his gnarled farmer's hands clutched the arms of his wheelchair.

'Don't ask me, Alain.'

'No . . . I'll ask the survivors of Auschwitz and Belsen. I don't think you'll find much inclination to forgive and forget . . . and I don't blame them. I can never forget.'

Albert looked round them sadly. His wonderful night of memories was deteriorating. It needed rescuing.

'I think it has depressed us all enough. Let us forget the war . . . even if it brought us all together. My friends, let us drink a toast. To Lifeline!'

The name was enough to jerk them back. They all raised their glasses, 'To Lifeline!'

'Absent friends.'

'Absent friends,' softly repeated as each mentally focused upon their own particular and private absentee.

# FOUR

The small rented Peugeot trundled between the posts and the new prefabricated huts that made up the border between Belgium and Western Germany. If the Passport Control Clerk registered any thought at the reading of the word 'Israel' on the two passports he gave no sign. He simply handed them back, smiled, and waved them through. Customs had not bothered to do more than glance at the vehicle registration. Mical let in the clutch, and the car moved forward again . . . this time on German soil.

The headlamps picked out the trees and the occasional small building on the roadside . . . even a garage or two, closed for the night, unmoved by the emptying tanks of visiting motorists. Ruth turned to Mical as a few spots of rain appeared and glistened on the windscreen.

'What are you going to do when you see him?'

'I want him to know that I know . . . I'll see how I feel.'

'Mical . . . it isn't funny any longer. You mustn't do this. Leave it to the authorities. After that programme they have to do something.'

'They won't do anything.' Mical's contempt for authority was not confined to kibbutz leadership. 'You will see. Just a few columns in a newspaper, maybe . . . then nothing. It's always this way.' She turned to Ruth, her eyes sad, and lustreless. 'It has nothing to do with you. I think it's time to split, Ruth . . . There is no need to endanger you.'

But Ruth wasn't about to back off now and leave her friend in the lurch.

'We're all "Children of the Holocaust" . . . remember? You might need some back-up. What the hell! I've got nothing much else to do. Well . . . have I?'

Mical smiled and silently concentrated upon the road

ahead, now obscured by the rain and the smearing of the badly-fitting windscreen-wiper.

The object of their seeking, one-time SS Standartenführer Ludwig Kessler, was pressing his argument with Rückert, ex-Luftwaffe Colonel, heavy with decorations and prestige.

'But why not? He may enjoy a certain popularity, but he is only a journalist!'

'It is too dangerous! It needs to be planned. The Organisation comes first.'

'And what about the individual? What about me? I have taken years to build up this . . . my industries. It is not a little thing.'

Rückert regarded him unflinchingly. 'It wasn't a little sum the Organisation contributed to set it up! It's time you went to earth, Kessler. Disappear for six months. Take a holiday. Close the house tonight and go to a hotel . . . your house in the country . . . anywhere, man!'

'I will do no such thing! I am due in London at the Trade Conference next week. I shall go as planned, and stay here until I go. Whether I come back immediately is a moot point. We'll see what happens.'

'And if the press pick it up and it becomes official?'

It was Kessler's turn for the cold, hard look.

'Then you, my dear Hans, would have to instruct the Kameraden to get me out. Which you will do because I have the key to the money-box. If I have to go it comes with me, Hans. With ME, and no one is able to touch it without me.'

Rückert's returned hard look quickly dissolved into his charming grin as he gently slapped his old colleague on the shoulder and helped himself to another large brandy.

In the vast organisation that is the Bundesrepublik Intelligence Bureau, Richard Bauer had so far found only one man he felt he could totally trust. Max Leider was, as he was, a convinced Democrat. They were both utterly loyal to their Germany, utterly convinced of a fundamental national sanity, and sadly aware that a very considerable element of their society had few feelings of guilt over their past, indeed would welcome back a National Socialism that gave them the euphoria they had felt under Hitler's Third Reich. The war defeat, and the subsequent revelation of Germany's culpability had already been forgotten, excused, exonerated. A bellicose minority had been responsible . . . and there was always the SS to blame. Mind you, very few of them had actually been members of the Nazi party . . . at least not within earshot. Older Germans who owned-up to being convinced Nazis, or even reluctant ones were as common as people with change on a flag-day in Aberdeen. But there were some, like Bauer and Leider, who would not permit that interwar madness to rise again, and who still felt shame and guilt for their nation's part in what came to be known as the Holocaust.

Richard Bauer had been unaware of it as anything but an ugly slander put about by Jews and Communists until, at the age of twenty, he visited friends in Toulon, and, purely by chance, saw a film by Alain Resnais called *Nuit et broule*. It shattered his young life and made him ask questions, look into what had been hidden from him. His shock and horror was unmitigated. His shame in being German unsupportable. As he matured he began to see and learn that all was not well within the economic miracle of Western Germany. There was still a sickness deep down, still given sustenance by world events, the advance of communism, and the desire of the Western democracies to forgive and forget. Occasional howls of injustice from Tel Aviv meant little until the abduction of Adolf Eichmann from South America and the subsequent glare of publicity in that glass booth in Jerusalem reawakened the conscience of the world to Nazi depravities, sharpened vengeful claws, and then provoked the cries of obscenity from well-meaning humanists declaring that the pursuit of war crimes was, at this late date, no longer tolerable.

That aspect did not exercise Bauer's mind overly nor that of his colleague. Their concern was hints and suggestions, snippets of information that implied that the old Nazism was dormant, not dead. Bit-by-bit they uncovered for each other a possibility, a suspicion, sometimes a certainty. The fact that both of them were with the Bureau, had long police and intelligence training, gave them an edge over most who concerned themselves with such uncoverings. It also gave them the practical common sense to keep their discoveries to themselves until they were in a position to blow the whole thing sky-high. It was one thing picking the brains of journalists like Hugo van Eyck . . . even assisting them with unimportant but sensational scraps of revelation . . . it was quite another to devise a combative strategy to deal body blows to these 'best laid plans' of a very powerful, and utterly ruthless organisation that seemed to have its tentacles stretching throughout the world and deep into the throat of government and authority. What were they doing? Why? What were they waiting for?

They read of Odessa, and other groups, real and imaginary, without too much credence. They both knew the basic premise was correct, but between the fiction and the reality there was a gulf.

Then one day in 1977, Bauer had been assigned to liaise with some representatives of British Intelligence, men from MI6 led by a certain Commander Deakin. That association had led to further liaison between the two, eventually leading to a frank exchange of views, and the handing of a British file for his eyes only. Bauer had learned quickly what had been kept from him by his own Bureau. He assumed they knew – they were good at their job. It was inconceivable that they did not know.

Bauer learned of the Kameradenwerk, the Nazi organisation formed and led by a man of brilliance, faith and determination. One who had arranged the escape of countless old Nazi comrades – men who had immediate need to leave Europe after the Allied victory. Men like Eichmann. That organiser had also made it a two-way operation. The getting out of so-called war criminals was one aspect only. The other was the restoration of a National Socialist hardcore to the new régime, both in government and in industry, in education and in banking, in every possible avenue that might have some effect upon the nation's thinking, and be poised – in positions of authority – to take over the nation when called upon. It also meant extricating huge sums of blocked funds set aside by the Nazi régime over the years of the Reich. Some had become notorious such as the art treasures of Göring and others which were returned more or less intact. The gold and jewellery set aside or looted in enormous quantities was diversified. Some was buried like Fafnir's hoard, and for years every likely lake in Germany was dragged and dived and fished for the legendary gold of the Nazis. It gave novelists material for bestsellers. But the real money . . . the real Nazi fortune had been lodged in Swiss banks and, when no claimant seemed forthcoming, forgotten and lost to the world.

Reichleiter Martin Bormann had managed to flee Germany in the very face of the Allied advance. He had remained undiscovered, but with as many reported sightings as the Loch Ness Monster. But Bauer knew, as several intelligence organisations knew, that Bormann had eventually reached Argentina by submarine, taking with him vast sums of money and gold. That fortune was quickly pounced upon by the rapacious Perón and his glittering wife, Eva – the 'Evita' of later years. The Pérons took approximately half of that fortune in return for permitting Bormann and his fellow exiles and refugees to remain in Latin America unmolested, unextraditable.

Bauer and his friend Leider had their suspicions about several members of the hierarchy still living comfortably and openly in Germany, but they were only suspicions. They suspected that the man who organised the whole Kameradenwerk, the man who had rescued most of the wanted Nazis from the new Europe and who had placed his trusted followers and colleagues in high places was none other than Germany's greatest war hero. A man whose position in Germany to this day is similar to that of Britain's Douglas Bader. The darling of his people, accepted and revered by even the Allied Air Forces, with whom he was a regular guest and honoured visitor. The man was Colonel Hans Rückert.

One of the men placed by Rückert, though in this case upon instruction from the fountain-head, Reichleiter Bormann himself, was ex-Standartenführer Ludwig Kessler, with instruction to place him where his own abilities could make him, with proper and large financial backing from an undisclosed source, into a key figure in industry. One day he would be needed as such, but also as something else. Something that Rückert only learned twenty years later.

Bauer, once he had got onto Dorf as a suspect Nazi of importance, had quickly discovered that he was quite possibly the Höherer SS-und Polizeiführer of Belgium and the Low Countries during the Occupation. That knowledge – or rather suspicion – plus certain other pieces of a jig-saw fed to him by Deakin in London from time to time, gave Kessler a special place in his uncoverings.

This morning, seated in his office poring over a purloined war-time file and other relevant information, Bauer was finding more pieces that fitted . . . even if the hole in the middle was still huge. Max Leider sauntered in, sat down and flicked a cigarette into his mouth with a childlike delight in the trick that ought to have been highly unGerman in the book of generalities.

'Why don't we go and eat?'

'Because I've got things unfinished and I can't keep all these papers much longer. Did you know that John Diefenbaker asked questions in the Canadian House of Commons in 1966 . . . and the then Minister of Defence, Paul Hellyer, admitted there had been a problem in a prison camp after an execution? Did you also know that a certain Oberst von Schalk, now living in Köln, admits that he knew the Wehrmacht officer was SS Standartenführer Kessler and that he was no longer in the camp on 19 April 1946, when prisoners were either confined or repatriated?'

'So it really does fit together. Can it wait? I'm hungry.'

The phone rang. Leider answered it casually.

'Richard Bauer's office. Who? Yes, hang on a minute. He handed the receiver to Bauer. 'It's from Brussels. Van Eyck.'

When van Eyck's voice was heard it was ebullient.

'It worked! The phones haven't stopped ringing. Half of

Belgium is ringing-in saying that Dorf is positively Kessler and that they have personal knowledge of him. I'm going to get another three programmes out of this, it'll put the wind up that bastard Dorf. Listen, the reason I'm calling is that that Israeli girl, Rak, wanted Kessler's address and so on. She started rabbiting on about young Nazis, which made me think there might be some mileage in it. You get my file if I get some dope on *them* . . . Okay?'

'We agree in principle. This Israeli girl . . . what does she intend to do?'

'Hell! How do I know? She breathed fire and Old Testament, and hurried off to spread the Wrath of God. Listen we have to meet for an exchange. Give me a ring when you have some bumph. Okay?'

The two Germans went to lunch and mulled over what the likely result might be. The result of that transmission, and how it might affect Kessler and ultimately themselves

The night was a dark one with very little moon and some light wind. Woxholt walked the grounds of the Kessler home with his Alsatian, unaware that he was being followed through night-sighted binoculars by a young, attractive Israeli girl standing on the roof of her Peugeot, which was parked well out of the way and concealed by a small copse. She dropped to the ground in her dark green track-suit, and made for the wall of Kessler's house.

To the rear of that house, sandwiched between the large garage and the workshop, was a guard-house. While Woxholt went on his rounds Franz took over in the guard-house. He smoked and read the *Krefelder Zeitung* until a gentle bleeping sound made him look up and see the flashing red warning-light above the surveillance system. Quickly he isolated the area, and flicked the switch that set the closed-circuit tv camera in motion, scanning with infra-red assistance the area between itself and the next camera scan Camera three picked up the crouching figure of a human being in a dark track-suit. Franz picked up the revolver from the drawer in the table, checked it was loaded, removed the safety-catch, and slipped outside into the dark night. He was wearing soft slippers and a dark sweater.

Mical crept nearer to the window of the house. The light was on and people moved about within.

She could just make out the top of the head of a man, sitting in a high-backed chair, a head she recognised from a recent television programme. Kessler had his back to her, but there was no doubt about the identity. Mical felt herself go cold. This man, balding, white-haired, had sent her family to be exterminated. People he had not known. People whose crime was to be Jewish in a world of Aryan supremacy.

Mical wanted to ask him, 'Why? How could this happen? What right did he hold that gave him the disposal of others?'

She was suddenly aware of hard breathing behind her, and swung round to find a Walther pistol pointing at her and a young Aryan face regarding her with amused confidence. Franz's expression was cold but approving of a pretty girl – Hebrew or not – as he asked her what she was doing.

Her lame excuse that she came to see Herr Dorf was treated with chuckling contempt. 'Legitimate visitors use the entrance. Turn round and put your hands against the tree. Do it, lady! There is a dog one hundred metres away who hasn't eaten yet. He's mean.'

He frisked her, with more than a touch of lasciviousness and found her passport, which he opened with a smirk, at the place which was 'marked' by her hotel registration card. His thumb moved across the slight indentation of the word 'Israel'.

'Mical Rak. Mmh . . . You Jews have funny names. Mical. Isn't that a man's name?'

'Mical was the daughter of Saul who became the wife of King David.'

The Biblical information covered her preparation to attack with a swift, hard kick between the legs. Franz collapsed clutching his genitals and gasping with the agony. He didn't even see Mical running for the perimeter, but the slight sound had brought the Alsatian scampering across the grass towards the activity. Mical reached her hired car before the dog reached her. She flicked the ignition, threw the car into gear and drove off with the engine protesting. It was eight minutes before the Alsatian gave up and found itself dodging traffic on the autobahn.

Franz was carried in by the guard, Woxholt, as Kessler came into the corridor to ascertain what was going on. Franz, in great pain and still doubled up, endeavoured to speak coherently. Ingrid wanted to hold him and comfort him with loving arms and kisses, for Ingrid had been Franz's mistress for upwards of three months, unknown to her father. Kessler would have neither approved nor permitted this, so the affair remained clandestine. She held back with difficulty and her face showed her concern.

'What has happened? What's going on out here?'

'I caught someone trespassing in the grounds, sir. A girl – name was Mical Rak. She carried an Israeli passport.' Franz gasped out the information in fits and starts.

But the word 'Israeli' had registered, and for a moment spread fear with the cold splash of ice-water. Ingrid suddenly forgot her lover's pain and turned to her father aghast.

'Israeli! Oh father!'

Rückert, who had remained with them for dinner, moved and bent down over the recumbent Franz.

'Did you find out anything else?'

'She was driving a small car with a Brussels numberplate. Woxholt ran out into the road. He saw her. She left this behind. It's the card from a gasthof, room number . . .'

Franz winced as he tried to stand, and gave up for the moment. Kessler remained quiet.

'Thank you, Franz. I am sorry you've been hurt. Ingrid, see that he is properly taken care of.'

He turned on his heel and returned to the study, followed by a thoughtful Rückert who went straight to the phone, dialled, waited.

'Maurer? Rückert . . . Listen carefully. An attempt has been made to enter the house of our colleague. Reason yet unknown, but we know it was an Israeli girl. Correct. Israeli. She was driving a car with a Brussels licence-plate. We know the number commenced with the digits 95. I agree. From

Brussels, it is too much of a coincidence. I suggest you do exactly that. She is staying at the Gasthof Venlo.'

Kessler was about to ask a question, but Rückert stopped him with a gesture as he listened intently.

'You've found who was doing the checks? Who? Bauer? No, the name means nothing.' He glanced at Kessler questioningly, but found only a negative shrug.

'No, nothing. Very well. Handle it your own way.'

Rückert replaced the phone pensively, then turned to Kessler.

'Why would they be after *you*? Israelis. You did not persecute them, as I remember.'

'I don't see that as a motive. No. the fact that this girl comes from Brussels implies a connection with van Eyck. I think it is time to attend to that man . . . once and for all.'

# FIVE

Bauer bent over his closed-circuit print-out, and scanned the information blinking at him in electric blue. The office, like most German offices in the Federal Republic today. was sparkling clean, technically efficient, well-designed and opulent. It all contrasted strangely with the pile of box-files on his desk and table, which looked like relics from another age which, of course, they were.

The top file was open and Max Leider was peering closely at the top print of a pile of photographs and photocopied documents. He handed Bauer the print.

'It's from the bank. It's the best lead we've had yet. It implies Kessler is a much bigger-wig than we ever imagined. Assuming Dorf IS Kessler – and only the proof is lacking . . .'

'But that IS lacking, Max. We don't *know*. We could even be wrong.'

'I don't believe it. As I was saying – if we bide our time and watch, Kessler will lead us to the Kameradenwerk centre, and we can break the whole damn thing.'

The phone on his desk rang, Bauer picked it up.

'Bauer, oh, hello, Tom. Yes, of course.'

He replaced the hand set at the end of his desk and brought forward the red scrambler-phone, muttering to Leider.

'Deakin, MI6.'

He picked up the red receiver, pressed the button, and waited a moment.

'Yes, Tom. Yes. It went out on BRT and caused quite a stir. I can't answer that one. I don't know. Let me return the call when I have some more information which might not be all that long. No, I have a meeting scheduled with van Eyck. Yes, I will. Goodbye.'

Bauer replaced the phone, halted *en route*, then dropped the receiver onto the cradle. He looked thoughtful. Leider glanced at him aware of a sudden silence.

'That scrambler is tapped!'

Leider felt his stomach sink a little. 'That means it has to be someone in this organisation, in this building.'

'Yes. I suppose I knew that. I could feel it on the back of my neck.'

He walked back to the scanner when the phone rang once more. Bauer glanced at Leider before picking it up.

'Bauer. Yes, sir. Not at all. I'll come straight away.'

Leider's eyes caught his own and held. 'That didn't take long.'

Bauer switched off his scanner, closed the open file on his desk, stared for a moment at the label which stated, in a faded, long-hand copperplate, 'Occupied Belgium 1942/43', and walked from his office.

The office of the Deputy Direktor was on the second floor. Spacious, well-appointed, carpeted not corded, and the large curtained windows looked out onto the landscaping and the fountain sculpture. Herr Deputy Direktor Maurer was looking at the fountain when Bauer entered, crossed to the desk and stood waiting. Maurer turned and looked at him, Bauer made the slightest of head bows.

'Sit down, Bauer.'

Bauer did so, and waited. Maurer resumed his seat behind the desk and crossed his hands before him on the desk top, assuming a pleasant and confiding expression.

'Bauer, I've been watching your work in this department with interest. You are keen and efficient . . . liked by your colleagues, and those with whom you co-operate in other countries. This is good. Excellent! But sometimes enthusiasm can persuade us to pursue a course of action which, for reasons unknown to us, is contrary to the wishes of our superiors.'

Maurer smiled encouragingly, and pushed the cigarette-box forward with his finger tips . . . Bauer shook his head. He didn't smoke – certainly not Maurer's offering. Maurer did. Bauer watched the thick-set, bullet-headed man with sensuous and cruel, insensitive features slowly and patiently light his Sobranie with a silver pocket-lighter.

'You have taken action in the matter of a certain Manfred Dorf. May I ask why?'

'He was put forward in a television interview as being an ex SS war-criminal, Ludwig Kessler. I considered it a matter for investigation, and simply made the normal investigative checks.'

Maurer made a face. 'Unfortunately, certain other departments in the Bureau are concerned with this and similar matters. They are, I'm afraid, somewhat angry that one of my staff should have – without consulting anyone – gone ahead and prejudiced their case by ill-considered and precipitate action.'

'I'm sorry. I didn't know. Isn't it our job to sort out these people?'

That was a try-on, and Bauer just couldn't resist it. He knew well enough that Maurer himself was not above suspicion, and the reference to 'these people' might just provoke him into giving himself away. It didn't.

'We do not pursue war criminals years after the Statute of Limitations was passed, surely? It is a pointless waste of time and money.'

'I was merely trying to keep the files up to date.'

Maurer beamed with overt good feeling to a subordinate.

'Of course, of course, my friend. But I do think it might be prudent to take a short leave . . . say, two months . . . until the matter blows over. Save us all embarrassment, eh?' His face became suddenly stern. 'As of tomorrow, Bauer.'

'I really don't want to go on leave, sir.'

Maurer stood up suddenly. His knuckles resting on his blotter in an ape-like posture.

'I am not "suggesting" you go on leave, Bauer. I am ordering you to! There is going to be hell to pay over all this if the minister catches wind of it, and I don't want my people on the carpet . . . do I?'

Bauer recognised dismissal when he saw it, and rose, bowed briefly with a mumbled agreement, and left the room watched by the glowering and suspicious eyes of his superior. Maurer was not a nice man . . . sometimes it showed.

Outside the Candide, in Brussels' Grand'Place, a taxi stood waiting, its motor running, and the driver leaning against the door. Albert had given them all an early lunch in his rooms, and they had all come early . . . just to snatch another few minutes with their old comrade, Monique, who was going back to England, to her husband, to her home, to her son, and to her life. This was no more than stepping back – for a moment – into time past. Monique's liquid eyes filled with tears very easily. They always had; it was her nature. But Albert looked at her with deep emotion. He had loved her more than he knew, and now it came properly home to him the enormity of his loss. There would be time for self-recrimination – after she had gone. Natalie and Alain looked at her, touched her hand, her dress, unwilling to lose the contact so recently recaptured, for they knew in their hearts they would never see her again. The reunion was a 'one-off'. Life happened that way.

Monique kissed Albert's cheek. 'It was lovely seeing you all again. I wasn't sure I ever would.'

'Come back. Bring Stephen and your son. There's plenty of room.'

Monique nodded rapidly, knowing she would not do so . . . not even mention the invitation.

Alain grunted and moved his chair forward.

'Don't stay with this old skinflint. Come out to the farm. I've got room, too . . .'

She looked at Natalie, fifteen years younger than herself, and embittered with lack of fulfilment. No one had replaced the boy she had lost during the Occupation. She had been in many beds of no consequence and tried to settle in one place. It didn't happen. Always it was time to move on . . . to seek more action of the sort known these days as para-military . . . always action . . . always anti-communist. Natalie had not forgotten.

Monique smiled at her sadly, and kissed her. 'It's been a curious few days, not quite real. Like pulling a curtain back and finding another one still there.' She frowned. 'Oh, I must go . . . Planes don't wait.'

She swallowed the lump in her throat and climbed into the taxi, busying herself with her handbag and overnight-case, only turning to look and wave as the cab drew away.

The others waved, then it all dissolved. The event was over, the relived past evaporated. Albert turned back into his café and just caught the headlines of a newspaper lying on the table before one of his customers. It told of the upsurge of indignation about an ex-Nazi who was still at large, someone who was the most hated man in Belgium. But it didn't seem to matter all that much . . . not any more.

The people who did care, to whom it did matter – the reporters, the media people, the sensation-seekers – were now making a bee-line for the Dorf residence outside Krefeld. Outside the gates of the substantial residence twenty or thirty journalists, several cameramen, and tv camera-operators among them, waited and made vociferous complaint. The guard with the Alsatian dog stood in the background and watched with hard eyes for the first signs of encroachment when he would release the animal. Meanwhile the housekeeper, the formidable Frau Reiss, kept them at bay.

'All I can tell you is that the Dorf family are not here. They are on holiday somewhere. No, I don't know where. I know nothing of Fräulein Dorf's political activities.'

On the fringe of the throng a young, dark girl in a small Peugeot heard what was being said, glanced at the closed shutters of the house and recognised it as likely. She started the car and pulled away from the rest. Half-a-kilometre down the road she remembered there was a telephone kiosk. She would ring Ruth at the Gasthof. Mical eventually got through and spoke to Ruth on the room extension.

'I'm not far from the Dorf house . . . but he's gone. No, I think it's true. the place is surrounded by reporters. I'm just going to check out the factory . . . but van Eyck said there was a country place. I've got the address somewhere. It's worth a try. Okay. You pack our stuff, and I'll be there in about an hour. Don't go to sleep!'

Mical replaced the receiver and set off again for the central industrial estate in Krefeld and the Dorf plant.

As the tiny Peugeot plied its way through the heavy, industrial delivery traffic of the estate, a large metallic-blue Mercedes was swooping across the hill country towards the Schleiden See. In the rear Kessler and Ingrid together read the daily papers gathered for them by the recovered Franz. Kessler was angered that the Belgian press should have given the matter such coverage, but what incensed him most was that several papers bore a photograph of himself, named as Manfred Dorf, alongside the wartime picture of an SS officer named as Ludwig Kessler. The resemblance was very considerable.

The Mercedes eventually pulled into the long drive that led up to Kessler's lakeside residence, used by him only once since the death of his wife. A place full of happy memories. Memories of a pleasant life now threatened by some fool of a television sensation-monger. But that man's days were numbered, or Dorf's name was not Ludwig Kessler!

Once inside the house Kessler crossed to the telephone while Ingrid and Franz supervised the carrying of suitcases into the hall.

'Direktor Maurer, please. Yes. Herr Dorf.'

He waited impatiently until he recognised the gruff voice at the Bonn desk.

'Maurer? Have you seen the papers? Has anything been done about this Israeli girl? No, my plans are unchanged, I am at the Schleiden See house, and Maurer, if there should be official interference, I may need an alternative passport.'

Ingrid joined him as he replaced the receiver. 'Do you want me to get a message to "The Pilot"?' Kessler merely shook his head, but Ingrid persisted. 'We should have more security. Heinz and Otto can only cope with so much. Franz must go with you everywhere now . . . please, father! There is one other thing. If anything happens to you, there is no one with access to the Swiss accounts.'

Kessler looked at her. 'Don't worry, my dear. I am not exactly new to living under difficult conditions.'

'No. But you are an old man now . . . and old men make mistakes. The Kameraden would not like that, father . . .'

'The Kameraden are *all* old men! But they still hold Germany's destiny and control more than you or anyone else imagines. Don't forget that. You would be foolish to do so.'

'And what happens if they DO get you? If they decide to make you a scapegoat? Who will make the money available to them? To US?'

Kessler's expression hardened, and he let it be seen that he was not amused by this turn of talk. It did not dissuade Ingrid.

'The contingency is taken care of . . . there is no need to concern yourself or your friends.' As an afterthought, 'Your friends do not come into it anyway.'

'Why not?'

'Because it is NOT THEIRS.'

'Stupid! Stupid! We are the only active organisation to lead Germany back to National Socialism. Do you think those old fools hiding in Paraguay and Brazil are ever going to DO anything? They are toothless old refugees pretending to be Hitler's Old Guard waiting for "Der Tag" that will never come . . . waiting for their Reichleiter to lead Germany back to supremacy. You are all so stupid!'

'You were happy enough to be part of it not so many years ago.'

'Oh, but it was, father! Light-years ago! There are young

men who are not talking about the old days and crying over their uniforms!'

'Is that what you think of me?'

Kessler's question was genuine, not rhetorical, nor inviting sympathy. Ingrid frowned at her own impetuousness and put her arm round his shoulders affectionately.

'Not YOU! Not "The Pilot"! You are both different. They all worship you and Colonel Rückert. Forget the old guard, father. Join the young ones . . . LEAD us!'

Kessler frowned and put on the dour expression she had seen so often.

'Ingrid, your friends doubtless mean well, but they are children without purpose, without faith. Throwing bombs, killing a few Jews, hi-jacking planes, and making hostages of old ladies . . . these are the trappings of foolishness. They are pointless, senseless, futile! Your brave young friends are no better than . . . and no different to the Baader-Meinhof lunatics. If you imagine a new Germany will grow from such beginnings then you are not my daughter . . . and I believe you are.'

But Ingrid was not happy. She was not convinced, and much as she loved her father she knew inside that he was blind to the realities of the day. He was beginning to live in a world of memories.

The Gasthof Vilno was unpretentious, and tucked away at the end of the street of old houses. Mical had just glanced at her fuel gauge to check that she had enough for the next leg of her journey, discovered that she could probably manage, and pulled up outside the hotel. She tooted, and waited.

No one came. She glanced up at the shuttered room, and tooted once more. After a moment's impatient waiting she climbed out of the car and entered the hotel. Ruth would have dozed off again . . . she kept doing it! Quickly running up the stairs to the first floor she inserted her key into the door of their room and entered. The room was in a relative darkness from the closed shutters.

'Ruth.'

There was no answer. Mical moved forward and promptly fell over something. It was a drawer from the dressing-unit. Mical looked quickly about her, suddenly feeling sick inside. The place was a shambles. Clothing and furniture strewn everywhere. The place had been ransacked. Fearful of what she might find Mical picked herself up and crossed to the tiny bathroom, the door of which was ajar. What she saw stopped her heart for a moment, and revolted her beyond anything she had yet known.

Ruth's body was draped face-down over the bath, her clothing torn to reveal the naked flesh of her back. She knew her friend was dead . . . she just knew. The exposed back had a hideous bleeding swastika cut into the flesh . . . Mical looked up through eyes that could not see properly. The tears wouldn't really come . . . and the sobbing was no more than a regurgitating of the abdomen. But her eyes saw the soap-writing on the mirror. The single word: 'Jude'.

The scream that came from Mical's throat was silent. The horror was the same as her parents and grandparents had known. Nothing had changed in the Rak family, the Nazis were still here, and their latest victim was her best friend, Ruth Liebermann, a sweet girl who wished no harm on anyone. She wasn't even hunting the maniacs who perpetuated this vicious insanity. But Mical was. Now she was. Now and for ever she was.

# SIX

Richard Bauer lived in a second floor apartment in the corner block of the Altenburg Strasse, over a tobacconist's shop, facing the eighty-metre stretch of uncovered river that flowed most of its way under the streets and houses of the city. Bonn had changed out of all recognition in the time he had lived there. Only his apartment hadn't changed. It still belonged to the age of Beethoven and most of the furniture might well have been wrecked by Bonn's illustrious son during one of his rages. There was hardly a single piece that had not been patched and mended. Putting up with it was the price Bauer paid for that eighty-metre stretch of river.

He looked across at it now as he entered the apartment house followed by Max Leider.

'He can't be all that involved with them. They'd never have given him the job.'

Leider's remark caused Bauer to pause as he inserted his key in the lock. They entered and closed the door before he replied, putting down the bag of groceries on the battered table.

'Have you considered who are the politicians and officials handing out the posts of authority? No . . . I mean it. Just think.' He held up one hand, and counted on his fingers as he ticked them off. 'There's Muhlfeld, once Gauleiter of Frankfurt, Malvezzi, naturalised-German, who was a prominent Fascisti with Mussolini. Volkmann, SS Stürmbahnführer in Denmark, who suddenly appeared from nowhere in 1956. Speth, Ritter, we know all about THEM. Why shouldn't they appoint Maurer? That way they feel safer.'

'And are you saying the whole regime is ex-Nazi?'

'Of course not! It isn't true. But there are enough. Every time they find another Eichmann there is always a reason to delay bringing it into the court. Another loophole in the laws to give them protection.'

'They also protect the innocent. Would you have different laws for some people?'

Bauer grunted, and moved across to the cupboard where he found a pan and a kettle, filled the latter, and plugged it into his supply, while he poured half the new bag of freshly-ground coffee into the pan. At the back of the same cupboard from which he extracted his pan were at least three percolators of various types that had been given him out of pity by his friends. But Richard was a creature of habit. He had always made coffee in a pan. He liked it that way. His taste was for mild, but full-flavoured, breakfast coffee from a blond bean, not the dark, burnt, bitter brew he was given by his friends, who seemed to prefer it that way. Hence the pan, and the unused percolators.

'What do you want me to do? Just accept it? I can't accept expediency as the answer to everything. I've just managed to get over the feeling of shame that I am German. I'm not ashamed any longer! "The sins of the fathers" and all that stuff. No, I've worn it long enough.'

Max Leider sighed and sat down. 'Haven't we all? It's just a handful, anyway. Does it matter all that much? We're beating our heads against a brick wall.'

'I'm not so sure it's just a handful. I was in Austria last year, watching a discreet, but unconcealed, celebration. Half the town was out in the cafes all toasting Hitler's birthday.' He looked sick as he said it. Leider watched him pour the boiling water onto the coffee in the pan.

'It isn't dead yet, Max . . . never mind buried.'

Bauer put down the full pan and crossed the room to his crock-cupboard and rummaged for mugs. Then he suddenly stopped, stood up, and looked round his room intently.

'The bastards! Someone's done me over.'

Leider glanced at him. 'You sure?'

'Of course I'm bloody sure! I know my own disarray. It's also my job to know.'

'You could be wrong. It's a long time since you were a field-man.'

Further speculation was interrupted by a persistent but discreet buzzing from Leider's paging monitor.

'Oh Christ! Can't they leave us alone for a couple of hours? Can I use it?'

He indicated the telephone with his head, and didn't wait for permission. They knew each other well enough to make the request superfluous. Bauer glanced round angrily, and paid scant attention to his friend and colleague as he dialled and started to talk. He was roused from his muttered complaining by Leider's finger snapping to attract his attention and urge him to write down something, with something, on something. Bauer thrust a notepad at him together with a pencil and Leider made his notes.

'Yes, thank you, Heinz. Be about twenty minutes.'

Leider compressed his lips and squinted at the address given before he looked up into Bauer's questioning eyes.

'The police have just found a murdered girl in Krefeld. They contacted me because they think it was political. She had a swastika cut into her flesh . . . and she's Israeli.'

Bauer felt the shock sink in as he remembered van Eyck's information. He crossed to the door, slipped on his jacket and stood waiting for Leider.

'Where d'you think you're going?'

Bauer blinked. 'With you, of course.'

'No you're not. You're on leave. I suggest if you want to call this place home you sweep every room for bugs. They don't just "look" – they "plant" '

'It takes ages,' Bauer protested, but Leider merely grinned, and closed the door after him.

The motorcycle messenger roared up the drive and rounded the lake skidding to a halt outside the house, throwing up a scatter of gravel as he did so. He dismounted, entered the porch, rang the doorbell and waited.

Kessler implanted his ring in the soft, warm wax on the envelope-seal and turned in his desk-chair to hand the packet to Franz who stood waiting.

'The messenger will deliver this to the Guestenhold Bank, Zürich, into the hands of the Manager, Ientropp. He will obtain a signed receipt which he will deposit into my bank in Bonn. He will enter Switzerland at Basel and depart by the same route. He will not declare the packet at the border. It is simply banker's instructions if he is asked, but he should not be bothered.'

The messenger took the envelope, placed it carefully into his voluminous inside pocket that was sealed by two independent zips and a button-flap. That, and the leather coat, would protect the document from most things. It needed to be protected. It needed to be secret. It was more important than almost anyone, even within the Party and the Kameraden, could possibly imagine. It was the first move in a pattern of predestined activity that could conceivably alter the face of the world. It had almost done so once and it could again. Much had been learned, much had been gained. Kessler was one of two vital links, in that chain of activation. The rest would emerge when he, and one other, were good and ready, and not before. But that time was at hand. Events were making it so.

The Gasthof Vilno was alive with police. Apart from the area squad the whole apparatus of the forensic, investigation, and senior administrative branches had been called in. It was, as Leider had said, tainted with political motives.

Inspector Millöker looked up as Leider entered.

Leider nodded. 'Dieter.'

Without comment they moved round the disarray, and Leider's expert eyes noted as much as the forensic pictures later confirmed.

'Why did you contact us?' Leider didn't look at him as he was interested in the handbag and papers of the occupant – presumably the deceased.

'Have you seen the corpse?'

Leider shook his head and followed Dieter Millöker into the bathroom. The now open shutters threw the cold light of day into the clinically simple bathroom. Ruth's skin looked less tanned in the white light, and the blood from the carved swastika had congealed into black. The whole thing had the appearance of 'soot-and-whitewash' that so many vicious crime pictures seem to have. Perhaps it was inherent in the subject matter.

The policeman muttered some obscenity and then continued. 'Not very pretty, though the girl is . . . was. I seem to recognise the symbol and the writing on the mirror.'

Leider glanced up at it. The smeared soap now shone in the daylight, and the word 'Jude' took on the significance of a firebrand. He sniffed through his nostrils.

'What do we know?'

Millöker produced his notepad, and read unemotionally.

'Ruth Liebermann. Israeli subject, native of Tel Aviv, age

twenty-six. Entered Germany yesterday from Belgium. Apparently a tourist. No known connection with any organisation – ours, or theirs. Travelling and registered here with a companion, another Israeli girl, one Mical Rak.'

'What do we know about *her*?'

'Name registered as Mical Rak, could be alias. We have no record of passport examination. We're a bit slack in these days of the EEC. It doesn't help *us*, you know.'

Leider made a face. 'Don't blame me. I didn't invent it.'

But Millöker wasn't being deflected. 'What d'you know that I don't, Max? Why are you people involved? And what's more to the point, who tells the Israeli authorities?'

'We'll do that. You just treat it as a police matter that has overtones out of your brief. Send me a copy of your report in the usual way, then send me under separate cover your FULL report: everything.'

Millöker sighed, fully aware that he was getting nothing more from Leider. The latter was already out of the door.

Bauer had managed to persuade two friends in the department to sweep his apartment while he attended to other matters. Time was all he had, and that was in short supply. He needed some things from his desk, some papers containing addresses and things of that nature. He found them untouched in his desk drawer, glanced round the office he was to vacate at least for a couple of months, and decided he would collect his bits and pieces the following day. Armed with his notes he set out for the garage where he kept his small VW, just off the Bahnhofsplatz, in the Wittingerstrasse. There was a large building project being worked on at this moment; the rumour was that it was to be a department store, but this was unconfirmed by either local newspaper reportage or a contractors' board. Whatever it was, it involved stepping off the sidewalk and threading round the fenced way over broken cement, chipped brick and the layer of builder's dust that settles everywhere. For Richard, whose rented garage was on the same side as the construction site, it meant crossing a narrow path over mounds of mud and rubble and circumnavigating the mechanical hoist.

As he picked his way through towards the hoist he was forced to stop twice by workmen wheeling barrowloads of rubble towards a skip, men whose great brown arms rippled with brute strength under the dirt and grey dust. When he reached the hoist he was, forced to stop and wait, his path ahead blocked by helmeted site foremen who gesticulated and indicated while grubby hands probed the paper specifications. Bauer waited patiently until a yell from across the street, and the sudden sixth sense of impending disaster, made him leap to one side. The sickening thud of the barrowload of wet cement that landed precisely where he had stood, made him feel physically sick and tremble as he stood up and brushed the mud from his trousers with even dirtier hands. The sort of nonsense action that comes with unthinking shock, and deflects momentarily the vomit that would otherwise probably rise in the suddenly constricted gorge.

His angry glance upwards to the cause of the 'accident' found no one remotely near the point of departure. The helmeted foremen advanced to assist him, muttering about inferior and inexperienced workmen leaving things lying about where anything could happen. Richard muttered excuses and got away quickly. He did not want to remain on the site, and mentally vowed he would not cross that area again while they worked upon it. Outside the Lorenzkirche he rested for a moment and regained his composure – then went for his car, by the other roundabout route.

Kessler was unaware that his daughter Ingrid and his manservant, Franz, were in any sense lovers. Ingrid was perfectly aware that her father would not have approved. He was straitlaced, even prudish. The whole slackening of restraint and revaluation of moral issues by the young made him indignant and very angry. Kessler responded to discipline, and approved of self-discipline above all. That, in itself, was the greatest of virtues to the curious, antiseptic mind that had been fostered by the SS. Homosexuality had been rife during the days of the war, which, for some quirkish reason, was not frowned upon to anything like the degree that heterosexual promiscuity was. Perhaps it all sprang from the leaders in the first instance. Roehm, the most blatant, gave men such as Kessler a justification for their putsch, the Lichterfeld Barracks, the night of the Long Knives – the Nazis' very own St. Bartholomew's massacre. It was a necessary 'cleansing'.

Ingrid had no such inhibitions. Few of her generation had, though perhaps it ought to be said that among the National Socialist elements sexual morality was higher than with most revolutionary groups. Franz even knocked before entering her room.

'Your father has sent a packet to Zürich by special messenger.'

Ingrid searched his expression. 'To the bank?'

'Yes, but not the same as the others. This one seems important. We used our own messenger, not the commercial service and it was not to the regular bank.'

Ingrid looked unseeingly at his face. Franz, feeling the time to be ripe and the surges of desire insistent, kissed her hungrily, but met with little response. Ingrid was thinking. She held back momentarily and let the strength in her arms imply the restraint she intended. Franz's face fell and he looked petulant. He was not used to rejection. Ingrid had hitherto shown the same lustfulness he had; neither had pretended to be in love, and were honest enought to accept the need for what it was.

'Not now, Franz . . . later. Tell me about the letter. Did you see who it was addressed to?'

As Franz reconstructed the handing over of the letter the house on the outskirts of Krefeld was being examined by a thoughtful man sitting in his small VW. Bauer recognised the house as either uninhabited or reacting to siege tactics. The curtains were drawn and the place had an air of lack of occupation, despite the handful of journalists picketing the main gate, more or less resigned to non-appearances, non-bulletins, non-news. They had not yet been withdrawn though they recognised that to be imminent. It was, after all, yesterday's news.

Bauer looked at the grounds of the neighbouring house which extended up to Kessler's house boundary. Wild garden and clumps of trees mainly. Bauer left his car and crossed the low fencing to circle behind the trees and approach the Kessler home from the side, away from prying eyes and nosy newshounds. He drew close to the house and made directly for the window facing him. The curtains were drawn, but not completely. He peered through the gap. Inside the furniture was covered by dust-sheets and gave every appearance of the family having gone away. He was about to move to the second window to confirm the impression when he sensed he was not alone and turned to see the guard, Woxholt, standing watching him, holding the growling Alsatian on heavy-duty, but quick-release leash.

At the sight of the bared teeth Bauer smiled awkwardly.

'I was hoping to find Herr Dorf. He seems to have gone away.' The lame apology sounded even worse as he spoke it and Bauer made an embarrassed farewell gesture as he backed away.

'The gate is this way,' was the laconic but firm directive. Bauer hastily changed course and walked with anxious tread towards the fence. Woxholt bent forward and slowly unclipped the leash. The dog bounced forward at the same moment as Bauer took to his heels. He was fit enough to leap the fence but, then, so was the dog. He reached his car less than two seconds ahead of the ferocious beast, and slammed the door shut after him. The journalists had scattered for their own vehicles the moment they saw Bauer running.

Inside the car Bauer fumbled with his ignition key and started the engine as the dog pawed and scratched his window and door-panel, its terryifying face and teeth constantly against the triplex glass now covered with smeared canine saliva. For a second his mind considered the ludicrous possibility of catching rabies from that window. He let in the clutch and the car jumped forward, stalled and slid back against the kerb while the dog infuriated by the sound of the engine became quite hysterical in its attack. Bauer silently prayed that Volkswagen used heavy-gauge metal in its door panels and restarted the engine. The dog suddenly turned, presumably in response to a hypersonic whistle, and without further thought for its quarry cantered back to its handler. Bauer turned his vehicle and went on his way. Twice in one day was enough for anyone. The easy and uncomplicated life looked desperately rosy from where he now sat. To hell with the Nazis!

'To hell with van Eyck!' were the words uppermost in Kessler's mind as he read the headlines and leader-headings in the papers handed to him by the pale-faced and obviously deeply concerned Rückert. The photographs of Kessler, as Manfred Dorf, were recent and well-printed. The articles were lucid, succinct, and demanded an official inquiry.

'Damn the man! Damn him to hell!'

'I should never have given that wretched interview in the first place. It was ill-advised, Hans.'

'There wasn't any alternative. To have refused would have implied either direct guilt or the wish to avoid publicity. It was a gamble that could have scotched the snake even if it didn't kill it. We lost the gamble.'

Kessler poured drinks for himself and the Colonel: large ones, undiluted.

'The man claims he has further revelations about the whole organisation . . . look at this . . . Bishop Hudal. The man is dead. How can he know about it?'

Kessler was referring to the Most Reverend Alois Hudal, one-time Bishop at the Holy See in Rome. The man most responsible for the cover and escape of hundreds of Nazis fleeing from the avenging Allies, who protected them, found mainly Vatican passports for them, and provided the 'underground railroad' that initially aided those seeking refuge. The underground route that helped Rückert himself, before he realised that he was not on any 'wanted list', and was revered as much by his enemies as he was by his own kind. Secure in that knowledge Rückert had returned as unobtrusively as he had left, to emerge when conveniently unearthed by the applauding military authorities. Pope Pius XII saw the Nazi opposition to Communism as a bulwark against what he most feared and withheld his condemnation of the Third Reich until the fall of Germany. This was Papal cowardice, but Hudal was no coward, and he was a convinced patriot.

Rückert's eyes clouded over coldly, 'I think it is time for M'nheer van Eyck to meet with an accident. We cannot permit disclosures about the Organisation.'

'I don't think . . .'

But Rückert cut him off. 'For once I am not asking you, Kessler. I am doing it! I am ordering you, in the name of our leader and the Kameraden, to leave Germany, at least for a while, and until we can be sure there is to be no official pursuit. You have perfect cover to go to London. There is the Trade Conference and your attendance has been announced publicly. You have reason to stay supervising the new factory installations. You will be strategically placed either to return unobtrusively or leave for permanent safety elsewhere. People have short memories, and governments only remember what it suits them to remember. We still have muscle where we need it.'

Kessler was silent for some moments. 'What will you do with van Eyck? He is known . . .'

Rückert was also silent before he turned his gaze and smiled upon the older man. 'I haven't decided yet. What shall we do about this girl, the Israeli?'

It was Kessler's turn to be enigmatic, 'She is now in the Promised Land with her Jehovah.'

Rückert nodded without showing any reaction and picking up his glass, emptied it. 'I shall leave now. There is one last thing, Kessler. If it means that you are to leave. We would not wish you to go "empty-handed".'

Their eyes met and held. Rückert did not emphasise his meaning. Kessler did not disclose that action had already been taken. They were old friends . . . but not blood-brothers.

'Is that the same coffee?' Leider's question was not flippant.

He wanted to know. Bauer had been making coffee just before he was called away. Now, a day later, Bauer was again about his brew with the same dented pan and brown fluid.

'Does that matter?'

'No. Just curious. We've kept tabs on Dorf. He's gone to the country.'

Bauer grunted. 'That much I already know. I was chased by the Fenrir's Wolf! Where?'

'He owns a house near the Schleiden See about fifteen kilometres off the road from Köln to Luxembourg.'

His eyes twinkled as Bauer thanked him. 'Good man. I owe you.'

Leider grunted and sipped his coffee suspiciously.

'You don't owe me anything. Just get the bastard so we can nail the pipe-line once and for all. If you'd seen the mess that Israeli girl was in you'd know why.'

'The Rak girl. Shame, I thought she was rather pretty.'

'No. Not her! She seems to have disappeared. No, she was travelling with a friend. One Ruth Liebermann, also from Tel Aviv. Now in another world, with a swastika carved into her back.'

'I didn't realise she had a friend with her.'

'Nor, presumably, did they. Have you seen the Embassy?'

'Mmh. They are going to ask some very unhappy questions. I think Schmidt will have to answer them himself. They won't be happy with anything less. It was the ancillary bits, not the murder. They don't like swastikas.'

'That reminds me, a message at the Bureau said van Eyck was arriving in the next hour, apparently to see you. Shall I channel him round here?'

'Please. I seem to have become accident-prone.'

'What d'you mean?'

'A barrow of cement just happened to fall off a building site onto me, if I hadn't jumped.'

The two men exchanged glances . . . slightly fearful, slightly concerned for each other, with enough warmth contained to imply the very real friendship they had.

# SEVEN

Kessler sat in his garden seat overlooking the lake considering his whole position. He did not want to leave Germany. His way of life, his position, his home, his friends, his outside interests all contributed to that reluctance, but none so much as his industrial empire. Kessler had become, over the years, a very capable industrial magnate. He enjoyed the power, the wealth, and the prestige. He also secretly saw himself as a lesser Krupp, and basked in that self-made opinion. From the very considerable resources made available to him by the Kameradenwerk controllers he had built up a successful business. But more, much more than that, he had shown his great gifts as an organiser and his grasp of essentials that made him what he now was: one of the four biggest industrialists in Western Germany. The vast manipulations of moneys and goods to and from South America concealed, very cleverly, the fact that he was repaying his original debt by channelling a portion of the profits from that industry back into the coffers of the Kameradenwerk. Coffers that ate up the surplus much quicker now that, with advancing age, the Kameraden were forced to employ others to do what they once did themselves. Money was dispersed all over the world and in very considerable amounts. It was what made them powerful. It was what gave the Kameraden their muscle.

Once it was human muscle, that of the comrades themselves. Now it was purchased – from sympathetic persons, to be sure – but it was no longer the same, and it cost. My God! How it cost!

Ingrid walked out to join him. She was not in a good mood. She had never enjoyed the Schleiden See house. It was isolated and there were no young companions, no one but Franz and he was showing signs of possessiveness that she didn't like.

'I am very cross today. Those articles have upset me.'

Kessler grumbled to his daughter, unaware that he was inviting retaliation because of her mood.

'You're only cross because they called you elderly and regard your military rank as insignificant.'

'There were no high ranks in the Gestapo.' Kessler showed an uncharacteristic streak of indignation. 'Some of the most powerful and feared men in Germany held military ranks the equivalent of "sergeant". They could still put the fear of God into a Field-Marshal! I should never have agreed to that interview.'

'Why don't we take a holiday?'

'There is no time. We are all getting old – those of us who are left. There is still so much to do.'

'Let Reichleiter Bormann do it! He controls the money and does nothing. Does he really think a new Germany will be built by inspecting fifty dagoes who fancy themselves in SS gear?'

Kessler swung to defend what he already doubted himself. 'The Reichleiter is still our leader. He has trained many younger men to take his place when . . .'

' . . . When he drops dead groping the middle-aged señoras whose husbands are too intimidated to object? Father! Why can't you and Colonel Rückert take command? Between you you know everyone and still have faith in the Reich. The young people look up to you both. They have never even seen Bormann! Who cares about him? He was never anybody! The others were *great*. He is nothing!'

Kessler looked at her coldly, his eyes steady to make his meaning deep-felt.

'He is *ALIVE*! That is not nothing!'

Ingrid bit her tongue. She had walked right into that one, and given her father a good reason to get up and avoid the detailed confrontation that she craved. He walked away angrily, leaving his daughter on the seat furious with herself for not minding her tongue. She would get nowhere in this manner.

The Israeli girl who was watching the interchange through her binoculars wondered what was exercising them so violently, just as she wondered how she could revenge herself on the man she assumed – correctly – had ordered the execution of her friend. Hitherto she had been content to see Kessler exposed for what he was, and brought to justice. Naïve it may have been, but it was what she expected and had a right to expect. Now it was different. Ruth's murder had been deliberate and vicious. And it was recent. The taste of blood was in the air for Mical, and it is a taste that most humans recognise and act upon. The predators of this world like their blood warm. Carrion wait for it to congeal. And man is the foremost predator of them all, despite his fine sentiments and veneer of civilisation.

London received Bauer's report that Dorf had gone to earth without much show of interest. They would wait. Dorf was due in London shortly for the Trade Fair, that would mean they had him on their own cabbage patch. It crossed Gidney's mind that he would suggest that the 'department of dirty tricks' might like to have a go at Dorf and play some games, see if they could come up with proof-of-identity by more certain means, however dubious their ethics. One didn't worry too much about ethics in this business, especially if the recipient was a criminal or a Nazi. He could wait.

Bauer was unwilling to wait, and was becoming decidedly edgy with the Belgian television man. Van Eyck was playing a very one-sided game. He had come to Bonn, ostensibly to deliver, but was now equivocating for an exchange. He was after everything Bauer had found out about Kessler's financial background, about his several accounts and his overseas companies, about the sum-total of his financial status, which was considerable. Bauer was also aware of discrepancies. Money that moved and disappeared. When asked what he was to get in return, van Eyck shuffled his feet and pleaded for time 'to permit his revelations to make their full dramatic impact upon viewers'. At which point Bauer protested.

'It is the business of Government departments to apprehend political criminals. This is not a publicity stunt.'

'Stuff that, Bauer! Governments haven't given a shit for the Nazis since Nüremberg, and that was just a sanctimonious circus to go with the Marshall-plan bread. It had no possible validity in International Law.'

Bauer bit his tongue because he couldn't argue that one too closely, and contented himself by pointing out that van Eyck ran a considerable risk in sticking his neck out.

Van Eyck sniffed contemptuously.

'Risk, my ass! They wouldn't dare touch a public figure. I'm known and recognised from the Mississippi to the Mekong. They just wouldn't dare!'

It was a good exit-line and Hugo van Eyck played it like the professional he was, with all the cynicism that had grown in him. Bauer watched him go, and breathed in deeply and sadly. Pride went before a fall.

Outside the apartment block, van Eyck crossed the road, skirted the river edge, and then made to cut through the housing project and its landscaped areas to get to the car he had parked – economically – down a side turning out away from the meters.

Two children ran past him laughing and making 'whoo' noises, while others played on the paths and the blue-painted swings and slide in the playground. A few residents walked and passed the time of day. Other pedestrians used the paths as a short-cut from Bahnhofstrasse into Schillerplatz and the office blocks. Van Eyck walked between two who were chatting volubly and pointing out the site peculiarities.

The shorter of the two was swinging an umbrella which caught van Eyck's leg in passing. The little man raised his hat and apologised, and went on talking. Van Eyck muttered under his breath and walked on, for at least thirty yards before the numbness in his leg turned to pain and then to agony somewhere round his abdomen. Hugo van Eyck suddenly stopped and yelled out in anguish. Several people turned to watch as he bent and hugged himself before dropping onto the ground, and twitching in spasm for thirty-five seconds. After that he was dead.

Mical Rak selected her purchases with care. She knew something of what she was buying. She was used to sleeping out and living off the land. In the Israeli Army, and even doing their guard stint on the kibbutz, she had learned how to make do with what was to hand. She also knew about weapons and how to handle them. That much was obvious to Herr Weinsacher who served her from his considerable stock. He was not offended when she regarded most of what he offered as toys and playthings. But the shotgun was a shotgun, and the shells good enough for what she wanted. She dumped her stuff in the back of the Peugeot, and went to get in the driving seat before she realised that the car had an occupant.

It was Max Leider. He showed his credentials and invited her to get in beside him, and simply drive about the town while he talked with her. After a few minutes she felt more at ease, and recognised that he was not 'the enemy' masquerading, but was actually police, or something, and was not enamoured of the Nazis. Somehow it was comforting – even nice – to find one German who did not secretly sympathise with the old regime. He told her what he thought she was intending. He told her about Ruth's death. He was right on both counts. Where they fell out was when he tried to influence her NOT to attempt to wreak vengeance upon Dorf. As he explained to her, they too thought that Dorf was Kessler. But they couldn't prove it, and they weren't about to let her go popping off shotguns at innocent German citizens until, at least, they had proof. But there was more. More he wouldn't tell her in any detail. Just that they, the police, or intelligence, or whatever, needed Dorf alive for reasons that were important, too important to reveal and they wanted her to lay off any attempt at killing the man she knew was Kessler. Indeed they would physically stop her if they had to. But they understood her feelings, especially after Ruth's murder, and would like her to assist them for the moment.

It was a good ploy. Mical fell for it, and decided to wait for her own purposes and help the legal boys bring the criminal to trail. It appealed to her. She was essentially law-abiding. Most Jews are. The Haganah were a very small and unrepresentative body . . . all those years ago.

Leider even gave her a camera and some film. It would keep her happy and stop her thinking about using the 12 bore. It might even give them some information as a bonus. Mical agreed to work with him, but only for two or three days, after which she reserved her rights. Leider smiled and went his way.

Then he telephoned Bauer and told him about the encounter and how he had worked it out.

'She'll probably take the shotgun along with her, but I don't think she'll use it. She's a nice kid. I believe her. You'll be there, just see that she stays out of trouble and keeps off our back. Okay?'

Bauer muttered about nursemaids and suchlike things but agreed to keep a watching brief. Then he left. He, too, was making for the Schleiden See.

'Snap!'

He said it to himself as he sat perched on the branch of a pine tree and swung his binoculars round to the other side of the lake where he found someone else perched in a tree using binoculars. It was Mical. Bauer noted, when she eventually lowered them, that she really was rather pretty. Not beautiful. Not overtly sexy. But there was a sense of character in the well-formed face and a likeable litheness in the movements of the body – athletic rather than nubile – acquired in the open rather than the bedroom.

He was distracted from further observation by the arrival of another car making up the drive towards Dorf's house. This time it was a green Saab with Bavarian plates. The man who got out was a large, brutish, unsavoury customer with a broken nose, and a tweed suit any self-respecting man would have avoided.

His name was Otto Dehmel and he was one of the organis ation's heavy brigade. A man who enjoyed the violence he was paid to inflict from time to time and revelled in the intimidation that was his stock-in-trade. One of the 'employed', not the Kameraden. With the bulk went a certain predatory insolence which manifested itself as Ingrid answered the door and led him in to speak with her father. She had met him twice before and disliked the appearance, the insolence, and the body odour he did nothing to conceal.

'The man Bauer has gone away. His concierge said he went to the Schwarzwald.'

Kessler grunted. 'And the television man? Van Eyck?

Dehmel smiled egregiously. 'The police agree it was a heart attack. They're sending the body back to Belgium.'

Kessler smiled to himself. 'I'm sure they're right. An occupational hazard, I imagine.'

'I was asked to find out if you have made arrangements to travel to England.'

Kessler looked coldly at Otto Dehmel. He was not intimidated by the man's size or the source of his instructions.

'I have made my own arrangements. Franz has gone into the city to pick up tickets at this moment. My schedule I keep to myself. It is safer that way. *I* decide what I am going to do, Dehmel. It is not decided for me. If the Kameradenwerk continues to require susbstantial funds it will continue to rely upon me and others to provide it.'

It was Ingrid who was provoked into retort. 'Unless Martin Bormann can be made to release the millions he is holding somewhere. Why has no one else access to National Socialist money? It is not his own!'

'The Reichleiter will do as he sees fit. The others would only squander the fortune in unbridled living . . .'

Ingrid laughed out loud. 'In their seventies? I find their idea of unbridled living hilariously funny.'

Kessler rounded on his daughter. 'They were not always old men! The fortune is secure because the Reichleiter has not parted with either the money or access to it. I should make it quite clear that he ALONE can do nothing and I have no intention of parting with my own contribution to any intermediary.' Kessler snapped the reply before he turned to Dehmel.

'While you are here I want you to take a look around. I want maximum security, and Franz is getting slack. He spends too much time about his own affairs.'

Dehmel nodded and left the room to do as bidden. Ingrid

was still smarting from the exchange with her father. It happened regularly, especially recently. It was something unspoken in the air. She turned a peeved face towards him again.

'What's it all FOR, father? *Tell* me!'

'In good time, my dear. Please try to be patient.'

'Patient! If your Kameraden are awaiting a "second coming", father, they are going to be as disappointed as the Christians!'

It was not an angry retort. More a sad one. Kessler watched her go with mixed feelings. Mixed, because in him, too, there was the beginning of doubt. The door closed softly. It was a heavy, well-made door with a good, solid brass handle and a plate-glass fingerplate. Kessler sighed and ambled across to the window and then turned and crossed to his large mahogany desk. He slowly drew out the top centre desk drawer, and rummaged about under the top papers, extracting a large manilla envelope with card-stiffened back. His fingers gently pulled out a glassine envelope containing black and white photoprints, and he gazed at them reverently, one by one.

Despite their pristine condition, for Kessler was the sort of man who looked after everything, it was obvious they were old photographs dating from the thirties and forties. His face softened as he regarded them with infinite love and pride. They showed him, initially in shirt and breeches, being decorated by the Führer himself. Another was a casual relaxed snap of Stürmbahnführer Kessler in sharp, neat SS uniform walking down the steps from St Sulpice in Paris with a colleague. The colleague was Heydrich, and it was taken three months before the latter was assassinated in Czechoslovakia. The last two related to his Brussels period and he wore the uniform of a Standartenführer. He was THE man in the Low Countries. He knew it, they knew it, and trembled. Kessler frowned at the final picture. It was, again, a picture of himself with a colleague. That colleague was a Luftwaffe Major, Reinhardt by name, with whom he worked closely in the last year in Brussels – 1943/4.

Kessler had few regrets in his life, regrets about his own

actions and decisions, that is, but this one was a source of continual anguish to him. He had had Reinhardt shot by the firing-squad while inside a Canadian POW camp. Shot, because it seemed to him at the time it was the proper thing to do, and he and the other inmates were incensed by the news of their Führer's suicide.

Later he had rethought the matter and decided that he had been unjust to a man whose loyalty to his Fatherland was unquestioned. It was a deep regret. He had even attempted to find Reinhardt's sister to see if there was anything he could do to salve his conscience, but shrank from the encounter when he saw her in the office in which she worked. She was so physically like her brother he had not the courage nor the effrontery to face her.

Kessler sighed and replaced the photographs in his desk drawer, and crossed once again to the window overlooking the garden and the lake. It had started to rain and the reflections in the window glass were already distorted by the rivulets running down. They acted like a mesmerist's fingers and Kessler drifted away into a different time.

The shouting rang in his head, in his ears, and made his spine tingle. '*Sieg-heil*! *Sieg-heil!*' The great roaring chant reverberating through the stadium was electrifying and uplifting as nothing else had ever been. This was what being a German meant. This was the way of National Socialism. This was the path of the Führer. These were his promises, and they were there, before the eyes and ears of mankind.

'*Sieg-heil*! *Sieg-heil*!'

The flags and banners fluttered and cracked in the breeze. The eagles shone like the imagined pageants of ancient Rome. Hundreds-of-thousands of men and women, their eyes aglow with pride and intoxication in their own splendour. There had been nothing like it since the beginning of time. Rome was poor by comparison. They really WERE the Master Race. Hitler had said so . . . now he proved it. All had come to pass and the world was their oyster, decayed, degenerate . . . ripe for the plucking by those strong and masterful enough to take it.

The canker in their bosom had gone! Jews, gypsies,

decadent intellectuals, inferior peoples such as the Slavs, the blacks, they had all gone, been erased, put to proper use 'somewhere'.

The triumphal marches that crossed and recrossed his mind's eye gave way to the clatter of tanks and the thunderous march of victorious armies – German armies. Again the Führer had proved their superiority. Europe had collapsed. One by one, the Danes, the Norwegians, the Dutch, the Belgians . . . even the huge armies of France, their traditional enemy, had sued for peace. Britain had been thrown out of Europe, her pathetic army a shambles. Soon they would capitulate and then the real enemy could be attended to – Communist Russia.

Kessler smiled inside himself as he conjured up that day in May when he had been personally invited to spend the afternoon in Berchtesgaden, an honoured guest of the Führer and Eva Braun. Himmler, Goebbels, Speer were there with Senior Vice-President of the Reichsbank, Emil Johann Rudolf Puhl, and a bank clerk named Albert Thoms who had taken Kessler to one side and thence into an inner-room where Bormann, Puhl and one other whose name he had forgotten told him of their plans for his part in certain eventualities, in case all did not come out as planned. It was the very first time it had occurred to Kessler that there was even the remotest possibility that Germany could lose the war. It was the first time Kessler considered that Bormann, and others of the hierarchy, unknown to their Führer, had contingency plans 'just in case'. It came as a shock, but being a realist he was not slow to accept the sanity of the proposals, and greatly flattered that he had been selected for such responsibility – a responsibility which he knew was not misplaced. Kessler was loyal to Germany, to the party, to his Führer, and to his beliefs.

'Father, father!'

Ingrid shook his arm gently. She had seen him go into these little trances of recollection before. It was a failing of old men to move into the past and dwell therein for as long as life would permit. The rain rivulets came back into focus on the window, and he turned round to face her.

'I'm sorry, I was far away.'

'Franz is back.' Kessler glanced over her shoulder to where the younger man stood in the doorway, respectfully not entering until requested.

'I have the flight tickets and the documents, sir.'

'Good. Was there any problem?'

'No, sir, except I think there is someone down by the lake watching the house through binoculars. He was there when I left, and is still there now.'

'It's a girl.' The statement came flatly from Dehmel as he entered the room unbidden. 'D'you want me to get rid of her?'

'A girl? Not Israeli, surely?'

'Could be. I didn't get close enough to ask. You want me to attend to her?'

Kessler pursed his lips. 'Not until tomorrow. Do it immediately after we leave.'

Mical Rak, still amid the trees near the lakeside, was unaware that people in the house, people she was watching, were talking about her and plotting her demise. Neither did they, in turn, realise it was the same girl that they thought had been eliminated at the Gasthof Vilno. Bauer knew it was. He was sitting in his car enjoying the sandwiches, bierwurst, and Pilsner that he had brought with him. It had not been a rewarding day so far. The only visitors had been a messenger, immediately recognisable as such, Dehmel – who they already knew for the brainless 'heavy' that he was. It was possible that he had been responsible for the death of Ruth. The carved swastika was the sort of touch he enjoyed. Time enough to cope with Dehmel. Max had tabs on that gentleman, and no way would he leave Germany without being picked up. Franz they knew as Franz Erich Melichar-Höss. The 'Melichar' part of the name Franz himself chose to drop, calling himself Franz Erich Höss. 'Melichar' had Jewish connotations that would have prejudiced his standing with the party, even though his neo-nazi friends were less sensitive to racial impurity than their elders.

Bauer sat back in the seat of the car and sighed, contained a belch, and rewrapped the remaining comestibles for later use. If he and Max were right, something was going to happen in the next thirty-six hours. Kessler was due in London the day after that. Something had to happen before. They wanted to know what, with whom, and try to decipher 'why'.

The rain had stopped. It was a warm evening. With any luck the night would be tolerable. He wasn't tired, nor were his eyes sleepy. If anything he felt more alert than he had done for ages. Fieldwork had its drawbacks, but it kept you on your toes and contributed to physical well-being. All those lovely plus-factors had been cancelled out in two years of desk-work, made tolerable by the continued close collaboration of his old field-chum, Max Leider.

# EIGHT

The mist lay on the lake as the morning light sifted through the trees and kept a steady grey pall around the house. Bauer sat half-leaning against the bole of an ash tree, rubbing his arms and shoulders to warm himself and relieve the cramp. The single blanket he had brought was draped round his shoulders and he stamped his feet upon the bracken and pine-needled ground.

Across the lake Mical lay in her sleeping-bag, the olive drab one she had managed to pursuade the reluctant vendor to search for instead of the bright blue or orange ones strewn about his shop. Her shotgun lay by her side.

Across the lake, facing the house, Franz was warming up the Mercedes, white fumes pouring from the exhaust. Dehmel carried suitcases from the porch and placed them in the boot of the metallic-blue saloon. He glanced quickly, scanning the other bank of the lake through narrowed eyes before he returned to collect the next pair of cases. Franz slammed the bonnet-lid as he closed it. That harsh sound woke Mical who quickly grabbed her shotgun and moved off, returning immediately to collect the borrowed camera. She reached the nearer shrubbery as Kessler and his daughter emerged from the house and followed Dehmel to the car.

She watched as Kessler climbed into the back seat, then spoke to Dehmel through the open window. The latter nodded and stood back as she heard the soft whirr of the motor that raised the window. When she looked back to where the Mercedes had stood, the man had gone. No sign of Dehmel, and the house door was locked.

Kessler's car crunched softly over the damp gravel and made towards the entrance as Dehmel crept round the lake in a wide arc. He assumed that the girl, Israeli, or whatever she was, would have remained if she was serious about her surveillance. If she hadn't, she wasn't, and therefore didn't merit attention. When he rounded the last of the rhododendron bushes with leaves that seemed coated with brown suede on their underside he saw the figure lying on its stomach some hundred metres away. The green anorak was unmistakable, as was the woollen hat, and the binoculars staring at the house. Dehmel smiled to himself grimly, and worked his way round silently to come upon her from the rear.

But the ground was not quite so damp under the trees and he knew his footfall was making more noise than he would have liked. He gritted his teeth, took the Walther pistol from his pocket and screwed the silencer into the barrel, took aim over the crook of his arm, and fired, three times.

The bullets thudded into the back of the anorak quite visibly, and Dehmel straightened up, only to be knocked onto the ground as a shape fell out of the trees above him. As he raised himself the smile left his face, and a hard, vicious look swept over it. Mical, who had fallen to one side, raised the shotgun and fired both barrels into his face. He didn't have time . . . or enough throat left . . . to scream. A red, pulsating splodge dropped out of Mical's vision.

She tried not to look at what had been the face of Otto Dehmel as she went quickly and expertly through his pockets. Among other things she found his plane ticket, and the hotel resevation at the St Vincent Hotel, Mayfair, London. She stuffed most of the pocket contents into her trouser pocket, and went to collect her anorak and hat.

Bauer heard the sound of the shotgun just as he was climbing into his VW. For a moment he hesitated, unsure whether to rush back to find out what, if anything, had happened to the damned girl who was in the way all the time. But Kessler was leaving. The Mercedes had reached the entrance and unless Bauer followed quickly he would lose him. He drove off after the blue car, and switched on the radio-phone he had installed in his car. He made his call-signal, and turned onto the drive from the concealment of the undergrowth.

'Fasan . . . Fasan . . . This is Ente . . . Come in Fasan.'

Leider's voice was unmistakable. The Stuttgart accent was accentuated by the radio mike.

Bauer dropped the damned thing on the floor and tried to steer as he bent over to reach it.

'Ente . . . this is Fasan. Our birds are on the wing . . . over.'

Leider, in his own car, watched the blue Mercedes streak past him as he replied.

'They've just flown past me on One-six-three. Am following . . . over.'

He let in his clutch, and pulled out into the highway as Bauer's voice came back.

'Stay with them. I'll catch up and double with you. Over and out.'

Bauer pulled onto the main road as he switched off, and then put his foot down pushing the accelerator onto the floor of the car. The VW shot forward.

In the woods Mical pulled the bracken covering her own hire-car into a pile by the side, then got in, started the engine, and bumped and shuddered over the terrain until she, too, had reached the road.

It turned out to be Köln airport. Leider watched Kessler's Mercedes enter the Arrivals bay and park. He muttered to himself that everyone else would be forced into the crowded Departures area that did not permit parking yet had no adjoining car-park, as had the Arrivals day. Kessler's driver assisted his master and master's daughter from the car and secured porterage before he attended to the rogue vehicle that was breaking every known airport bye-law.

Inside the concourse Kessler made for the Lufthansa desk and stood to check-in for the London flight. Ingrid came to speak to him. Leider, who was watching, realised that she was not travelling with her father. At the desk itself Kessler indicated that he was hanging onto his hand-luggage and declined a label. Leider noted that he was a First Class passenger – of course. Ingrid kissed her father on the cheek and left, presumably to rejoin the car and driver. Leider stayed with his quarry who made for a seat in the departure lounge next to a man in a grey overcoat (crombie cloth and tie-belt) wearing a soft, old-style fedora. Leider crossed to the telephone bank, stuck his head under the plastic canopy, and dialled.

Kessler stared straight ahead of him, apparently unaware of the quiet voice at his elbow.

'The ticket for Zürich is on the seat at your side. You are already checked-in. I should leave when the London flight is called, but instead of the direction go to Gate Eleven and wait for the Zürich flight. You will be met.'

The man in the crombie coat stood up and walked away towards the bookstall. Kessler remained immobile. Leider watched from the phone-booth where a close observer would have seen that he was not talking into the receiver but into a walkie-talkie mouthpiece.

The gentle chimes were followed by the soft, mellifluous voice of the announcer.

'Lufthansa announce the departure of their flight LH351 to London. Will passengers please go to Gate number Seven.'

Leider turned and watched as Kessler picked up the folded newspaper at his side and held it with his small case as he walked towards the Gate entrance and turned with the other passengers for the short walk to the departure gate.

Bauer, in another phone booth outside the building, where he had watched Ingrid get into the Mercedes with Franz and drive away from the airport, heard the reported movements of Kessler relayed by Leider, then hung-up his walkie-talkie receiver, detached the actual phone, and dialled an overseas call.

After a moment a voice answered in English.

Bauer replied in English, 'Four-two-seven-six, please. Thank you.'

The voice that was eventually heard was Deakin's.

'Richard Bauer . . . Bonn. Yes, our subject has just left Köln on Lufthansa Flight Number LH351 for London, Heathrow. No sir, it was a pleasure. Er . . . look . . . I am on suspension at the moment. They call it "leave", but it isn't. I would like to come to London and follow it through. Does that go against anything you have in mind? . . . Fine . . . No. I will make contact . . . I look forward to it . . . Thank you.'

# NINE

The black taxi-cab drew up outside the very superior Hotel St Vincent. One of those exclusive hotels in which London and the European capitals excel. Not too large, not too obvious. The St Vincent was obviously a hotel – not like some in Paris and Rome that one had to know about, have an introduction to, in fact, before venturing between the portals. It was very expensive.

Kessler stepped out and paid the driver without looking at him. The Commissionaire attempted to take Kessler's small case, a service firmly, but politely, resisted by the older man.

Inside the entrance, by the reception desk, Ingrid was sitting anxiously awaiting the arrival of her father who had left Köln exactly three flights before she did, and was only arriving in the hotel now. There were guests on the stairs, in the lifts, and in the corridors, so that she did not give vent to her worry and frustration until the door of the room was closed behind them.

At the exact time Kessler checked into his hotel, British Airways flight 259 was taking off from Bonn Airport and heading towards London. In the forward, non-smoking part of the Economy area, Mical Rak sat with her book open on her lap. She wasn't reading. She was weighing up in her mind what to do next. She knew where Kessler was staying, or rather, she knew where the man, Dehmel, who she had killed, was supposed to be staying. But what to do? It is not all that easy to shoot a man in the streets of London – not if you intend to get away with it. There were problems.

Franz brought the drinks to the table in the corner. He and Ingrid had been prevented from talking openly because some woman in a ferocious, floral-print dress had sat down at the table they were using in the lounge and showed no sign of moving. When the corner was vacated they moved.

Ingrid was uptight. Franz knew that boded ill for any love-making that night.

'Franz, my father is taking money with him. I don't mean in his pockets but arranging transfers. I know about his own money. That is transferred the same way as always. But there's something else. It's just different! Did you know he has transferred a million marks from his own account. That implies he intends to stay wherever he is going . . . at least for some time.'

'What about the factories? . . . and the house?'

Ingrid made a curious face. 'There was a time when I assumed he would leave all that to me. I would be very rich, and very powerful, sought after by all the jet-set as a suitable spouse . . . I know that isn't the case now. Oh, he will see that I am well cared for. He loves me. I know that. But there is something he loves more and is waiting for . . .'

Franz grunted as he downed his whisky. 'It won't come from that bunch in South America!'

'I am frightened that it will not come at all.'

Ingrid paused, she did not want to give voice to the thought inside her, that her father was actually ready to move the great Nazi fortune that they had all heard about, yet knew nothing about. She and her young friends feared that when the old guard died access to the fabled moneys would go with them. It would sit in the Zürich vaults and accrue interest over the years like the wealth of the Czars, for ever and ever, amen.

'If you think I am going to take on the Kameradenwerk you can think again.'

'You're frightened of them!'

'Too damn right, I am! Anyone who isn't, is a fool. They may be old men but they have long arms – younger arms – and they are everywhere!'

'They play games . . .'

'So they are old man playing games but it's one hell of a game, and they're good at it. Oh boy . . . are they good!'

Ingrid glowered at him. 'So are we!'

Franz looked at her, his grey-blue eyes fearful and urging her to take it easy. 'Ingrid . . . we are amateurs! They have an organisation IN DEPTH! It goes back, layer after layer. D'you know who is one of them, and who isn't? I don't. But THEY do. It's like something that is branded into them. Something not quite normal. Bigger than life. It scares the hell out of me! And I work for them.'

Ingrid didn't reply. She remained quiet as they drank. She was silent and uncommunicative throughout the meal with her father. They ate in the hotel, which had an excellent restaurant, but nothing seemed able to give her appetite. Kessler assumed that she was still piqued with him over the deception of the Zürich flight. It would wear off.

Bauer was met at Heathrow not by Deakin whom he had expected, but by Commander Gidney. They had spoken twice on the phone but otherwise knew little of each other.

'I hope you don't mind me meeting you instead of Tom Deakin, but now that you've all arrived in the jolly old UK it is really my lobby. We've got your man under surveillance, though he wasn't on that wretched plane, the one you said.'

Bauer looked at him quizzically. Gidney continued in the dry, rather bored voice he affected.

'No, anyway he was spotted arriving in Zürich. I like the Swiss, you know. People say things about them. We've found them very helpful. He had some business at a Bank.'

Gidney looked out of the cab window and muttered something about the traffic piling up that might affect his homeward journey that evening, then continued.

'One of the first things he did when he arrived in London was to trot along to the city. To Becker and Seeburg, London Wall. We found he has quite a lot of assets in the UK . . . about three-and-a-half million quid in DM's actually. I could use that sort of money myself. Curious thing was that, as late as last week, that was *all* it was. As of three hours ago it was nineteen million. Interesting isn't it?'

Bauer withheld the whistle in his mouth . . . when in Rome . . He glanced at Gidney.

'Old Nazi money from Swiss banks?'

'Could be, dear boy, could be. Personally I think not.'

'He may try to move it.'

Gidney turned a disbelieving look upon the German.

'Wouldn't be a lot of point in watching it if he didn't, would there? No . . . you see . . . WE think it's on its way to swell the coffers of the dear old Kameradenwerk. Question is, where?'

'Do you know where Kessler is?'

Gidney gave him another of his curious glances.

'Didn't I say? How remiss of me. The St. Vincent, Upper Berkeley. You probably know it. His daughter is with him and a rather pretty young Aryan chap. He's with *her*, I fancy . . . but you can never tell these days.'

Bauer sensed all was not on the table and caught a slight evasive inflection in Gidney's manner.

'You aren't being quite open with me, Commander. Are you?'

Gidney grunted rather than blustered, and looked once more at Bauer as if to size him up. Apparently the consideration had been favourable as Gidney sniffed noisily and continued.

'Look here, Bauer. There is a bit of a problem. Her Majesty's Government are not in any way committed to the pursuit of War Criminals. It's all too far back in the dim distance to bring any votes today. But we like to keep our files up-to-date.'

Bauer assumed by the 'we' Gidney was referring to MI5.

'We can't officially do anything, but we will nibble a bit round the edges . . . just to see what's in the centre, if you follow me. Our Great Panjandrum thinks it would be a good idea if we encouraged YOU and gave whatever help . . . on the side . . . that we could legitimately give within the confines of our brief.'

Bauer recognised that the situation graphically described by his American friends as 'the eight-ball' was upon him. He smiled to himself. These British, charmingly hypocritical as ever.

'What d'you want me to do?'

Gidney beamed as he would to a player who had agreed to go in to bat first. 'Good man! We're after the Johnny who runs the Kameradenwerk. We think we know who it is. I'm sure you think *you* know who it is. We can't prove it, and he is too well-known to risk a scandal. Kessler will lead us to him, one way or another, and one way or another we will nail him *in flagrante delicto*.'

The remainder of the journey was passed in small talk and inconsequential shop talk. Gidney took him to a small short-let apartment they had rented for him just off Portman Square, and handy for most things . . . especially surveillance on Kessler which was about to commence for Bauer. It had already commenced for Mical Rak.

This time her hire car was a small white Fiat. When she objected the Hertz people assured her that in Britain there were more WHITE Fiats on the roads than any other colour. She hadn't time to argue or go elsewhere. Time was of the essence.

That white car was her undoing. She should have listened to the voice inside her that said 'pick another colour'.

Franz was taking delivery of their own hire car, which just happened to be white. He had been called by the reception desk to come down and sign the hire form, check out the vehicle, and pick up the keys. He was outside looking at the car, noting a small scratch down one of the rear doors when his attention was caught by another white car parked across the road from the hotel where the driver was attempting to feed a parking meter. Instantly he recognised the girl who had temporarily crippled him in Krefeld. You don't forget those sort of things. Not overnight. He signed the form and turned away, walked back towards the hotel entrance, and ran up the stairs to the room occupied by Kessler.

Kessler was hanging a jacket in the wardrobe when Franz was told to enter.

'Well?'

'Herr Dorf, the Israeli girl. The one from the house, she is outside this hotel, watching.'

Kessler snorted, and didn't even bother to turn round.

'Nonsense, man. The girl was eliminated.'

Ingrid was writing a short note by the window when her father made the admission. Something she had not known. There was a cold callousness about the remark that suddenly gave meaning to Franz's comment of the previous evening. Yes. There was reason to be fearful of the Kameraden. Even her own father.

Franz was not to be put down. 'With respect, sir. It was I who was in direct personal contact with this girl. I have no doubt that this is the same girl.'

When Franz stood up to his employer there was a very good reason. Reason to believe that he might be right. Kessler looked at him, and Franz held the look. Kessler then crossed to the bedside phone and lifted the receiver. He waited for the hotel desk to reply.

'Seven-eight-two . . . three-four-six-three.' He waited patiently until he heard Rückert's voice answer.

'Provider, here. There is a problem. The Israeli girl has reappeared. Apparently not. It may have been the wrong one. I wish to deal with it, now.'

Rückert considered, then gave permission for Kessler to act upon his own initiative. Kessler turned to Franz.

'Give me the car keys. It is ME she is after, I think, then *I* must be the decoy.'

Kessler walked to the lift and pressed the button. When it came it was half-full of guests returning from lunch. Several spoke German. It was, after all, a favourite hotel with West Germans of means. Even the receptionists spoke German as a second language, flawlessly. In England that was something

Without looking to left or right Kessler crossed the foyer, nodded discreetly to the doorman and stepped out into the early afternoon sunshine. He stood a moment as if taking the air. Long enough for anyone watching to see him without fail. It would be most unlikely for any potential assassin to shoot him on the steps of the hotel. Even so, Kessler was pleased to note that his courage did not fail him. He had always been able to keep a cool head and discipline any fear that might have risen to loosen the bowels of a weaker man. His grey well-cut Savile Row suit testified to his status and his white hair gave him dignity. Franz had told him where the white car was parked and where to look for Mical. He saw her out of the corner of his eye, hovering, about to get into her own car yet not doing so.

He walked to the hire car and fumbled with the key, watched intently by Mical. Too intently, for she entirely missed Franz coming up from behind until she suddenly felt the hard tip of the gun muzzle in her back, and heard the whispered word to walk ahead of him and get into the car, the door of which was now being held open for her by a smiling Kessler.

He got in after her and held her firmly, with her face in the upholstery until she felt the sharp prick of a needle in her forearm. Within seconds she passed into oblivion.

She woke heavy-headed to see and feel movement over rough ground. The car edged past a large sign stating that the site was being developed by Dorf Industries Ltd – Chemical Division – and would provide employment for eight thousand workers. A boon to the area, obviously. She did not notice the site watchman walking towards the car which had stopped, but she heard the door click shut after Franz got out and explained to the watchman that Herr Dorf was interested in one of the new construction techniques and had come to see for himself. Kessler nodded politely to the man as he glanced across at the car and touched his cap

The car lurched forward again over the rough ground, and eventually came to a stop outside a semi-finished building that would, eventually, become a laboratory testing-unit. Mical was dragged inside and thrown down into the corner by some crates, still metal-tied and showing their straw packing. She wanted to scream, and then realised it was not the numbness of the injection inhibiting her, but a large piece of sticking-plaster across her mouth.

Mical's recollection of the next two hours was hazy. She knew she had been beaten, punched, and mishandled . . . she knew she had been questioned about her accomplices and said . . . as far as she remembered . . . nothing at all. Then it was all vague until she felt repeated pricks in her arm and consciousness left her.

In the hotel Ingrid waited with the newly-arrived Colonel Rückert. He had been visiting a Bomber squadron of the RAF as their honoured guest. He had been wined and dined, and swopped stories with the older officers who remembered the war days. Had been fêted as the legend he was by the young men, and charmed them all, as he always did by his natural dignity, his humour, and his willingness to let bygones be bygones and embrace his old opponents. Hans Rückert was a success wherever he went. Even the artificial arm and lower leg lent him a mystique shared only by one or two others – most of whom were there to greet him.

He had left after dinner, and was now waiting for Kessler.

'I do not understand, Colonel. We thought Otto Dehmel was taking care of the girl at the house by the lake. Are you saying it was the same girl that father thought had been eliminated earlier?'

'I am saying exactly that. She is a formidable lady, this Israeli. Otto Dehmel is dead. His body was found in the woods by your father's house, more or less minus his face. We must assume this girl is not as helpless as she might sound . . . or that she is not operating alone.'

'But why should she be after my father?' Ingrid was upset, and showed it. She was beginning to worry about her father. 'He is of no consequence to the Jews. He was not one of the racial tormentors. He never baited Jews.'

'I agree.' Rückert was as puzzled as she was for a proper reason. He checked his wristwatch then stood up. 'I will be in touch later, I will not be available at the number he has until after seven tomorrow morning.'

Ingrid nodded as he turned to go, then spoke quietly but firmly.

'Colonel. Why won't you work with my friends? We need your guidance.'

Rückert turned at the door and looked at her. That was all. He said nothing, just looked, coldly, and without a flicker of recognition. Then he left.

The bars had closed on St Katherine's Dock and the night-life seekers had moved into the West End before the white car slid silently down the lane towards the river. The black, oily waters moved and occasionally rippled against the dark timbers of the jetty. Kessler assisted Franz as he lifted the slumped form of the Israeli girl from the rear seat of the car and unceremoniously tipped her into the river.

The splash was surprisingly slight. She almost slid under the surface and was whisked away downstream into the darkness.

Kessler sat in the front of the car this time. Franz lit a cigarette and Kessler decided he too would smoke before they moved on.

'She will simply drown. In that drugged state she has no chance. The marks on her arm will indicate to the police, when they eventually fish her out, that she was an addict and fell in the water while incapacitated.' Kessler paused. 'That leaves only the man Leider, whoever he may be. She was unclear about that. Police, perhaps, but I would imagine a colleague of the other one . . . what was his name? Bauer, Baum, or something. I will telephone Bonn when we get back to the hotel.'

He nodded to Franz, who started the car and quietly crept back onto the road that circled the Tower and led back through the city

# TEN

The first thing that Mical Rak remembered with any clarity was sitting inside the tiny cabin of the Police River-launch, wrapped in a couple of blankets, and having hot coffee and brandy poured down her throat by none-too-gentle hands. They did not want to be rough but this was urgent.

Vomiting had brought up most of the filthy, oily river water, the scum of which held greater danger for the girl than the volume of water she had swallowed. A combination of circumstances had contributed to saving her life. First, the fact that she was drugged to unconsciousness meant that her breathing was minimal. Second, his care for neatness and propriety had made Kessler instinctively zip up her track-suit and pull the sleeves to wrist-length where the elastic held. It meant that she went into the water with a quantity of air trapped inside a near airtight suit. She remained on the surface. Thirdly, a greater knowledge of London's river would have told Kessler that they had picked an area near the HQ of the Port of London Authority, and one that was patrolled of necessity with great regularity.

She had, in fact, been in the water less than four minutes.

Bauer's phone rang in the furnished apartment he now called 'home'. This time he gave nothing away and answered with a simple, 'Yes?'

Gidney identified himself, 'Did you know that the Israeli girl, Rak, was in London?'

Bauer was suitably surprised. 'No. Has she made contact?'

Gidney's sigh was audible. 'Not exactly. The police have just hauled her out of the river, alive, but only just. It would appear that she had been doped and dumped.'

'I suppose you are ruling out local criminals? London does have mugging doesn't it?'

'Don't really believe that, do we? Anyway, I'm sending her round to you. You'd better keep an eye on her in future.'

There was no opportunity to protest. Gidney hung up with alacrity. Obviously he intended to avoid protests from anyone.

That attitude was shared by Kessler on re-entering his hotel where he immediately crossed to the bathroom to wash his hands. Old habits never die. Ingrid had often wondered if her father was merely hypersensitive to soiled hands or whether or not it had a deeper significance for him. The Pilate syndrome.

'You're sure about her now?'

'The way to be sure is to do it oneself. I am sure.'

Kessler dried his hands on the small handtowel bearing the hotel initials. Ingrid took the opportunity to nag her father yet again, and unforgivably bring in the attitudes of her mother. Kessler never accepted that and dismissed his daughter roughly. Enough to make her seek consolation from the ever-willing Franz in his own room.

The arrival of the ambulance caused no stir. Neighbours seemed not to notice, and the depositing of Mical was carried out in quiet and the minimum of fuss. Bauer stood in the background unobtrusively, and said little. It wasn't his place to. He was a guest in the country and, for the moment, at least, in MI5's debt for the apartment. He watched in silence as she was placed in the bed in the tiny bedroom. Mentally he reconciled himself to the settee for several nights.

'Is she all right?'

'No. She isn't. They've been rather unpleasant about it and very expert. She is badly bruised and will experience considerable pain. Our medics were concerned about possible internal rupture, though there are no broken bones. X-rays seem to imply she's got away with it.'

'Is she still drugged?'

'No, again. That's our people's sedation. She should be coming out of it shortly.' Gidney handed Bauer a paper bag he was carrying awkwardly. 'Top her up fairly regularly. Hot toddy. D'you have that sort of thing in Germany?'

'I don't . . .'

Gidney made a noise as if to say 'these bloody foreigners don't know anything'.

'Hot milk with a goodly splash of whisky, put in some sugar. Honey's better, if you have it. Personally I like it with a touch of cinnamon . . . Langdales?' But he sensed it was hopeless, and muttered only that Bauer should keep an eye on her and keep her out of the bloody way – for good.

'Her belongings imply she is not short of money and the supply of travellers' cheques is what one might term "goodly". Buy her a ticket for Tel Aviv and send her on her way, there's a good chap.'

Mical actually surfaced some half-hour after they left. Her first reaction was one of excruciating pain. She moved. The gasp she uttered brought Bauer running from the other room. She looked up at him with just a touch of fear in her eyes.

'You're quite safe. Don't worry and don't move. You'll be all right, but it will take a few days in bed.'

'I can't stay in bed!'

'Suit yourself.' Bauer sensed it was the appropriate attitude to take, as indeed it was. Mical tried to move and promptly fell back on the pillow with a cry.

'I did warn you. Look, there's nothing to worry about. I shall be in the other room. Your clothes have been washed and are drying . . .'

'My clothes?' Suddenly she realised she was naked under the hospital dressing-gown she was wearing, and blushed slightly. That, if anything, endeared her to Bauer. It was the first thing that had. He, like Gidney, wished her miles away, and that quickly. He looked at her face, pale and taut under her natural tan, and decided the time for a helpful overture had arrived. He returned a few moments later with a mugful of hot milk and whisky, with sugar.

'I'm told this is a British panacea for all ills. Smells good. Come on . . . knock it back while it's hot. Apart from the cold you can get pneumonia from shock. Did you know that?'

Mical obediently sipped her toddy, and nodded like a

subdued child. Bauer noted that her eyes were heavy again. Sleep would heal more than he could. Best to leave her.

It was after nine the following morning that Mical joined the living world again. Again Bauer was at the bedside with a tray of breakfast things. He smiled down at her and offered the tray.

'English breakfast? Bacon, eggs, toast, marmalade? The coffee is really good. I made it with beans I ground myself.' Bauer looked childishly proud of the achievement. Why not? He spent half his life making coffee, or so it seemed, but had never bought himself a grinder.

The enthusiasm was enough to convince Mical that even if she was not really ready for such a repast at nine in the morning she would, at least, make the effort, if he would help her to sit up. He did, gently and with consideration . . . but in doing so the dressing-gown parted several inches and revealed something of her body. Bauer could not help noticing, and his face registered the anger he felt. The poor girl's flesh was black and purple in appalling patches, not yet yellowing, but viciously angry in appearance. Whoever had done it had meant to hurt. She saw his eyes on the bruises, and blushed once again.

'I'm sorry . . .'

'My God! They certainly did you over. Was it meant to make you talk?'

'Yes. And I did, I think. I don't remember very much, but I think I told them what they wanted to know.'

'Which was?'

'That I was not part of an Israeli organisation. But I seem to remember I sensed what they were frightened of . . . and I added several names for good measure. I told them about that television man . . . van Eyck and my cousin, Adam Giered and a German policeman called Leider, anybody.'

Bauer looked quickly at her. 'You mentioned the name Leider?'

'Yes, I think so. Do you know him?'

'Yes. Yes, I do.'

Bauer was pensive for a moment, working out the possible repercussions of that statement.

'Following Kessler is a dangerous business.'

Mical stopped eating and looked at him. 'Is that what you're doing?'

He nodded. But she came back, 'Are you Jewish, too?'

'No. I'm not. As a matter of fact I'm German.'

He went into the whole bit. Perhaps, if he was honest, to proclaim to a Jew that all Germans were not inherently anti-Semitic, and really did want to set the record straight. She accepted it, with reservations no doubt, and went on to tell him of her own background of how her parents died, how her family were killed. Why, in fact, she was there. Bauer still wanted her off his back . . . but he understood and sympathised. The mid-twentieth century was no time to be a Jew. Is there ever a time? The State of Israel changed nothing. It was a home, a refuge, to which they had a tenuous right, but one day . . . one day . . . there would come the reckoning. Mical knew that, as did every thinking citizen of that State. They got to know each other enough to accept each other's reasons and to be free of strain.

Max Leider had considered the implications of Dorf being out of the country, with his daughter, his man-of-all-work, and doubtless others he knew nothing about. Colonel Rückert had also gone abroad. The police were not all that imaginative but they were thorough. It occurred to Leider that, as no one who held authority was about, it might be a propitious time to do a little exploring. Then someone found the body of Otto Dehmel.

It was Max's opportunity. He arrived at the Schleiden See house with the police who wanted to make their routine checks. The elderly housekeeper, Frau Gerhardt, made the journey from the village specially to let the police look around the house. It was something she could not properly avoid.

There was one man, separate from the others, who seemed to have special authority. He wanted to probe around the rooms. Why? Frau Gerhardt reasoned that if a man was killed in the grounds, searching the bedrooms was an unnecessary extension of duty, and argued either un-German enthusiasm, or something quite different. But, then, she couldn't object without casting suspicion somewhere and implying there was something to hide.

But she watched Max as he solemnly opened every drawer and cupboard and went through desk papers and took some of them out. She didn't like that. They were private papers belonging to Herr Dorf. Herr Dorf would really not like it either. He was a very private man, and he was a very important man. Frau Gerhardt respected him enormously. Her late husband had been an officer in the old SS – lovely men! So strong and handsome in their uniforms. It wasn't like that any more, and more's the pity. This man Schmidt seemed all right but he didn't have the panache of the old ones. Even Adenauer had something German about him. Schmidt could be anyone. Hitler had it . . . Ah, the Führer had everything! Frau Gerhardt mentally sighed, and peeked through the crack in the doorway. That policeman was going through the desk again. He was lifting the papers and feeling about underneath. Perhaps Herr Dorf had things he wished to hide. She would speak to Herr Deputy Direktor Maurer, who visited from time to time.

Max Leider found the envelope under the papers. He knew it was important, and he knew that he was at risk. His own sixth sense warned him. After leaving the house he went into the village where he knew the local policeman. He was seen leaving half-an-hour later, and posted an envelope about ten inches by eight.

It was two hours later that Max Leider's body was found in a burnt-out car on a side road leading away from Bonn. The men responsible had also persuaded the postman to permit them to retrieve a largish manilla envelope they had inadvertently posted in error. It was found to contain photoprints, and was addressed to a Mister Arkwright in Central London, *Poste Restante,* Trafalgar Square.

Mr. Arkwright never did call at the Trafalgar Square Post Office. He was going to, but made a duty call upon Tom Deakin in Whitehall on the way. Gidney was there with him.

Indeed it was Gidney's office they used. He was a stickler for the proprieties. It was an MI5 matter now that it had all come into his backyard, and MI6 were only involved as a matter of courtesy.

But it was MI6's news that shook and saddened Bauer as he accepted the cup of tea offered with condolences. His hand shook slightly when they told him of Leider's death. They also handed him a white envelope containing photoprints which had been handed in less than twenty minutes earlier by their courier from Germany. That envelope had been handed to him at Köln airport by one of their German people who had got it from the German police, who had in turn received it from the hands of a village policeman. It had been one of a pair of envelopes with identical contents – photocopies that he, the village policeman, had made for Herr Leider. He was an amateur photographer and an old friend. There was also a report handed in by the local postman that an envelope addressed '*Poste Restante*, Trafalgar Square Post Office, London', had been claimed back by two men. The German reports were quick and thorough, and Bauer received that compliment with mixed feelings.

The photographs had already been scrutinised by MI6 before being handed over. There was no doubt any longer in anyone's mind. Manfred Dorf WAS Ludwig Kessler, late of Hitler's SS. Leider's sacrifice had given them that much.

Gidney now began to question Bauer about Mical. She was progressing . . . she was recovering quicker than hoped. She was a delightful young lady, and no, there was nothing developing between them, and all the proprieties had been observed.

The *Poste Restante* desk in the Trafalgar Square office is situated at one end of the several counter positions. It was perfectly possible to read a paper, fill in countless telegram forms, or even football pools, while keeping a weather eye on the counter. The manilla envelope had been forwarded (less contents) and the surveillance was round-the-clock. After three days no one had come to claim that envelope. Rückert decided that it was time to reassess the situation. Something was amiss It was also about this time that Kessler felt the hairs on the back of his neck stand up from time to time. An old feeling. He knew it well. 'Pilot' and 'Provider' met in the hotel room once again. They were short and to the point. Kessler was addressing the international delegates to the Trade Fair that afternoon, as Herr Dorf, of Dorf Industries, of course. Only one London paper had bothered to question the TV disclosure about Dorf/Kessler. Nobody cared. It was all a long time ago, and even Nazis have to live.

That meeting voiced the doubts and thoughts of both men. Kessler complained that he was being followed. That his hotel was under surveillance. He felt it. That was enough.

The conclusion drawn was that authority was moving its leaden feet, shuffling – perhaps no more — but there was activity, and that boded no good for anyone. The uncollected envelope gave strength to the argument. The contents they had intercepted were prints, after all, copies, by implication. Rückert decided the time had come to call upon old British friends in high places and sound out the ground. One evening was enough. James Croggan, who was 'involved' with the Home Office, quickly imparted the information that MI5 were interested in one of Rückert's compatriots. Not a respected Luftwaffe chap like him, of course, but one of those wretched Nazi fellows we had all thought dead and forgotten.

It was enough. Rückert passed on the information he had gleaned, and made his plans. Kessler was persuaded that if the matter were being investigated, however cursorily, by British Intelligence, for whatever reasons, the net result could well be searches instituted by the German Federal Republic because public and world opinion would force their hand. It was not acceptable. It was to be avoided by evading it.

Every vehicle parked outside the St Vincent hotel was a potential surveillance vehicle. Every waiter and bell-hop was a member of MI5, or should be regarded as such. Once more Kessler's room in the hotel was the scene of a meeting, but this time Rückert brought with him a detection device for bugs and other electronic equipment. He swept the suite before a word was uttered. Only one device was found, and that in the bedside telephone. It re-routed calls incoming, and recorded those outgoing, but it did not eavesdrop. Kessler wheeled the trolley of tea-things out into the corridor, and turned on the radio as an added precaution. He and Rückert crossed to the open window and looked out over the trees and fine houses of Mayfair. Rückert reprimanded Kessler for keeping his photographs. They had sentimental value, nothing else, and Kessler should have known better. They had now been burned, but there was ever the suggestion that at least one other set of prints had been sent. Whoever had them KNEW Kessler and Dorf were one and the same. The decision to move was taken. It had to be. The Kameraden were at risk once more as was their 'Provider'. Together they would make escape, continuity, and eventual triumph possible.

Mical risked a short walk on the fourth day. She was still in some pain, but the bruises were no longer tender, and the discoloration not as bizarre as had been envisaged. A friendship between her and Bauer had developed. Bargains had been privately agreed. Attitudes exchanged. She had made no attempt to leave and pursue her vendetta. He was solicitous and reported the greater part of what he had done, what he had found, what their quarry was about. Only the visiting Rückert had been logged. Every other move Kessler made was either personal shopping, banking business, or connected with the Trade Convention. He had given no indication that anything other than his business interests occupied him. The reported loss of Leider had been confirmed by telephone enquiry to Bonn, to mutual friends. Bauer kept his sorrow and sense of loss to himself. Mical sensed his grief but avoided the issue and Bauer was grateful for that.

The morning of the Tuesday saw Bauer admitted to the entrails of MI5's administrative block. After he had shown his identification and signed some forms he was eventually shown to Gidney's sanctum. After the muttered exchanges Gidney told of their own surveillance progress, and how the matter was moving out of MI5's hands into more lofty circles, and might, just might, be a matter to be raised with the German Ambassador. He could report that Deakin had been informed by one of his people in the right place in German Government circles that the Israeli Embassy had been mollified following their not unnatural concern over the death of Miss Liebermann. All was quiet, if on the edge of the hob, but no longer simmering.

'By the way . . . where is your . . . er . . Israeli lady friend at this moment? Would you know?'

'She's gone shopping. We do have to eat, you know Supplies had run out over the last few days. Time to restock.'

'I shouldn't get yourself overloaded. My instinct says that our friends are ready to move. We have hinted that they are being watched. We let them find a bug or two, and tailed them obviously. I think they have the message.'

The telephone rang. Gidney frowned after answering and looked accusingly at Bauer. His tone was of indescribable surprise.

'It's for you!'

Bauer took the call . . . went pale . . . asked a few pertinent questions, and then swallowed hard before returning the instrument to its cradle.

'I really do not think you should have given this number Bauer. It's not on, you know . . . May one enquire who, and what?'

Richard Bauer looked directly at him. 'It was Mical. Miss Rak . . . the Israeli girl. She was telephoning from Orly Airport, in Paris. I gather she had followed Kessler and his daughter to Heathrow . . . managed to board a shuttle behind them . . . and is about to take a flight to Buenos Aires after them.'

Gidney's face fell. 'Good God!'

# PART TWO

# A Place in the Sun

# ELEVEN

Mical looked down from the window seat of the Boeing 707 The city below was Asuncion, the capital city of Paraguay with a population around quarter-of-a-million. Sandwiched between Bolivia, Argentina and Brazil, Paraguay had some of the emptiest, most forbiding territory in Latin America. Flying north from Buenos Aires over Santa Fe and the Corrientes the low-lying marshes and jungle areas give it a lushness from the air that gives way to the pitiless plateau that becomes the Mato Grosso of Central Brazil. North of Asuncion one could see an area of dry, desert scrubland – the Bahias and the Alazar.

The thunk of the undercarriage dropping and locking comforted Mical. The old 707 was a luxury she had not expected. Warned of the DC8s flown between Asuncion and Montevideo by a well-meaning traveller trying to appear seasoned she had accepted the 707 flight to Bogota, via La Paz and Asuncion, as an omen. Now below her stretched the city where she hoped to find Kessler and his colleagues. Enquiries at Buenos Aires had elicited the information that Herr Dorf and his family were flying to Asuncion by private, chartered, executive plane. She had watched them being driven out to the small expensive turbo-prop job and seen it take off. There was a chance she would find Kessler again, but it was a chance, no more, until she found that her 707 commercial scheduled flight would arrive at Asuncion at roughly the same time that the executive taxi did. Despite the lag in time before her take-off the jet speed of the scheduled flight would catch up.

The descent was smooth, the touch-down hairy. Not the pilot's incompetence she realised very quickly. The runway was like the suspension test-course for Range Rovers. There was even a four metre hollow in the tarmac which felt like the Boeing was on its knees suddenly. Then it was over and soon the disembarking passengers shuffled down the tin steps onto the baking ground of Paraguay. The heat of the atmosphere hit you like a hot flush as soon as the exit hatch swung open.

President Stroessner Airport was neat enough, a little too big for its own importance, and riddled with police who all seemed to suffer from weak eyesight . . . or had seen too many movies. Their dark glasses, unmoving pose, and facial expression were a cliché within ten seconds of rounding the palm-studded, wire-fenced terrace, but there it stopped. Everything stopped. Only one small door was open with only one man officiating. The luggage was piled onto trailers and disappeared into tin mouths with bits of leather hanging loose. The Guardia, or whatever it was called, was divided into two distinct, uniformed organisations. Mical reasoned that one was Polizia, one Militar. You could guess which was which, the Polizia were greyer, the Militar khakier. Equally uninviting.

The line shuffled forward towards the door. The heat intensified. The gasoline fumes became stronger and more pervading. Heads turned to watch another scheduled flight land. This time it was a DC8, and it bounced.

Then a private jet – a two seater with room for six dogs and maybe a racehorse – taxied to a prominent place on the apron where it was met by airport officials. Then it was Mical's turn to get out of the heat into the shade of the building, except that it was hotter inside than out. Somewhere down the concourse there had to be a restaurant. The smell of tortillas and chilli sauce was unnerving, especially when it was tempered by an equally virulent, intensely sweet perfume forced into the atmosphere through the air-conditioning vents. Eventually Mical was only six away from the military gentleman who was perusing passports so intensely. And that was when she saw the executive taxi coming to a halt on the apron. She recognised the plane and mentally urged the wretched Passport Control to speed up and let her through in time to rent a car and tail whatever vehicle picked up Kessler. Through the tinted glass of the window facing the apron she saw Kessler and Ingrid being assisted from the small aircraft by Franz, as a large Dodge sidled up to the plane and stood waiting. A Customs Officer with manifest-papers and clipboard saluted respectfully and smiled his acquiescence to whatever the wealthy German people desired. He did not even glance at their bags, but saluted again and held the door of the car open. Mical couldn't move back or forward and just had to watch helplessly as the Dodge sped along the edge of the apron and disappeared from her view. An hour later she was still waiting for her rucksack to come trundling round the luggage-conveyor and end up on the carousel. When it did she had another hour to wait until the Rent-A-Car people returned to their desk and told her they didn't have a car available that week or the next: 'You see, señorita, it is the Ascension, the Fiesta of the City.'

Like most of the cities of Central and Western South America, Asuncion divided into two sections. A reasonably affluent business community, with stores, city streets, public transport and most civic and community facilities which rapidly petered out into streets that wound through old areas and recent rehousing, which already looked part of its period neighbourhood. Overhead-wiring, whether electrical or telephonic, is the disease of Latin America. Nobody puts wires underground, so there is a permanent network of cables down every street and on every wall. The taste among the poor is for bright colouring – you can't blame them for that – and regular painting of walls hides the cracks, the peeling plaster, and the bits that somehow never got finished by the civic authority. The cobbled streets alternated with trodden earth, but the narrow twisting lines of humble dwellings were relieved here and there by decorative iron balconies, brackets, and street lamps from a more elegant age. The churches were fine, mostly of warm stone that held the sun's heat and didn't disintegrate too quickly. Traffic was elderly by European standards, and largely of American or German manufacture. A Military Zone terminated the spread in one direction, industrial development in another. The River Paraguay divided at Asuncion, or if you prefer, the capital was the junction of two rivers, which eventually flowed on through Argentina into the estuary of the River Plate.

The beauty of Paraguay to Germans seeking asylum was primarily the welcome of its regime, and the fact that huge areas of the north and west of the country were almost inaccessible and unpopulated. When you are pursued by zealots that matters.

Mical was not overly impressed by the outer appearance of the Hotel El Paradiso, but the tiny square opposite – the Plaha de Piedra – was charming. The hotel had been suggested to Bauer by Tom Deakin, implying that it was a useful place for visiting policemen who wanted to remain undercover, and he had communicated the address to Mical, and agreed to join her there as soon as he could organise his own transport, probably a day behind her.

Mical opened the door and stepped into the cool of a small hall, with a tiled floor and a central winding metal staircase. A staircase that was really a fire escape painted white and pale blue, but served adequately to get its guests to their rooms on the two floors above. Apart from a desk cum counter the hall was unfurnished. Behind the counter, sitting back in a cheap swivel-chair reading a much-thumbed paperback, and resting his head against the telephone switchboard which looked at least eighty years old, sat the proprietor, José Garriga. Garriga was slightly swarthy, of average build, and sported a neatly trimmed moustache on his upper lip. He turned to see Mical and remained with his mouth half-open as she approached.

'Señor Garriga?'

'Si.'

'My name is Mical Rak. I telephoned from the airport.'

Garriga beamed. To say it was like the sun coming out would not be true. Rather was it the revealing of Montezuma's treasure. El Dorado was in his mouth. Jose Garriga's teeth left much to be desired, but what nature had taken artifice and the skill of some dental goldsmith had amply replaced. But the grin was unmistakably friendly, the expression anxious to help and be of service, as well as an expression of masculine approval of the young lady before him.

'Ah, si. Señorita Rak. The Herr Bauer makes a reservation for you . . . ye-es.'

Garriga left his seat with unexpected alacrity, and came round the counter, seemed surprised that there was no baggage apart from the blue rucksack, but gallantly carried that as he preceded her up the iron staircase, pointing out the amenities as he led her.

'This way lead to the verandah that goes round the courtyard. Is pretty, also useful, yes?' He kicked a door in passing. 'Is bathroom.' Kicked another. 'Is los retretes . . . er . . . W.C.' Then beamed expansively, and pushed open a room door revealing a small, neat, purely functional room that owed nothing whatsoever to the thinking of Hilton. It was a very Spanish interior. Cool tiles, brass bedstead, mended lace coverlet and dark, cheap, but ornate furniture, such as it was. Latin American 'black wood' furniture is the equivalent of the mass manufactured 'white wood' furniture so beloved of British landlords.

But the effect was pleasant enough and Señor Garriga hastened across the room to push out the shutters and let in the bright sunlight from outside. It burst into the room. Garriga shuddered and replaced the shutters three-quarters closed.

'Is too much . . . I think.'

He left Mical to work herself into the room. Unpacking took four minutes. She had so little with her. Then she crossed to the window which led onto a tiny balcony, not big enough to do more than stand on, but overlooking the Plaha de Piedra.

The phone rang. It took her three minutes to find the ancient receiver, which was housed on a shelf under the cane bedside-table and half-hidden by what seemed to be an antimacassar.

'Hello?'

Garriga's voice informed her that there was a call for her from Rio de Janeiro.

'Hello?' Again. 'Is that you, Richard? Look. Can you speak up, the line's not so good?'

Bauer was checking that she had arrived and found the

hotel. He informed her that he would be arriving late that afternoon on a DC8, and would find his own way to the Hotel El Paradiso.

'You can get a 707 if you make noises. I got one.'

'That's from Buenos Aires. I'm in Rio. I couldn't get a flight to Buenos Aires before tomorrow, so I came via Brazil. It's hot as hell here. What about you?'

Mical smiled to herself. 'It's hot, I suppose. About the same as Israel.'

Bauer's sudden silence implied that he understood that he, the Aryan, was the one out-of-court. She helped him out by continuing on a new tack.

'I lost Kessler. He came in by private plane. I saw him, but I got stuck in Passport Control. How do we find him, Richard?'

'We have one lead . . .' Then the line went dead.

She tapped and 'hello'd' but it was dead, and she was suddenly frightened. Being isolated, totally alone in a place like Paraguay was unsettling. She acknowledged a sick feeling in the gut that wasn't there half-an-hour ago. Loneliness does that. But it sets the adrenalin moving like nothing else except terror. Time enough for that.

Outside of Asuncion, following the river towards Rosario, the main road, which is considerably better than half the roads in Latin America, winds across the river valley and then moves northwards for twenty kilometres. After the road leaves the valley and mounts the higher country and scrub-land there is a dirt road leading off to the east across the scrub, through areas of cactus and stunted Joshua trees.

The black Dodge moved on its exaggerated suspension across the baked earth, down the track, until it entered what seemed to be an open drive with planted orange trees down one side, and marshalled rows of cacti on the other. It ran over the rise to where, in a small depression, stood a yellow-painted hacienda.

The adobe structure with its spaciousness and classical architrave, plus the rather fine ornate ironwork over the windows, and the surrounding border of shrubs, bougainvilia, and indigenous herbaceous plants all showed it's previous status. The building was not dilapidated in any way, but the shutters were all closed. There was an air of the unoccupied about it.

Kessler looked out of the Dodge window and nodded involuntarily.

'Nothing has changed.'

Rückert sitting next to him merely grunted and reached for the leather handle as the limousine drew to a halt. Both men got out into the brilliant sunlight. Kessler screwed his eyes against the glare. His shrewd, experienced glance, plus the knowledge of previous visits, guided his eyes to pick out here and there the merest indication that guards were suitably posted.

'Hola!' Rückert's voice of command rang out and was immediately answered by the clatter of booted feet. Two sullen-faced men rushed from the building entrance and came to a stop before the arrivals. Both gave the Nazi salute, and both arrivals returned no more than a nod. Rückert stalked away after barking in German-larded Spanish demanding that the bags from the boot be brought in, and that the heavy luggage was to be collected from the airport.

Kessler followed Rückert into the house as the clatter of an approaching vehicle was heard bounding along the track and the sound of raucous laughter echoed across the still, hot forecourt. An open truck skidded to a halt and deposited its load of eight brown-shirted young men, all sporting swastika armbands, and all slightly the worse for their morning beer. Their levity fizzled out when one of the luggage-carriers muttered and indicated with his head that Pilot was back and Provider was with him. This was big time.

In the shuttered hacienda Kessler followed Rückert down the remembered corridor and into a small room at one end.

The room was spartan. Barely furnished with simple, wooden folding-chairs, bunk-beds, and a collapsible table. The wooden lockers would hold overnight gear, and little else. Kessler looked about him.

'Nothing has changed.'

'What did you expect?'

'Nothing . . . something. I don't really know.' He sighed inconclusively, 'How long will I be here?'

'Two or three days. There are meetings to arrange . after your interrogation.'

Kessler swung round and stared at Rückert.

'After my WHAT?'

Rückert realised he had been clumsy and backtracked slightly. 'Kessler . . . you know it is necessary to examine every aspect of what has happened. The Kameradenwerk is at risk. Let us examine that risk. It is our way. It has made us survive for almosty forty years. I made it so. I shall keep it so.'

The determination and dedication of the Luftwaffe Colonel was apparent to his old friend. It was, in a way, touching in its simple, single-minded guardianship. Kessler was honest enough to admit that it was his pride that was hurt, nothing else. The big European industrialist who travelled first-class, who snapped his fingers and everyone jumped, was affronted at being treated by his comrades as a comrade. He blushed inside himself before Rückert eased the path for him by a conciliatory smile.

'It is necessary, Ludwig. Once you would never have questioned it.'

Kessler breathed in slowly, and straightened up as he faced Rückert. 'I am sorry, Hans. I do not question it even now. Forgive me.'

It was late afternoon when the DC8 touched down at Stroessner Airport. It was the last plane of the day and had only seven passengers for Asuncion. The customs officer had already changed into his best uniform for the trip home. He liked the blue uniform, crisp and important looking. It impressed his girl friend. It didn't impress Bauer as he shuffled through and waited for the man to finish picking his teeth with a matchstick, and make up his mind to chalk meaningless hieroglyphics all over his two bags without even opening them. The passport control was less cursory. They looked at Bauer for a long time, compared his face with the likeness on the inch-square print affixed to his passport. They even asked him to look up so that they could see his face better, held the exchange of looks, then beamed and returned the passport with the comment that German guests were always welcome in Paraguay. Bauer muttered some hypocritical pleasantry, and mentally calculated that as there were upwards of two hundred thousand German residents (not all of them Nazis) in Latin America the statement was unnecessary.

He found a private car with TAXI scrawled on a piece of blue card stuck against the windscreen. After a haggle in broken Spanish, larded with German and English words, the price was agreed and partially paid, at the driver's insistence, and the old banger lurched into the highway from the airport parking lot.

He reached the Hotel El Paradiso as it was getting dark. Registered with the smiling Garrigo, spent half-an-hour talking with Mical, and dropped into his lumpy bed gratefully. He hadn't slept for over fifty hours, and there is nothing like air travel to debilitate and disorganise the time-clock.

The following day was cool for the season – at least the morning started that way. There was a breeze from the north which brought the jungle smell of the Mato Grosso with it. After a good breakfast, which he ate in his room, Kessler walked round the hacienda to refresh his memory. The photograph collection, some framed, some merely pinned to the wooden walls, was second to none. It was the most complete and intimate record of the Nazi hierarchy from the years 1932 to 1945. Most photographic libraries would have given their eye-teeth for that collection. Many autobiographies and military memoirs would have to be revised if ever they came to light. Kessler walked from one display to the next savouring the revived memories with particular pleasure. He was at the age when such things bring joy, and the conviction that the 'old days' were indeed golden. His interrogation had been set for eleven-thirty, and he filled in the two hours after his breakfast by wandering. He renewed his acquaintance with the stables at the rear of the hacienda, talked briefly with the men whose task it was to attend to the horses and vehicles. He questioned them as to their daily activity and about the visits of contingents from Chile, Uruguay, and Bolivia, where the movement was most effective. There many groups of young neo-Nazis who, guided by resident members of the old guard, met and drilled and exercised, wore their uniforms, their swastika armbands, paraded their flags and plotted great deeds they did not have the courage nor the experience to carry out. It was a gigantic, pathetic boy's game . . . and Kessler knew it.

Their counterparts in Europe did not play games. They threw bombs, killed, and maimed, and demanded blood money which the fat-cat world of the West invariably gave them, thus confirming their belief that the democracies were impotent and decadent. Which they were. They always were, and always would be. That much Kessler recognised himself, as his Führer had done. Democracy carried with it the seeds of its own destruction. That had been shown in the beginning, when in Ancient Greece the demos had been destroyed by that very freedom and belief in human rights they sought so repeatedly to restore. The tyrants of the period were right. In that respect, if in no other, most tyrants had always been right, even when the word changed its connotation. Nothing ever happens by committee, and by the time all rights and conditions have been legally complied with, and the misguided concerns of humanism have been mollified the enemy is already in the citadel.

He sighed and walked the perimeter, mentally noting that the guard positions were exactly as he remembered them. It flattered his memory, but questioned the wisdom that had not seen fit to make a variation. He checked his watch as he glanced at the makeshift, open area landing-strip behind the hacienda, then crossed to the highest position of the surrounding scrubland and looked over the domain. Somewhere over the rise, out of sight but no more than twelve kilometres, if that, was the city of Asuncion. Only Bolivia had shown greater sympathy for the expatriate Germans – at least since the halcyon days of President Perón and little Evita. Kessler had first come to Latin America towards the end of the first Perón regime. He confessed to being surprised at the situation. Having been attuned to the pan-European-Soviet attitude to the survivors of the Third Reich he had come to regard his colleagues within the parameters of the term 'War criminals'. He did not necessarily agree with that assumption, but it was difficult not to have the picture coloured by his surroundings. To find them not merely alive and well, but positively flourishing, blatantly flaunting their persons and beliefs in the New World, behaving with typical Teutonic overbearing insensitivity, heel-clicking, prideful, domineering, was amazing to him. Bormann had bought his place in Argentina, and while he was able to do so, his compatriots and Nazi colleagues were safe and preferred. The moment Perón toppled, things changed. Many went underground, many changed names, nationalities, Bormann stopped being the Godfather. Those who had hitherto depended upon his largesse found themselves knocking on his door, cap in hand, for whatever miserly pittance he cared to hand out. That was before he 'disappeared' and became inaccessible – even to his colleagues and personal friends. He still had some – then.

Kessler had by this time built his industrial empire, and considerable profits from Dorf Industries and other companies began to flow into the coffers of the Kameradenwerk where, under the control of Colonel Hans Rückert, the needy were given enough to exist upon. Those in danger from extradition were moved, housed, and given new identities. The Kameradenwerk rebuilt its strength under Rückert's guidance and, as so many of the comrades were approaching late middle-age, younger men were employed, at great expense where ideology held no water, to further their activities.

Then it all went wrong. The world had time to look at old wounds, time to stand upon its dignity and righteous indignation, time to find the scapegoats for the pillory that had to fill the place vacated by the Jews – for the Jews were no longer quite so pliable, no longer quite so available when

Israel existed, and a sense of guilt was still with the West. The time had come to turn again to the threat of Nazi terror, the fascist demon. The Israeli hit-groups formed and struck. Eichmann was snatched from his home and placed in the glass booth for the world to shake its fist at, and cry 'Vile!' Schwend was arrested. Stangl extradited. Herbert Cukurs, the 'butcher of Riga', was 'executed' by Jewish avengers in Montevideo. Barbie, safe – as he thought – as Klaus Altmann, the guest of Bolivia, friend of fishing-tycoon Luis Banchero Rossi (who was murdered), was exposed to the astonished press of the world. Mengele was sighted, Doctor Josef Mengele, 'The Angel of death' of Auschwitz, wanted only one fraction less than Bormann himself.

Bormann, of course, was dead. Hadn't he perished in Berlin in the last days of the bunker? Even his skull had been found and identified by experts. His grinning skull that sported such obviously identifiable teeth, was so conveniently discovered. But Dr Hugo Blaschke, his former dentist, was not sure, after all he had no records to compare it with and memory plays tricks. But the skull just sat there and grinned as few skulls have ever grinned.

Attorney General Dr Fritz Bauer of the State of Hesse who had pursued an unflinching course after both Mengele and Bormann suddenly died in 1968. The loose ends were being tied. But Bormann was sighted, photographs of himself and his friend, Adolf Hundhammer, in Bolivia were printed, rumours grew, novels were written – after all, he was unlikely to sue so he was anyone's game. The hunt was up. Tally-ho! The jackals of journalism moved in. Rückert tightened his grip, and the visitors were discouraged. Fatality *is* discouraging!

Kessler glanced at his watch again. He stalked purposefully towards the hacienda. The guards saluted and smiled politely at this venerable figure who was so important, some said vitally important to the whole movement. They watched him as his walk faltered momentarily. He had to bend and use a helping hand to circumnavigate the rocks. But then he was an old man, wasn't he? Hadn't he known Hitler personally, and been in at the very beginning? He had even been on the Gleiwitz raid that precipitated World War II – that was something!

The 'old man' reached the flat area round the house and walked quickly to the rear doors. Inside it was cool. The shutters of the house hadn't been opened since they took up residence there in 1972. Of course it was cool! Kessler walked down the corridor to the double-doors of the main room, and entered.

Inside the room the arrangement of folding-tables and chairs was that of a military court-martial. The resemblance was not lost upon him, nor the irony. The black cloth covering the main table was of felt, and hung stiffly over the edges. Already seated were Rückert and three others. Two he recognised as old timers, Erich Gehlenand Viktor Kempke. The third was introduced to him as Udo Reiner-Lingens.

'I am sorry this looks so formal, Kessler, but it is our way, and it applies to everyone.' The apology was genuine. The manner deferential. Kessler waved it aside.

'There is no need to apologise. I agree with it.'

Kempke indicated that Kessler should occupy the 'hot seat', which he did with a certain formality and dignity, sitting bolt upright in the chair provided.

'May one ask who is to head this enquiry?'

Kessler looked directly at the central empty chair as he asked the question. Rückert turned to him.

'Doctor Mengele.'

Kessler stared at his colleague for a moment before the fury rose in his gorge. '*I* am to be questioned by that sadistic mountebank? He is *nothing*!'

But Rückert was not to be drawn. 'He is the most wanted criminal of all – after the Reichleiter. The "Angel of Death" of Auschwitz is not nothing.'

It was said with a cynical smile, which itself managed to mollify Kessler's initial anger, 'You used not to be so squeamish.'

Kessler shook his head. 'Not so! I have always held that the end justified the means. Mengele was merely a butcher for his own perverted amusement!'

The conversation was terminated by the increasing roar of a helicopter engine descending.

Kessler curled his lip, 'Can he afford to fly these days? Last time I was here he was scraping for pin-money.'

Rückert was irritated by Kessler's attitude and showed it.

'He is the Reichleiter's choice. Almost the only contact we have with him outside of Yqueras. It is Bormann's helicopter.'

'Why can he not pick someone else, someone worthy?'

'Because he feels safe with Mengele. Together they are the most wanted men in the whole world. Who would *you* trust?'

Rückert's eyes blazed as he glowered at Kessler. The situation was not one of Rückert's seeking. He knew the score. He knew step-by-step what had happened. The interrogation was quite unnecessary, and Kessler was understandably affronted, but he would have to accept that their way of doing things knew NO exceptions. And if orders were to that effect, so it would be.

The sound became deafening as the chopper sank to the patch of ground behind the house, throwing up clouds of dust in all directions. The motors cut, the overhead blades slowed and the hatch was lifted to permit the grey-suited, grey-haired, moustached, tall, lean figure of Mengele to emerge and drop to the ground. Bending slightly he walked under the blades towards the house and the men meeting him, shook hands with one and entered the rear doors.

The heads in the room turned as the footsteps approached down the corridor, halted, and the door handle turned. Mengele stood framed in the doorway, his hard eyes glanced round the room quickly, appraisingly, as if he was planning his emergency exit as a matter of course. He did not even acknowledge the others, but made straight for Kessler.

'Kessler!'

'Josef . . .' Kessler's reply lacked the forced enthusiasm of the opener, but the two men embraced slightly. Not a bear hug, merely a holding of each other's arms, and a close search of faces. Possibly there was a grudging respect for each of them as two who have survived.

'*Lieber freund*, please forgive this, but it is necessary that we know. You understand . . .'

Kessler nodded and resumed his place as Mengele touched hands with the others and sat in his central chair facing Kessler. Rückert handed him his own report and Mengele read it carefully, pedantically . . . re-read passages, then turned to Rückert and asked that they begin the interrogation.

Rückert did not stand, but lent an air of formality to the proceedings by the solemnity of tone and correctness of procedure. Gehlen acted as stenographer, as he could manage shorthand and speedwriting in equal distortions, but claimed he could understand his own jottings. He would provide the transcript to be forwarded to the Reichleiter. Rückert questioned. Kessler answered and elaborated. Mengele nit-picked. Clearly this was going to last for hours

# TWELVE

They were enjoying some home-brewed coffee, and talking about their sole 'contact'. The name 'Yqueras' given to them by Deakin at MI6 before Bauer left London. The claim was that this Argentinian was a millionaire industrialist who had been a friend of the Nazis since the thirties, was a trading partner with West Germany still today . . . particularly with Dorf Industries. Deakin had opined that Yqueras was the link man with Bormann himself . . . if the 'old bastard' still lived. It was their only link.

The knock came on the door at exactly ten-fifteen. Immediately Bauer hid behind the door and Mical warily answered the knock to find the grinning Garriga standing before her.

His request was that he might be permitted to enter and talk with her and her friend who was standing so suspiciously behind the door. He seemed harmless enough. What did he want?

The little man entered and smiled once again as Bauer emerged, only his pride deflated. Garriga explained very simply and quickly that he was a contact man for MI6 in the sense that he 'put up' visiting 'firemen' and did small tasks for his British friends, who paid him money from time to time. He had been warned to expect problems with his guests, and was here to see how he could be useful.

They accepted him for what he was, and asked him what he knew of someone called Yqueras, millionaire.

'Don Julián? Oh, si, everybody knows this man. He is very, very important.'

'You mean you *know* him?' Bauer insisted.

'Eh! Who knows El Presidente . . . who knows the Queen Elizabet? No, señor . . . I know OF him. He is a big, big man. He has a hacienda near Cardusa, I think . . . but he moves about very much, I think. His home is in Buenos Aires.'

They pumped him about a Nazi meeting place. Anywhere known to be associated with the Nazis. But Garriga knew very little. There was gossip about such things. There were foreign journalists who came looking for such things. Most went home empty-handed . . . others went home in wooden boxes. It was not a good thing to be interested in. But he would enquire carefully, and find out where Yqueras lived. That would not be so difficult.

Garriga was as good as his word and returned to Mical's room some two hours later. He advanced into the room sheepishly and handed Mical a bunch of flowers he had either bought in the market or picked in the Municipal Gardens. The gesture was Latin, flamboyant, rather sweet, and accompanied by the most golden of grins. Mical laughed her pleasure and rewarded Garriga with a kiss on the cheek which obviously meant they were almost betrothed. He also said he had found Yqueras' address, and handed them a piece of paper. When Bauer implied he wanted a hire car to go to Cardusa and spy upon Yqueras' household Garriga clicked his teeth and made a pained face.

'Señor Bauer . . . is not possible. The place is guarded. Why you wish this thing?'

'Because I need to find out where Kessler is. What he is doing and why . . . and who the contacts are.'

'This Kessler . . . he is important to you too, señorita?'

Mical nodded. 'Not quite the same way. I want to kill him.'

Garriga looked at her in momentary disbelief, then shook his loose hand in the air. 'Aye-aye-aye!'

He glanced over his shoulder then spoke quietly.

'We are needing to know and eavesdrop – is right word? I learn from Englishman, deceased – You have money, señor?'

'Why?'

'To bribe the servant of Don Julián who is standing outside this room now.'

Bauer looked at Mical, and she smiled, then looked at Garriga. The latter obviously took it for a sign of approval and returned the grin before admitting the tall, po-faced Indian who waited, cap in hand. Garriga rattled off some patois which drew monosyllabic replies.

'He say is possible. He will be needing some money – fifty American dollars.'

Bauer fished some notes from his pocket and gave Garriga the fifty. The little Paraguayan divided it into two, gave his friend half, and pocketed the remainder. Seeing the questioning look on Bauer's face he explained. 'My frien' speak only Spanish. Is for the translation.' Again the golden grin.

The wall clock had ticked away five hours before Mengele closed the file on the table before him, and opened the second one. He extracted a photo and handed it to Kessler.

'This is the girl?'

Kessler took it, and stared at the face of the young Israeli girl. He handed it back and nodded.

'It is the same.'

'You are absolutely sure?' Mengele leant forward as he asked this question.

Kessler frowned. 'Of course. I dealt with her myself in London. There is no further danger.'

Mengele's eyes took on the heavy-lidded stare Kessler had seen so often before.

'That photograph was taken here in Asuncion yesterday at Stroessner Airport.'

Kessler felt the breath leave his body as he stared at the unmoving face of Mengele. Rückert had turned to Mengele questioningly. Clearly he, too, knew nothing of this.

'I do not believe it!' Kessler was indignant.

'It is true, if you look behind the head you will see the time and date on the wall behind. There is no doubt. These are routine pictures taken by the hidden camera operated by the passport officer on duty. We pay them quite a lot of money to photograph EVERYONE who enters the country . . . at the airport . . . at the border crossings. That way we feel safe. Come along, Kessler. It is your money that pays for it.'

'I dealt with her myself,' Kessler was plainly puzzled and exasperated.

'Then you should have been a little more thorough, and seen that she was dead! Ten years ago it would not have happened. You are getting old.'

Kessler stiffened, and one could see his hackles rising. 'We are *all* getting old, doctor. I am far from being the oldest man round this table. Like Thor we cannot fight old age.'

Mengele made a face to imply a misunderstanding.

'No, no no. This is not personal, Kessler. Please do not take it so.' He narrowed his eyes and became pensive in the mean, shrewd way that was peculiarly his own. 'The girl was Israeli. They could be intending to start up their terrorist kidnapping again. That is what concerns me . . . what concerns us all. We do not wish another Eichmann. Where is the girl?'

The gentle, but barbed question was turned on Rückert.

The handsome face remained solemn as he spoke.

'I can't tell you. I did not know of this.'

For the first time that day Udo Reiner-Lingens spoke in a soft Austrian-accented voice that Kessler placed as around Linz and the Danube valley.

'Since we knew of the existence of this girl and bearing in mind what we had been told by Colonel Rückert prior to his arrival here, we checked with our police sources. The girl has not registered. She is, therefore, either no longer in Asuncion, or is staying with friends, colleagues, anyone who makes it possible for her NOT to register. That – in my opinion – makes it already suspicious. If she is a tourist or merely pursuing a personal vendetta against Kessler, why is she not staying in a hotel? No. This argues that she has accomplices who have made arrangements for her, and possibly others, to lie low in Asuncion undetected. I leave it to your imaginations as to why. It is a risk we cannot take. We must assume she is part of a group and act accordingly.'

Rückert shook his head. 'Without more evidence I am not going to order an evacuation. I have put some of the men on alert, temporarily, but I still maintain that this is not an Israeli hit-mob.'

Silence fell on the room. No one seemed to wish to make addit- ional comment. Mengele stood up and turned to the others.

'I think we may now excuse our colleague. Forgive the necessity of this, Kessler. We must consider well.'

Kessler recognised that he was being dismissed and stood, half-bowed, and turned on his heel. When the door had closed after him he went to his room and sat waiting . . . for what he did not know. Eventually he called for coffee and biscuits and stood, saucer in hand, looking out between the shutter slats at the dry and ungrateful landscape round the hacienda. He noted again how without crispness and pride the guards moved. Their shirt and breeches uniforms hung about them, and they moved with truly Latin lethargy. Something inside Kessler ached at the sight. His own shirt-and-breeches days were so different. Then there was electricity in the air, pride and fulfilment just round the corner to be made manifest by their Führer . . . as indeed it was.

The knock on the door was quiet but insistent. Mengele poked his head in and beamed egregiously at Kessler.

'May I come in?'

He did not wait for an answer and none was forthcoming. Mengele entered and sat down in the larger of the two chairs, his feet thrust out before him. He was smoking a long, thin cigarillo.

'What is happening? Anything?'

Kessler's question was not rhetorical. He felt the sudden need to demand that something should happen.

Mengele was evasive. 'You must understand that resources are so limited. The Reichleiter insists that we have to wait to be invited . . .'

Kessler snapped his reply. 'There is no invitation coming! Germany is not interested in us. We are an embarrassment!'

Mengele thumped the table at his side in anger.

'No! I will not hear defeatism! They are already facing a slump. The communists are everywhere. There will be a call. You will see.'

Kessler turned to face him and thrust forward his neck. The expression was porcine, and intended to imply no argument.

'There is NO SLUMP! Germany has NEVER been more prosperous. The communists are contained. There will BE no call. We can only make moves to influence by our example, and by using what power we have to gain control. Nothing has changed for us.'

Mengele made a 'closed' face and puffed his cigarillo irritably. Kessler turned and looked out of the shutters once more.

That afternoon, in the city, his daughter Ingrid and his manservant, Franz, walked together to a prearranged rendezvous. It took them past the great, brown church, built like a minor cathedral with two ornate bell-towers either side of the porch. The square in front was broad, and paved with pink-and-white patterned stone. Amid the casual citizens taking the air, passing the time of day, or coming from the church, were two that incited the interest of the Germans. A peasant woman and her son, Indian extraction with the distinctive faces of Incas, presumably in the city from the distant country, were at the opposite end of the square facing the church. They were on their knees, hands clasped in front of them as in prayer, the woman muttering her Indo-Spanish chant like some mantra; the son, fifteen or sixteen years of age, in faded blue jeans and red cotton shirt, was slightly behind her. On his face, instead of the mystic, totally involved devotion of his mother, was the slightly stupid look of non-understanding bemusement one sees on peasant faces throughout the world. The two figures hobbled forward. They would cross the square and hobble on their knees right up to the altar as an act of abasement and contrition, a showing of their humility and unworthiness, and they would both ignore the blood on the dress-hem and the jeans, and return to their village in the warm ecstasy of having communicated. The pain in their knees would somehow have reached to Heaven and pierced their Saviour, shown Him their Faith.

Ingrid watched them for several minutes before she took Franz's arm in anger, and forced him from the scene

'Ignorant cretins!'

Franz found it amusing . . . foolish, colourful, even exotic. To Ingrid it was the mindless self-abasement of an idiotic mind that had abdicated all human pride and self-respect. It simply proved the racial implications that the Führer's theorists had hatched, half-baked, from puerile generalities.

They crossed the Calle São Paolo and entered the maze of coloured streets, tiny shops, and corner bars that form the edges of the economic centre of Asuncion. One bar stood apart from the others, simpler, more primitive, it was more a fonda than a taverna. Franz parted the bead curtains with his hands and held them back for Ingrid to enter. Inside the atmosphere was of stale tobacco, coffee, beer, cheese and the pervasive smell of tamales. They moved through to the rear section, almost a separate room where the locals did not venture. It was a place for the 'others' who came from time to time. The heavy-jowled proprietor watched the Germans come in as he stood and wiped his glasses and coffee cups. He was one of the few patrons who offered pulque as well as beer and Brazilian wine. It made him popular with Indians and made his customers very sick.

At the table in the corner of the rear room four young men were sitting. The one nearest, smiling at their entrance, was blond, blue-eyed and handsome in an over-bred way. The other three were Latins, one possibly of Indian descent but with fine dark features. The blond, and one of the others, stood up as Ingrid approached the table.

'These are my colleagues: from Brazil (the thick-featured one nodded) from Chile (the Indian face smiled) and our leader in Asuncion.' The last did not even move a muscle, and the eyes were cold.'

'Franz you have already met. This is Fräulein Dorf. The key person in our planning.'

The Brazilian nodded again. 'I have met Fräulein Dorf before. She once had my vote,' he grinned apreciatively 'When she was Miss Fourth Reich two years ago.'

Ingrid made a tiny smile in reply, 'Six years ago.'

The Brazilian shrugged. Why did these Germans not understand? He knew it was six, seven years ago. He was flattering the lady. Do they know nothing?

Ingrid talked to them for ten minutes about what was being done in Europe, what the Neo-Nazi youth of Bavaria, Austria, Swabia, Saxony were preparing to do. She explained yet again how the war had affected her nation, how the young generation of post-war Germans had rejected, revolted from, and totally dismissed their heritage. They were ashamed, guilt-ridden, and servile. The second generation were not. They held their heads high in a Germany already superior to its conquerors, ready to be reawakened to its proper greatness and point the way to others, to their Latin American brothers, to the New Order that would do what the Third Reich had failed to do. She outlined the need for huge amounts of money and the waste of this upon the Old Guard in their midst.

She implied something was afoot, that somehow her own father, the industrialist Dorf, was a key figure, and that – in her opinion – the great Nazi fortune was about to be transferred.

The blond German looked at her for a moment and then spoke in awe.

'You mean – THE account?'

Ingrid nodded. The Brazilian lifted his eyes to look directly into her own.

'Do we know roughly how much is in this fortune?'

Ingrid stared him out. 'Yes. I do. Forty-eight billion Deutschmarks.'

This was received in the silence it deserved, broken only by the Brazilian turning quickly to the waiter hovering near the blond German.

'Hey! *Azucar*! *Vamos*!'

It was only by thus drawing attention that Ingrid realised the pretty, dark, young man who waited on table in the fonda was not merely hovering round Vinding, the blond. The boy was coquettishly showing himself to the handsome German who, presumably had already given indication of his tendencies.

The 'sugar' made a pout, and minced from the room as the fine-featured Chilean young man spoke to Ingrid.

'What is to happen to this money now?'

Ingrid sighed and confessed that she didn't know. She also said that was why they needed to talk. It was necessary to get to someone who would work with them, the young, against the old regime, the Kameradenwerk, but who was totally trusted by them. There was only one such man: Don Julián Yqueras.

The Paraguayan representative opined that the Don would not agree. He was too much part of them. Wasn't he, too, an old man? But the Chilean did not agree. He knew Don Julián Yqueras personally. Yqueras would ride with anything that preserved his wealth and his position. He would try.

When Ingrid and Franz left the fonda they walked back to their hotel through the streets, passing down the side streets of humble dwellings where children and women were sitting outside the doorways of their homes tearing coloured paper into flags and torn-paper patterns. The women fixed them to lengths of string and tape.

'What are they doing?'

Ingrid smiled. She had lived in Paraguay for two years and knew about the Fiesta.

'It is Ascension Day in two days' time. There is the festival, and they are making flags for the streets. Asuncion takes its name from that Day when it was founded. You will see, it is very impressive.'

She laughed, and didn't divulge exactly HOW it was impressive.

Mengele was still with Kessler, complaining of how weary he was of the whole wretched continent.

'You have seen more of it than most, Josef. They tell me you know every nook and cranny, and can disappear in thirty seconds.'

'Always there is someone. They hate me, Kessler. They want to kill me, but they never do. They end up on the cold slab themselves.' Mengele's eyes glinted. The cold, utterly ruthless look chilled even the marrow of Kessler's well-inured bones.

'What was it you really wanted to see me about, Josef?'

Kessler knew very well what it was, and had had enough of pussy-footing. Mengele breathed in through his teeth and turned a smarmy smile upon him.

'My dear old friend. You must understand how we live here. It is not good. The Reichleiter is becoming difficult. He is getting old.'

'Aren't we all? As I said earlier.'

'Indeed, indeed. But you, Kessler, remain young. Look at you! I am so envious. You have your beautiful daughter with you?'

'Yes. As I am sure you already know. She is staying in Asuncion.'

'This is so good, so nice. I have no children, as you know. I would like to have given life.'

'The world is full enough, Mengele, and, besides, the deficit you created more than compensates for credit entries in the Great Book of Life, does it not?'

The sarcasm was not wasted, Mengele's face fell once more, and the scowl of utter hatred was there momentarily before he forced himself to chuckle and appreciate Kessler's barbed joke for what it was.

'Enough of that! I want to ask you, my friend, would it be possible for you to make a small personal advance to me?

From your own resources, of course. Life is becoming so expensive here. They bleed us! And Bormann is so tight-fisted. He always was. He has no right to keep us all deprived. He knows that we depend upon his party funds. I cannot take employment of any permanence. I have to be ready to move at a moment's notice. I have been on the run for thirty years, Ludwig! I am the most wanted of all the so-called War Criminals, because I served my Führer in exterminating his enemies, and benefiting medical science. But they come, and they come, and always they want to kill me.'

Mengele had just the trace of a wildness about his look – not insanity, for no one was more sane than Josef Mengele in the medical sense – it was an animal's look, an animal constantly on guard against predators. Then he smiled.

'But it would be so nice to enjoy a little of life's luxuries. Just a little, for whatever time there is left to us.'

Kessler pursed his lips and looked directly at the outcast. 'What happened to the Grand Design, Mengele? Are we not to reassert ourselves in the world? Is that not what we are here for?'

Mengele was anxious to cash in on his personal need, anxious not to give wrong impressions. 'But of course. I did not mean anything. Just that, now – for the immediate moment – I want more than beans and tamales. It is all right for you, swanning around Europe in the best hotels, your own home . . . respect . . .'

The ire was beginning to choke the man. Envy and bitterness would not let him remain coherent, but Kessler was cold and unmoved.

'I earned what respect I have. I did what was necessary for the Fatherland. I did not *enjoy* myself in sadistic, bloody debauchery that achieved nothing.'

'If you are going to live here, too, I suppose you have provided yourself with ample funds. Oh, yes, it is easy for some!'

Kessler did not reply for some moments and watched Mengele put out the cigarillo on the saucer, where three stubs already lay. Suddenly he took out his cheque book and wrote out a cheque with great speed, tore it out, and handed to Mengele, whose greedy eyes had suddenly become interested.

'Here you are, Josef. That will buy your cigars and little girls for at least another year. I have made it out to "Bearer". There will be no need to declare identity or sign anything. You may cash it in safety.'

Mengele read the amount, folded the cheque and put it in his pocket. For a moment he seemed about to say something, but didn't. He grunted and walked from the room. Kessler watched him go then he himself walked to the small hand-basin and carefully washed his hands.

# THIRTEEN

Don Julián Yqueras owned several farms and modest haciendas throughout Latin America. His home was Argentina, of which he was a proud citizen, but he spent much time in Paraguay, Brazil and Bolivia attending to business interests. He had intended to spread his interests into Chile after the war in Europe, but two attempts were made on his life, and he drew the inevitable conclusion that he was not welcome in that country. The Casa Pertegaz was a small delightful hacienda of great charm and architectural quality, out of all proportion to its modest size. It was, if anything, the favourite of Yqueras' homes. It was situated outside the small village of Jil, which was on the Rutas Romanicas leading from Cardusa into Asuncion. The capital was thirty-six kilometres away.

Don Julián himself was a tall, lean man of dignified bearing, aristocratic features and manners, and very considerable wealth. He belonged to an old Spanish family that had come with the Conquistadores, intermarried early with Inca aristocracy, and consequently held respect and following from all sections of the community. He had come to the head of the Yqueras empire at the age of twenty-two when his father fell from a horse and broke his neck. Don Julián enjoyed his position and his wealth, which was why, in 1934, he had aligned himself with fascist causes in Europe and turned his economy in their direction. Franco's Spain was a natural ally and Don Julián supported that cause with funds and imported arms. He quickly embraced the Reich of Hitler, as it seemed to him that only by that support was property and position to be retained by those who had it. The Comintern threat was very real . . . not least in Latin America. The dictatorships of Perón and others found in Yqueras a staunch supporter for those same reasons. He had no particular brief for Germans as opposed to French or British (though he admitted that he could not stand the upstart Mussolini and refused to assist the Italian in any way. That was too much.)

His trade with Germany had grown in the thirties into a trusted partnership, so much so that it was to Don Julián Yqueras that the first Nazi hoard was entrusted prior to the breaking out of hostilities. That hoard he had guarded and invested with great profit. He had been the intermediary with Juan Perón when, in the late forties, the Nazi hierarchy who had escaped the Allied clutches needed asylum. Yqueras' personal bribe to Perón was estimated to be over a million dollars. El Presidente extracted a much larger share of the Nazi booty when Bormann himself, under assurances from Yqueras, arrived in Buenos Aires by submarine.

After Perón's fall the new regimes were not quite so sanguine about the Nazi presence on their soil. It was Yqueras who mollified and bribed their continuity of asylum or perhaps one should say, relative freedom from harassment and extradition.

Don Julián's wife, Donna Maria, had died in 1953. The couple were childless, and Julián went back to his earlier days of short-term mistresses, courtesans, film stars and jet-setters. Women were necessary to show he was normal – nothing more. They did not interest him in themselves.

Don Julián had two passions in life. He adored good cigars, smoked abstemiously but fulsomely, and delighted in watching the faces of his smoking friends when he offered them a superb corona from which he had removed the paper band.

The other passion was his piano. He played well for an amateur. He was a natural pianist. Had he so wished in his youth he could have trained to be a very considerable concert pianist. His long, strong fingers and broad hand gave him every natural advantage. He had the leisure to practice *ad infinitum,* and from time to time he did. Then left it for six months, and resumed his international playboy existence coupled with stringent control of his business interests. Just as suddenly he would return to Cardusa and continue his love affair with his Bechstein – of his five pianos this was the one he cherished. It was his voice because it responded to his touch and his interpretation better than the others. The Steinways were magnificent but sonorous and velvet-like. The Bösendorfer was not quite so fast in action, and somehow, 'cushioned' his touch. No. It was the Bechstein that gave his Bach, his Schubert, his Beethoven the sound he wished. His taste was for the classical purity and brilliance of Mozart and Haydn, whose keyboard works Don Julián considered vastly underrated. He also liked Ravel and Debussy.

When the car arrived at the gateway to be admitted by the openly-armed guards, Don Julián walked onto the terrace to greet his guests. He knew Colonel Rückert and Kessler as old comrades. He respected the former enormously, and actually liked the latter. Kessler had endeared himself to Yqueras as almost the only German in Latin America of his acquaintance who actually 'liked' music, and played the piano himself . . . not well, but with love. They stepped from the Dodge, and crossed to shake the extended hand of the Argentinian.

'Colonel, Kessler! It is good to see you both. Please.' He motioned them to the table and chairs on the terrace where coffee was waiting them. By the side of the table the white-coated waiter stood like some Nubian slave, deaf and mute, merely there to serve. The man looked quite different from when he appeared in the doorway of the hotel to face Bauer and Garriga.

Rückert declined the offer of coffee. 'Too much coffee rusts my ligaments, Julián. They lubricate with strong liquors. Some of your excellent brandy, for example. May I?'

The Luftwaffe Colonel had noted the decanters and glasses on the side-table and made towards them as Yqueras urged him to help himself. They talked pleasantries for twenty minutes before Yqueras suggested that they remove themselves from the midday heat and go into his study to talk of their affairs. They followed him, and the servant followed them bearing the tray.

The study was Yqueras' personal domain. Decorated with Japanese austerity, European treasures, and unobtrusive Latin luxury, it was sparsely furnished. Little more than tables to take his sculptures, plus his desk, his considerable library, and his Bechstein. The walls were hung with half-a-dozen paintings of great worth and distinction. No dealer had picked out investments for Yqueras. He knew, and chose for himself. They were superb.

'Why do we always come in here?'

Rückert asked the question. Yqueras smiled quietly and inclined his head towards Kessler.

'Because it is my favourite room, and because my friend has been anxious to reassure himself that the Bechstein remains in my possession. It is the only room that I have anywhere that is finely tuned to a set humidity and temperature. My piano and my cigars demand it.'

The servant brought canapés, more coffee, a box of cigars and Rückert's glass and decanter. Then he discreetly withdrew, though a keen observer would have noted that the door was not properly closed.

They talked of the financial transfer, the usual one, that is, and Yqueras hedged around the possibility of something else before he came out with it. Yes, there was to be a major transfer. Yes, it was 'in hand'. No, there was no assistance required other than the arranging of a meeting with the Reichleiter.

Yqueras was not too pleased that he was not party to the transfer, nor, in fact, knew the extent of the money involved. Bormann, too, had been cagey, but he kept to the routine. No one could arrange a meeting except through Yqueras, and no one would be present other than Mengele, and he only to introduce. Nothing had changed. Yqueras implied that Bormann was more nervous; he also hinted that Kessler might find him 'changed'.

The arrangements for the meeting were memorised carefully by the servant standing outside the door in the corridor. He would report it to his friend Garriga (and the European who would pay him) as soon as lunch had been served and his afternoon break began.

# FOURTEEN

Bauer and Mical listened with rapt attention as Emilio, Yqueras' servant and Garriga's brother-of-a-half-cousin-once-removed-who-had-married-his-sister's-uncle reported on what he had overheard. Garriga paid him the balance of the money owing and the man went away happy enough, anxious to overhear anything that the 'señor' wished.

Mical frowned. 'So we know Kessler has a meeting with someone important at a place called Casa Dos Caminos. That's about *all* we know, isn't it?'

Garriga shrugged non-committally and sucked his golden teeth, 'I think I am knowing this place. It is on the edge of the Alazar. It belongs to the Doctor Mengele.'

Bauer looked up quickly, but it was Mical who spoke, with a catch in her voice, and a sense of shock.

'Did you say, Mengele?'

'Yes.' He gave a curious sad look. 'It is the man you are thinking. Very bad medico. Many people try to kill this man, I think. But they always have the accident. Mengele is still here. Many people know him, but he is not in one place very long. This Casa Dos Caminos, it belongs to him.'

Bauer was silent for some moments. 'How do we get there, José?'

Garriga bent over the coverlet on the bed and made channels with his finger-tip: a rough map, in effect.

'Here is Asuncion. Over here is the Alazar. Fifty kilometres of baked, bare sand and rock . . . maybe more. Is not good place. Is high, like the Sierra. Here . . . I make the line . . . is rough track along the valley. Here . . . is where it divide into two roads: "Dos Caminos". There Mengele has his house. He can see anyone coming along the valley ten miles away. There is only the road. No, if you want to be there you must go round.' He made a sweeping gesture with his arm. 'Across the foothills. You cannot take the car. It must be horses. I think it is possible to look down upon the Casa from here, maybe quarter-of-a-kilometre away, I do not know. Is possible.'

The decision to go there had to be immediate. Garriga told them that it would take seven or eight hours of riding to reach the vantage point. If they were to do it unnoticed then it was necessary to leave that afternoon, make camp at least half-way, and complete the distance immediately after dawn in order to be in position, unobserved by Mengele, before Kessler arrived. The little Paraguayan would find horses for them with enough gear to make their trek reasonable. Mical asked him for guns. For money it was possible. For money all things were possible.

She did not make the request secretly. Bauer heard her ask, and said nothing, merely added that a revolver with ammunition would be useful for their personal protection. Garriga looked from one to the other, and smiled his huge smile. For a moment Bauer wondered exactly what he thought of the strange foreigners who wanted such curious things and had such peculiar errands. Bauer had been in the field for the Waffenschutz for two years, but on relatively unspectacular assignments. His forte was basic policework which he knew inside out. His employers knew it, and used his abilities intelligently. There was only that one thing. His personal fixation upon the still-living Nazis, and his fear of a new uprising of fascists in the land he loved. He had no sentimental delusions. Germany was not all beer and Black-Forest gâteau. It was not the picturesque mediaeval streets of old Nuremberg. It was not 'Meistersinger', nor was it the land of Beethoven and Brahms, Goethe and Schiller, any more than Switzerland was all yoghurt and cuckoo-clocks. But what he knew, what he had grown up in, despite the initial devastation, was HIS land, HIS home, and it made warm sense to HIM. He wanted it to remain sane, prosperous, and proud. A nation of hard-working, well-intentioned, cultured human beings whose past remained the past, and gave them no more cause for shame than did the past of any nation.

But he saw enough. He sensed and was cynically aware. The past was NOT dead. The future was NOT assured. He, and any German who felt as he did, must take their own, concealed, surreptitious steps to eradicate and render impotent the latent dangers that threatened his country. His quiet, unassuming policework had borne fruit in many directions. He had enough contacts in various areas to help. The German banks had been specially helpful and, though the Swiss were not quite so forthcoming, there was enough anti-Nazi feeling in that curious nation to permit of searches that would not normally be permitted to ANY police or intelligence operators. He knew more than he told, and suspected more than he dared speculate.

Mical had gone shopping for bits-and-pieces. Garriga had gone to find horses. Bauer stood on the tiny balcony and looked across the square, over the rooftops of the small coloured hovels of the back streets, punctuated by the warm stone towers of the churches. Even the great campaniles of the Cathedral could be seen across the expanses of buildings and the skeletal, neon-sign hoardings. Asuncion lay before him. Bauer speculated how many of the simple inhabitants of the city were aware that the Germans in their midst were not simply tourists, or refugees from war-torn Europe. How many even knew that a long time ago unspeakable things had been perpetrated upon men? But his sigh implied that he suspected they knew well enough and cared no more than a little. Why should they? It was a long time ago, and a long way away. They had their own problems of survival and cruelty: their own police, their own politicians, their own injustices. Who cared about Germany, or Europe, or anywhere else but their own backyard? And who was to say them 'nay' and accuse them of indifference?

Mical returned with her purchases, and found him silent and preoccupied. She suspected it was to do with her, and her request for firearms. It was an issue to be fought over, at best argued over. She did not want to. She liked Bauer. He, in turn, did not wish to offend her. He, too, found that he liked this small, almost impish Israeli girl with her infectious smile and sparkling eyes that clouded over into sadness so easily.

Garriga staggered into the room with his equipment and purchases (all secondhand, and doubtless greatly overpriced. Probably by half-cousins-of-married-nephews-who-knew-someone).

The wide-brimmed hats were tried on solemnly until Mical started to giggle at Bauer's enormous headgear.

'It looks bloody silly, doesn't it?'

'I think John Wayne's memory is safe enough. You really want me to wear this, José?'

Garriga put his head on one side and made a face.

'Is necessary, señorita. The Alazar is not a good place. The sun makes the hills into desert. You do not wear the hat you, too, become sand. Is true!'

Then came the unwrapping of the large sacking parcel. Inside was the revolver, a Walther pistol, standard issue to Bauer's colleagues. He knew it well. The rifle was pounced upon by Mical who picked it up, and handled it with the assurance of practice. He had not thought of her in terms of the Israeli Army, but recognised that it was inevitable that she had served. He spoke to her quietly.

'Can you handle that thing?'

'Oh yes. It's a French standard F1 sniping-rifle. It's been modified a little . . .' She tried the bolt-action quickly.

Garriga beamed at the expertise she showed, and tried to become part of it.

'It has an effective range of eight-hundred-seventy-five yards.' He almost chanted, then smiled sheepishly. 'Is what they say. The sights make it good, I think.'

Mical nodded, 'Is there ammunition?'

Garriga looked slightly unhappy. 'Three ten-round clips. Is all I could get, señorita. Is no time.'

They talked rapidly of the necessary information basic to their purpose. Garriga pointed out that Mengele was known as a man paranoid about his safety, with reason, of course. He thought it would be likely that he would have made certain provisions to guard his rear and flanks, maybe they should watch out for buried mines. It was possible.

He looked at Mical with his slightly bulbous eyes devoid of any trace of white. 'Please, little one, be so careful . . . eh?'

The concern was genuine, and Mical could only smile and kiss his dark cheek, which obviously pleased him no end. The horses were kept at a stable on the edge of the town. They found them already saddled-up and waiting. Not exactly the finest of hunters, but adequate for their needs. Neither was an experienced rider, and they took it very easily for the first half-hour.

Garriga went ahead by car showing them the way out of town and to which country road they should keep. They steadily plodded up the slow-rising road. Several long-distance haulage lorries passed them without a glance, and one or two cars, before it became quiet. Ahead they saw Garriga's car pull up on the earth at the side of the road.

He pointed towards the hills they could see over the grass rise ahead.

'I have to leave here. You go over there. Go straight towards the sunset. Follow the river bed . . . is dry, but you can see . . . I think there is broken-down old building, maybe seven kilometre on the side of the hills. I have not been in the Alazar for many, years. I was hunting when I was young. Make camp and go on when it is light again. Good luck, señor Bauer, señorita.'

They watched him drive away, and suddenly felt very alone and vulnerable. Without speaking they urged their horses forward up the slope. Quarter-of-an-hour later they reached the ridge and there, spread out before them, was the massive, seemingly never-ending landscape of the Alazar Hills piled up upon each other into a great, dry, parched Sierra. No suggestion of grass, weed, or cactus, just a great, red-brown emptiness of lunar landscape. They both quailed inside at the sight but said nothing, and walked their beasts down the slope towards the river bottom, or where intelligence told them the river bottom would be if there was a river. No doubt at one period during the year it would be in full flood, quite possibly the valley itself would become green and flower-covered for two weeks, before it became dry and arid once again.

The horses picked their way between the stones. Not once did one stumble. They knew the land, they knew its hazards. Mical wondered about snakes. José had said nothing. She even had thoughts of buzzards, mountain lions, cougars and became subdued. Soon it would be dark. They would make camp and try to sleep.

Kessler walked from the simple, basic ablutions – he couldn't in all conscience call the room a bathroom, with its matchboard walls and its cracked, white, porcelain sinks of American manufacture, dating from the early nineteen-hundreds, and its grey 'composition' floor. He held his towel round his neck. Curiously, something he never normally did, yet had always done when in military barracks and quarters. It had seemed to be the way. It came as a matter of course. The trousers and shirt-sleeves even had something of the army bunkhouse about them, despite the quality of the trousers and the cloth of the shirt, both purchased in London's St James'.

He entered the room he was sharing with Rückert. The latter was sitting on his bunk-bed polishing his boots. Kessler walked across to his own bunk.

'Nothing ever works in this God-forsaken country! The taps give a filthy brown trickle. Surely it is not beyond us to organise a proper supply?'

Rückert continued without looking up. 'Kessler, this house is ready to vacate at very short notice. It has to be. We do nothing that will imply habitation of any permanence. There is a basin in the corner, over there.'

Kessler looked up and saw the elderly galvanised bowl

standing on a tea-chest. He crossed to it, examined the water, which was clean, and started to wash his hands and face.

When he finished he turned round to find Rückert regarding him curiously.

'Kessler, DID you bring money with you?'

Kessler continued drying his hands as he spoke. 'I did not BRING it. No one carries that sort of money. It is a perfectly normal bank transfer. We've done it before many, many times as you know . . .'

Rückert interrupted. 'I'm not talking about that . . . and you know it!'

Kessler breathed in. 'The other I am not permitted to discuss in detail, but since you ask. Yes, the initial moves have been made. Transfer can be effected once the proper security measures for withdrawing have been satisfied. It can only be withdrawn by the Reichleiter and myself. In my own case, *alive!*'

Rückert chuckled. 'You're a cunning old fox. No wonder they never caught you. Are you taking this Israeli thing seriously enough?'

The last question was an afterthought, or so it seemed. 'Any one who does not take an Israeli threat seriously is a fool, and his days are probably numbered.'

Kessler looked at him solemnly, 'Why should they concern themselves with me? What am I to them? No one looks for a pfennig when there are marks lying about. If they want any one surely they want Mengele. Isn't he the ultimate choice as well as the obvious? "The Angel of Death" from Auschwitz? There are enough survivors of that wretched place to make life eternally frightening for Josef.'

'Mengele will outlive us all. He has more to fear, I grant you, and his cunning has grown accordingly.'

'He is the Great Hyena of the human race. When I think, Ugh!' Kessler could not bring himself to talk about it. He was not a squeamish man. He had no particular conscience about the appalling revelations of that Final Solution. But it was, to him, unnecessary, would bring the Reich into disrepute, and availed nothing. He found it distasteful, he was even a little revolted at what had been revealed. Not that he had really suspected less, but the reality is somehow more shocking than the thought. He changed the subject.

'Hans, you must understand the movement of money is not difficult until it becomes vast in quantity. The sheer amount of money to be transferred has to be done, in this case, through more than one party. It means that at least three separate quarters are aware of that exchange. That must be done, therefore, with extreme care. We have to trust each one of those who know. I have asked the Swiss to channel it all through our friends in New York, then to Rio where Julián's co-operation is essential. He must assist the bank with foreign currency holdings of his own. He has agreed to do so. I assume you trust him, as I do.'

Rückert nodded his head wistfully. There was a shade of reluctance, almost amounting to resentment, about Rückert's expression. Kessler noted it and wondered, then crossed to his bunk and removed his shoes. Rückert lay down on his blanket and Kessler reached out to switch off the light. They lay in silence for quarter-of-an-hour. Neither voiced his thoughts, yet both felt the communion of old friends unspoken. Kessler heard Rückert reach for a cigarette, and saw the momentary glow as he lit it, then watched the tiny pin-point of red glow recede regularly.

At length he spoke to the handsome man he had known most of his adult life.

'Is it all over, Hans? Do we delude ourselves?'

A moment, then the rough voice coughed, and spoke.

'Not yet. What is it, Kessler? There is something. I've felt it since we arrived here.'

'It is not "anything". Just the late realisation that the dream is not to be fulfilled. There is no Fourth Reich. There never will be.'

There was no denial from Rückert, no protestation such as Kessler was aching to hear. When the words came they were conciliatory, and evasive.

'Time, Kessler. Time. It will come.'

Kessler's heart shrank inside him as he heard it. Rückert of all people. The foremost campaigner for the survival and revival of what Hitler's Reich stood for. Was it now merely 'survival'? Kessler lay his head back on the cheap pillow-ticking.

'Do you think about the old days, Hans? I think of nothing else. There were mistakes, stupidities, excesses – but the Führer was right. He saw to the horizon and beyond. Greatness was there for the taking. A whole new concept of the destiny of mankind, not only Germany, and WE could have led that resurgence, Hans. My God! It would have been so wonderful, so beautiful . . .'

The tears had formed in his eyes and he sniffed, and turned on his side. The light-spill in the room from the moolight outside made slatted pools on the floor of the room. One was by Rückert's bed. Kessler watched the hand stub out the last of his cigarette on the saucer by the bed. Then a quiet shuffling, and a hand placed something gently on the floor by the side of the bed. It was an artificial limb.

The moonlight looked down upon the towering adobe walls of what had once been a shelter for animals – wild horses, brought in to be slaughtered as meat. Now only the walls remained except for some poles and broken pan-tiles at one corner. The small fire flickered and flared, throwing up a glow into the face of Richard Bauer, as he prodded and fiddled with the embers to keep them alive. Outside the silence of the desert was absolute. No living thing made any cry, or gave a hint of its presence.

Mical lay on one of her blankets and rested her head on the saddle. It was much colder than she had expected. Used to the Israeli and Syrian landscape round the Golan heights, even the bare nothingness of the Gaza strip, she knew how cold desert areas could become at night, but not quite the same as here in the Alazar. The temperature had dropped and dropped as the sun sank below the high plateau ahead. The grey embers at one side of the fire coughed and fell to powder. The side nearest to Bauer cracked and sparked momentarily. She looked at the German hunched over the glow, and raised herself on one elbow.

'Richard. What are you thinking?'

'Disconnected thoughts . . . common subject. I don't know.' He sighed. 'If I'm honest I started this Nazi witch-hunt because I didn't like the innuendos that were made – everywhere – about Germany, MY Germany. I and my friends are not responsible for what was done fifty years ago by maniacs in the name of Germany. But I deeply resent that I am German and my government has failed to pursue the criminals that are still among us. The "sins of the fathers" and all that bit. But it's not like that now. What started as a crusade of principle is now something else. I found things out. Things have happened to me, to friends of mine and others that I cannot just equivocate over. It has become a personal thing. I see an evil that I have to stamp out – because the authorities are hidebound, and unable to do anything – even if they could – before it is too late. It is now URGENT.'

Mical looked at him, puzzled. 'Why do you think this? Is there something you haven't told me?'

'Not much. It's more a feeling than anything. I have some information from Germany, from London, even from Switzerland, worrying snippets that nag away at me, and seem to fit into a pattern I sense rather than see. For decades those Nazi millions have lain dormant in Bank vaults, lost to the world, or so it seemed. Suddenly it is moving. Why? Why, Mical? What is it to be used for?'

'This is all part of why you do not want me to kill Kessler, isn't it? Is he part of it?'

'I believe he is very much part of it. Perhaps it is better if he is killed. My flesh is beginning to creep and the hairs on my neck will not lie down. There is a terrible fear gripping my guts. You know?'

She looked at him, suddenly cold herself. 'Armageddon?'

'In a way, yes. Did you know that in Central Africa half of a nation – I can't remember which one it is – has been leased to a private company who have built rocket-launching sites? They have all the necessary technology. Anyone who has the money can go and pay for a satellite to be sent into orbit, no questions asked. Many of the scientists working there are Germans. I just wonder what sort of Germans.' Neither spoke then Bauer added quietly, 'I am more frightened than I have ever been.'

He walked to his corner, lay down, covered himself with a blanket, and closed his eyes.

# FIFTEEN

It was the sudden sound of a stone exploding in the embers of the fire that woke Bauer. He didn't sit up, merely opened his eyes and looked quickly in the direction of the sound. It was almost dark still, but the suggestion of dawn showed above the wall on the east side of the hut. He realised that someone was standing against the wall, near what had been the window and was now merely a hole in the wall. It was Mical, looking calmly and steadfastly across the landscape towards the lightening sky in complete silence. She did not look round as Bauer joined her at the opening. He followed her gaze to the distant horizon where the light was behind the silhouetted hills of the Alazar. They both recognised the awesomeness and beauty of dawn and waited for it, silent and respectful. The sun was about to top the ridge, then, suddenly a single shaft of brilliant, laser-like light streaked across the landscape towards them. One could almost hear it.

'The Dawn reacheth even unto Hebron!'

Mical's quiet childlike voice spoke simply. Bauer felt a lump in his throat. He didn't know why. It was just simple, innocent, truthful. He put his arm round Mical's shoulders, and rested her head against his chest. They stood there for several minutes when Bauer sighed and touched her cheek with the finger of his hand that was round her shoulder.

'We've still got a dozen miles to go. We'd better move out.'

Mical went to attend to the horses while Bauer stamped out the fire embers, swilled out the coffee-pot, and generally tried to leave the place as they found it.

Dawn was observed by Ingrid as she lay on her side in the hotel room and watched it through the window. Franz was sharing the bed with her, as he usually did when her father was absent. Franz was dozing. Ingrid, however, had been thinking for the last two hours.

'Franz.'

The young Aryan grunted, and moved, but remained otherwise unaware. She dug him sharply in the back, and he turned sleepily to protest.

'I've been thinking. Julián Yqueras is sympathetic to our cause. We must move . . . now. He is the one to do it. I want you to telephone him, and tell him that it is vital he does something today. Tomorrow may be too late. He will understand why and that my father is to remain *alive*. That is essential, in case he does not already know.'

Franz frowned in disbelief and ruffled his hair as he sat up.

'You want me to telephone NOW?'

'Yes, not from this room. I could do that. I don't trust Rückert. He could well have this hotel phone tapped. He doesn't trust us either. Go down to the Post Office round the corner. They have special pay-phones that accept credit-card charging. Go on. Do it now.'

Franz muttered to himself but did as he was bid. He put his jacket and slacks on and went.

Bauer checked the sun, his watch and the compass, and decided they were about where they ought to be. Which did not impress Mical especially as there was nothing whatsoever to be seen in any direction apart from baked earth, more foothills and dry gullies, and an endless unfolding of more and more of the same. The sun was quite high in the eastern sky. It must be approaching seven-thirty, maybe even eight, though she did not want to question the German's competence. He was a nice man, gentle, and despite his calling, with an air of uncertainty that was immensely likeable

He had dropped from his horse, and laid a stone on the reins as he walked to the edge of a gully, then turned smiling.

'I think we've just about made it. The valley is down there, I can see part of the road. My guess is that the Dos Caminos place is about half-a-kilometre from here . . . over that ridge probably. I think it might be sensible to do the last bit on foot. It's less obvious if anyone happens to be watching.'

Mical dismounted and together they picked their way to where the foothills fell away to the valley, the valley that was really the edge of the Alazar, for they had made a large arc to reach their objective. In ten minutes of stumbling and leading their horses the rock outcrop softened into the dried mud of a gully, and thence along a ridge. Suddenly below them the hills dropped away and revealed the single-track road, little more than a dust cart-track. At the point where the road divided into two was a small house, set, as it were, upon a triangle of mud and stones, an island from which it would be easy to see across the valley in all directions and have a commanding view of the Alazar foothills. Between them and the house was a cultivated area, mainly down to orange groves, with one tilled field which showed no special crop, other than a proliferation of white stones.

Mical looked at Bauer with a touch of admiration in her eyes. His amateur dead-reckoning was faultless, and she felt oddly secure in his company.

They found a suitable shaded area in a gully to tether their horses and unload their gear before creeping forward to a vantage point where they took up position and waited.

Kessler checked the time on his wristwatch. He had done so three times in the last ten minutes. He was sitting on his bunk-bed eating his breakfast from a tin plate placed on his knees. Rückert was doing the same on his own bed. They had been given a substantial breakfast – military style – frankfurters and mushrooms, with half-a-loaf of peasant bread and a tin mug of coffee. Both men had eaten heartily. Kessler put the plate to one side as he picked his teeth with the tip of his tongue, then took a swig of his coffee. For a moment it could have been any barracks, anywhere, anytime in the last forty years, and Kessler mentally noted how 'comfortable' and 'at home' he felt. The army years never leave the average man. They implant a pattern and memory upon him which is, in varying degrees with the man himself, more natural than hindsight cares to admit. An admission repellent to the more liberal humanitarian thinkers of our time, but a fact for all that.

'How long will it take me to drive from here?'

'An hour-and-a-half . . . once you are out of town. There shouldn't be a lot of traffic today. Everywhere is closed and preparing for the fiesta. You've been to Mengele's house, haven't you?'

'Not this one. When I was last here he lived in that dilapidated, wooden farm-shack not far from the border. I don't think he had been there long, either.'

The two men exchanged smiles. Rückert fastened his black glove at the palm, covering the metal and wood that served as a hand.

'Josef never stays anywhere very long. He is allergic to being established and who can blame him?'

They fell into light conversation, inconsequential but informative. After all Kessler had not been in Latin America for many years. He needed to catch up.

'What happened to Eichmann's family? Do they still live in Buenos Aires?'

'Yes, still in San Fernando. His son, Horst, you remember him? Insists upon flying the Nazi flag every year to commemorate his father's execution in Jerusalem.'

'And Pfeiffer?'

'We don't really know. He left Santiago – under pressure – as you must remember. The Reichleiter used to visit him regularly. Now? Who knows?'

Rückert sighed. Every one of his flock who left the security of the Kameradenwerk blanket to fend for himself was a comrade lost. Every death reported was a hole in the ranks. Rückert's 'army' of old comrades was dwindling year by year, mostly through old age and sickness, although on average they were a strong, fit and long-lived bunch. Good comrades. Together they had seen, achieved, and suffered much. Their time would come again. That certainty, or delusion of certainty, was what strengthened Rückert's resolve. Even he felt tired sometimes, but not the disillusion that was now sickening Kessler as he sat and sipped his coffee. He must have shown something of it, for Rückert leaned forward and slapped his knee.

'Courage, *mon vieux*! All is not lost!'

Kessler looked solemnly at him. 'It is to Germany, Hans. Even you resort to French to bolster me up. Where IS Bormann? Why is he not giving us the word?'

'Ask him yourself, Kessler!' Then he softened again. 'The Reichleiter is eighty, my friend. Where is he living? Bolivia most of the time . . . but he, too, moves about. He, too, is nervous. That is what he and Mengele have in common.'

Kessler was not satisfied as he sipped his coffee again and glanced up at his comrade.

'Hans, why have you never allied yourself with the young activists? You are their hero. The most decorated flier of the war. The handsome, dashing Colonel Rückert. They would follow you anywhere. Why, Hans?'

Rückert snorted. 'Because they are a disorganised rabble. Their National Socialism savours of anarchy. WE exist "forty years on" because we ploughed the field well. We sowed well. Ludwig, what matters a few tares? The crop was splendid!'

'I hope you are not going to say we were beaten by the weather. No joking, my friend. the life is in *them*, not in this charade here.'

Rückert shook his head as if to dispel ugly thoughts and restore the balance of sanity.

'I was only partially joking. They ARE a rabble, and they ARE basically anarchists. This is the Bakunin thinking . . . it has more to do with THEM, than with US! Their pretence of loving their Fatherland is a front to make their terrorism palatable. There is no substance in them, Kessler. And besides . . . they like niggers!'

Rückert's 'Aryan' prejudices were always just beneath the surface. The bonhomie and charm no more than a veneer of the ruthless, fascist fanatic that was the real man. Kessler was not all that different in his thinking, but he was a sentimental man, as are most Germans, and Rückert was not. Possibly that made Rückert the more honest, but less palatable. The hyprocrisy of sentimentality is a coinage accepted by most civilised nations as a convenience of social behaviour that avoids the overtly unpleasant.

Kessler sighed and shook his head slowly.

'We have remained the way we are for too long. By behaving like war criminals we have accepted that we are just that. Why? I do not consider myself a criminal, "War" or otherwise. I did my duty, as I saw it, to my Fatherland and my Führer in whom I had, and retain total faith! Where is my crime? In what way are you different from the much-lauded Air Aces of the RAF? Your war record is greater than any allied airman's. What is the difference?'

'They pretend they fought in the name of democracy and freedom. We fought for supremacy. A supremacy that was ours by nature.'

There was a knock at the door.

'*Herein!*'

The German barked command came instinctively before it was softened by the Spanish.

'*Venga!*'

A dark-skinned orderly appeared, and spoke directly to Rückert, as courtesy demanded.

'The car for Standartenführer Kessler, sir.'

Rückert nodded, and both men stood up.

'Will you be here when I return?'

'I imagine so. Let me warn you about the drums, if you have forgotten.'

Kessler smiled. 'I have not forgotten. Perhaps we can go to the Fiesta together.'

Outside the hacienda the air was fresh and highly-scented from the red cactus flowers that had proliferated in the last two days without either warning or apparent reason. There were also small clumps of a thyme-like herb that grew between the cacti and gave to Central America and the higher plateaux of Latin America the same pervading sweetness that the maquis gives to the Midi and to Corsica.

The saloon car waited, the orderly holding the door open

for Kessler as he stalked into the early morning heat. Already the sun was up and flashed and probed through the tree that centred the courtyard. Rückert watched him drive away from the shade of the open doorway. No raised arm in a wave, no happy smile of encouragement. It wasn't like that. It never had been.

Franz returned to the hotel after almost half-an-hour's absence. Ingrid was still in bed and waiting impatiently.

He reported that Señor Yqueras had not been displeased at the call, that – although awakened – he had seemed most happy to be consulted. He implied that he would do as he saw fit, and would be in contact, and Ingrid was to be assured that he fully understood that no harm was to befall her father.

'Why did you add that?' Clearly Franz was not assured of the necessity of keeping his master alive, but – as he knew the latter's daughter rather well – he was puzzled that she should have been so specific.

'I love my father, didn't you understand that? I also know that people are expendable in certain causes. His removal would gain us nothing, Franz. I have been around him enough, have overheard enough to know that. I have listened to him and the banker, Leitgeber, talking. There is something about father being there – in person – and alive. I suspect it is either a facial scan, or maybe his hand, I don't know. He must be alive for that to register. To prop up a dead face, or whatever, does not work. The electronic device does not operate if the facsimile is not alive. There is also something else, a device, a token, something that he must have at the same time. Whatever it is it is kept by Reichleiter Bormann. If we want that forty-eight billion Deutschmarks we have to have that "key" intact. I think Don Julián knows all this . . .'

'But it could all be happening today! The Don said there is a meeting with Bormann today. What do we do?'

Ingrid considered. She was a hard, observant, intelligent female. She had watched her father closely over the last two weeks and something in her was stirred.

'We do nothing. Let my father's disillusion be complete. Then he will come to me or I shall approach him. You will see.'

Franz sighed, mentally and emotionally champing at the bit.

'What do we do now?'

Ingrid turned her smile upon him, and her eyes betrayed exactly what she intended to do 'now'.

The sun was beating down unmercifully on the Alazar and the valley bottom. Bauer glanced up at the great flaring orb in the sky.

'It's going to be hot as hell itself out here in another hour.'

Mical smiled widely at him. 'You're forgetting I am Israeli. It is hot in Israel, you know. You should come and visit us sometime.'

'I didn't imagine Germans were very welcome in Tel Aviv.'

Mical's face clouded momentarily. 'No. It is all right now. We don't bear grudges. You were not to blame and you are fighting them perhaps more than we are now.'

Bauer looked at her child's face and changed the subject. 'One of the problems of being Aryan is that you're inclined to turn pink and become parboiled rather than tan gracefully. That bit was left out of racial superiority. I suppose a tan was half-way to the touch-of-the-tar-brush they so despised.'

Mical giggled, and they both turned back to look down on Mengele's tiny house. Nothing stirred, there was no sign of life. Behind the house a flat field of grassy scrub was hidden from their view by a clump of trees which gave the house its much needed shade. Bauer thought he caught the glint of metal as from an automobile, or vehicle of some sort, but nothing was really visible through the foliage.

The heat made him slightly drowsy and the sweat poured down his forehead and cheeks, despite the hat Garriga had bought for him. Thank God he had! Mical had brought the sacking wrap with her. It contained the rifle, sights, and ammo.

In Asuncion the shops and offices remained closed as on a Sabbath. The city was quiet, waiting. Fiesta and the time of the Ascension was at hand. It merited respect.

José Garriga was about his business as hotel proprietor, by which he meant sleeping in the small 'office' in the main hall and stairwell, instead of in his apartment behind the main building.

In Room 464 Franz had fallen into another sweaty slumber after excelling himself in sexual athleticism, and leaving a contented Ingrid purring on the flowered sheets. It was very hot.

Inside the small house atop the earth ramparts of the valley two men sat in relative silence and waited. One – the owner of the house – fidgeted and kept wandering from window to window and looking out keenly through binoculars. The other sat in the shadow and chain-smoked Turkish cigarettes he had specially imported from Buenos Aires to Bolivia where he lived – most of the time.

Along the tarmacadam of the Route 17 that sped from the capital straight as an arrow northwards, a Packard saloon was being driven by a white-haired man who was mentally rehearsing what he was going to say to his superior if the situation turned out be be as reported. It was hot in that car, less hot possibly than it would have been in an open vehicle, but Kessler perspired, and felt his shirt sticking uncomfortably round his arms and abdomen. His back was wet and caught the draught from the open window so as to make it actually cold. It made Kessler frown. He didn't like draughts . . . even in this climate.

Bauer felt a hand touch his own, and blinked his eyes open. Mical nodded to his right, and Bauer came to life and brought the non-reflective binoculars to his eyes. In the great distance a small cloud of dust implied the movement of a vehicle.

That cloud was immediately picked up by Mengele inside the house as he watched carefully and waited. His companion said nothing . . . merely lit another cigarette from the butt of the last one.

Mical was already unwrapping her rifle and fitting it together with silent and unemotional expertise. Her eyes met Bauer's who was watching her.

'I have to, Richard.'

He nodded. 'I think I want you to . . . now. Can we just wait till I see who is in that house? Then you can have him . . . and good luck.'

She nodded rapidly and continued preparing.

The windscreen needed to be wiped halfway along the dirt road, and the water container was dry. The wipers smeared, white dust, but made enough channels in the arc to give vision of sorts Anyway, there was no traffic. He needed only to be able to see the track. Kessler peered intently through the streaks and made out the approaching building that could only be Mengele's house. As he slowed down he saw the door open and a single, tall, lean and white-haired man emerge. He recognised the medico, and smiled grimly to himself as he saw with what nervous intensity Mengele was glancing about him, almost behind every tree of his orange grove.

Through the binoculars Mical watched Kessler emerge from his car, straighten his jacket and tie, and follow Mengele towards the entrance. Her glance shifted quickly to take in the hard, unpleasant face of the 'Angel of Death'. This was the man who had 'worked' upon her mother in that unspeakable place. This was the man who had 'selected' her grandparents for extermination. Walking behind him was the man who had evicted them and sent them to the concentration camp in the first place. This man, this Kessler, who had tormented her soul from that moment of revelation. It did not matter that he had not soiled his own fingers with the deaths, the torments, the horrors. It was upon his word, unmindful of the consequences of that word. The other, the so-called doctor, was just vermin. The ire, and shame, and passionate hate rose in her throat and she gripped the rifle. Bauer gently touched her arm and looked at her soothingly.

He smiled. 'On the way out, later.'

She nodded quickly, repeatedly, as if to calm her own nerves, for she knew that in the emotional state she was in she would be a worse marksman. Time. Time to pause and collect. Time to calm.

The military flags hung limply against the wall of the big room in the hacienda. The tables and chairs remained in the positions of the court-martial that they had been set in two days ago. Rückert sat at the central table signing letters, and sealing them in envelopes before handing them to his aides who stood waiting as he issued orders, and generally behaved as if an operation was in existence.

'Post this batch here. But *these* are to be delivered by hand by my selected personnel. Clear?'

Rückert's aide was a young German called Emil Krebs who had been with them in Paraguay for seven years and was trusted by him. He was a university graduate from Silesia who had fled the Soviet bloc and made for the Federal Republic as soon as he could see the wood from the trees. Krebs laid the last envelope before him and Rückert signed and sealed it, then turned to him.

'Krebs. Take this to the airport. Ulrich Stangl will meet you there on the tarmac, by the plane. You will hand it *personally* to his passenger after he has shown you his green card. You will NOT enter into conversation, no identification will be made, but you will doubtless recognise the passenger. He is a very well-known Head of State. You will say nothing to anyone of his identity, or I, personally, will cut your throat. Is that understood?'

'Perfectly, sir.'

Rückert stood up and addressed the eight men in the room, only one of whom was not German by birth.

'You must all be aware that we are now on the brink of what we have been waiting for for so long. Consider this as being "*Der Tag* - minus - three months". You will give no indication, nor word of implication, by bearing or by personal excitment, that today is any different from any other. There is enough wild speculation among our Latin friends as it is. I want no more of it. This is official, and it is a military order, as everything will be from this day forward. That is all.'

The heel-clicks, the head-bows were textbook. The training had been excellent. Rückert was a good officer.

'Krebs, before you go. I want the entire unit on stand-by. The guard has been increased as you know. I want it doubled as from sixteen-hundred today. Rankl will take four men into Asuncion and make contact with our friends in the Polizia. Double-check all arrivals during the last ten days: passports, registration, and most of all the photo-bank. See if there is anyone suspicious.'

'What are we looking for, sir? It would help if I knew.'

Rückert sighed. 'An Israeli hit-group. They may, or may not exist. I think they do and I am taking no chances. Not at this moment in time.'

'And if there is suspicion?'

'Kill them. Don't ask questions. Just eliminate them.'

The telephone rang. Rückert frowned and picked up the receiver himself.

'Yes? Ah, Julián! Yes, our friend left on time. He should be there about now. As agreed, indeed. If you wish, certainly. *Adios*.'

Rückert replaced the receiver thoughtfully, frowning still as if asking himself a question.

'Inform Señor Yqueras when Standartenführer Kessler returns, will you? He would like to know exactly.'

The men departed leaving Rückert alone in the room. He lit a cigarillo, and sat back in his chair with a pensive expression. About him the air of a dissatisfied man quarrelled with the latent sense of security he had felt for a long time. He was honest enough in his thoughts to recognise the latter as the comfortable, unruffled calm that he, as an old man, wanted to seat for ever in his bowels; but his mind, his ego and his training grasped the former as the friend for whom he had long waited. He stood up and crossed to the long, wooden cupboard against the wall.

He opened the door and took down from the rail the coat-hanger on which hung his Luftwaffe uniform, much-decorated. He slipped it from its hanger, and put it on over his shirt and tie. Then looked at himself in the mirror on the inside of the door. Still the handsome Colonel Rückert with the cigarillo in his mouth and the famous smile on his lips. He reached up to take down the case on the shelf and opened it. Inside the Knight's Cross with Oak Leaves, Swords and Brilliants, shone and sparkled. The unique neck decoration given to him, the favourite aviator, by the Führer himself.

Mical slowly raised the rifle to her shoulder and peered through the sights.

'Mengele,' was all she said. Then, as if in warning, a gust of wind blew her hair across her face. She bit her lip and lowered the gun, took a handful of dust and threw it in the air four or five times, cursed under her breath.

'We have only the one chance. There is too much wind suddenly. We'll go down there.'

Mical indicated a ridge some fifty feet below them, sheltered by a sudden finger of rock. Bauer nodded and slid down the first part of the slope, took the rifle from her and gave what assistance he could. She didn't need it. She was fitter than he was. She could see Mengele hovering on the doorstep, and then suddenly Kessler stepped out and turned, talking to someone.

Bauer, too, stopped, and held his breath. It had to be, but he needed to be sure. A hand came out of the doorway and Kessler shook hands. A second later another hand passed Kessler something small which he immediately pocketed. There was a sudden 'thunk' and Bauer felt as if his leg had been severed by a blow. He fell down, and rolled forward clutching his leg in agony. Mical saw him fall, release the rifle which he was carrying. It dropped and slid down the slope – out of sight.

Mical's first inclination was to go after the rifle, but she realised Richard was hurt and bent over him. The jaws of a great, iron man-trap had closed on his leg just below the knee, and his trousers were torn and blood-soaked. Together they bent and used every ounce of strength to prize open the jaws. They got it open enough, and jammed a rock between the teeth as she lifted out Bauer's shattered and bloody limb.

Below them at the Casa, farewells were being said. They had heard nothing at that distance.

Bauer looked at her. 'Never mind me! This is the chance, Mical, take it.'

She looked into his eyes and saw that he meant it. She slithered down the slope to the ridge, and fished the rifle out of the scree. A quick inspection showed that it was still clean and intact. She slid the bolt and took aim.

Kessler had left the man at the door, and was walking with Mengele towards the car. The shot rang out with an echoing clap that reverberated right across the valley. The windscreen behind Kessler shattered, and both men ducked and took cover.

Bauer watched through the binoculars and bit his lip. Mical had reloaded and waited. Kessler moved towards the door and her second shot rang out. The window of the door shattered. Kessler kept his head down and gritted his teeth. Mengele wriggled across the road behind the vehicle to seek shelter behind the stone and turf wall of the mound. There was no way he could get back into the house without making a dash for it. That was exactly what Kessler then tried. He dived for the half-open door of the Packard and wriggled inside, below the dashboard, as shot after shot ricocheted off the metal bodywork, and broke more glass in the windscreen.

Kessler started the engine, and braced himself for taking the initiative. He yelled out to Mengele.

'Josef, show yourself!'

Mengele may have been careful of his life, but he was neither a coward, nor paralysed with fear. He did as bid, and Kessler let in the clutch, and did a very tight, three-point turn as shots divided between the car and the wall near Mengele, then stopped. There were ten shots. The clip needed renewing, possibly. He stepped on the accelerator and chanced it, speeding away down the straight road with as much meander as he could manage in the confined space. At the same time Mengele made a dash for the house entrance. Bauer understood what was happening, and was prepared enough to fire the revolver to imply a continuity of shooting, and let them know there was more than one person firing. The bullets fell short, of course, and were wildly off mark. But, then, a revolver doesn't pretend to hit at anything but point-blank range. Not even a Colt .45, whatever the Westerns claimed.

Mical had replaced the clip in three seconds flat, but decided to better her position, and reach the mound behind the orange grove. She moved down, and then became aware of another engine starting. They were making a dash for it.

Suddenly the engine noise, hitherto muted, roared into full volume as the helicopter swept up and over the rooftop of the house, and made straight for her position. She lay back and fired four times. From above two faces, one pale and angry, one swarthy, Italianate and curiously bland, with a cigarette between his lips looked down on her and searched the ground to find who else was there, before it wheeled up into the sky and was gone. There was only the echoing 'chopper' sound gradually fading into nothingness, then silence. In the distance a small cloud of white dust rose to show the escape of the Packard saloon. Mical's face looked down as she sank her chin onto her chest, and sobbed to herself for a moment.

Bauer lay back on the hot, dry ground and tried to think of something else but the pain in his leg before he gave in to it and passed out. He had managed a handkerchief tourniquet with a pencil from his pocket and a stone from the ground. It worked, but Jesus! it hurt! Then, suddenly, it didn't hurt any more and the sun wasn't hot, and it didn't matter.

He was lying on a simple bunk-bed when he came to. He realised he was inside Mengele's small house. It was relatively cool, and someone was moving about near at hand. He turned his head and tried to sit up. The pain shot through him like an arrow, and seemed to go all the way up his spine. His trouser leg had been torn off, and the flesh was bandaged with cloth, and just beginning to show pink rims to the torn edging as the blood seeped through.

Mical joined him and gave him some brandy she had found in a newly-opened bottle. The place stank of Turkish cigarettes and body odour. Outside in the shade of the trees, the two horses were nibbling the grass and the orange leaves they could reach. Mical told him she had managed to get the horses down the gully and round below where he was lying, and somehow she had half-lifted and half-dragged him and got him across a horse and over to the house.

Bauer looked at the small girl with admiration, gratitude, and not a little amazement. She was no bigger than his sister's child who was only eleven years old, yet she had done all this. That left only the problem of getting back to Asuncion and a doctor who would attend to his leg. The fact that she was five-foot nothing, and female, and ought to be helpless was what finally got him onto that horse. He nearly passed out again with the pain, but refused to give in in her presence. They'd make it. Somehow.

# SIXTEEN

Kessler dumped the shattered Packard on a derelict lot on the outskirts of Asuncion. There was no point in attracting attention. He removed the licence plates and dumped them in the river and checked that the engine number had been chiselled off. It had. The Kameraden were usually careful. All documentation removed.

He then walked to the hotel where his daughter was staying. It was late afternoon when he arrived, and he went straight up to her room. Luckily she was in, and concerned when she saw him. It was not like her father to be nervous and disturbed.

He told her what had transpired, and she realised that the unease was not personal fear. He was an old man and would obviously react differently to his younger self, but it was more than that . . . something quite different.

'We must stop these Jews, father. Franz will get some of his local friends . . .'

'No. It is better left to Colonel Rückert, I assure you. Please.'

She put her arms round him and kissed his forehead.

'Are you sure you wouldn't like some tea or some coffee? A brandy? You're upset and very tense. I can feel it right through you. Your whole body is tense.'

Kessler did not reply.

'Will you drive back here this evening, and have dinner with me? I would like that.'

Kessler smiled at her, and indicated that he would do so, but she would have to rent a car for him. She telephoned the concierge, and a car was arranged.

'Why don't you move into the hotel, father? Why must you stay out there? I have never been, I don't even know where it is, but it can't be very comfortable for you.'

'For the moment it is best and certainly safer.'

Ingrid looked at him coldly. 'For whom, father?'

'The Kameraden, who else? Probably for me, too, as I seem to be this month's target. It is therefore safer for you, my dear. And that matters to me very much.'

The sudden earnest look on his face was something she hadn't seen since the death of her mother. A look of love and desperation at the thought of anything happening to her. She realised that he loved her very dearly, and tears sprang to her eyes. She threw her arms round him and hugged him tight.

'Oh . . . Vati!'

The embrace was long and sentimental for both of them. Probably the greater for having been so long delayed. When they parted he stood up and smiled at her.

'Now I must report back. I will see you this evening.'

He walked out, straight-backed and dignified. He was Kessler again.

She left half-an-hour later and joined Franz in the fonda that was their meeting place. Franz was trying to extract one of the cool, highly-coloured soft drinks from the Vantas equipment on the counter. Equipment that had been installed in 1926, with a great glass bulb emerging from the box shape and levers. In the bulb was chilled water. By selecting the lever the colour of the drink could be chosen. It didn't make much difference what the colour was, the taste was more or less identical. Very sweet, yet curiously acidic. Obviously totally ersatz, and the very white, fine-textured froth was added by spoon by the dispenser. The colours, when ranged along the counter, reminded one of stained glass from some European cathedral, the early period of the middle-ages when glass had colour and quality, before it became debased.

Nothing was working for him, but Franz persisted. She watched him after taking her seat. Watched his body as it bent and moved, trying to work the wretched thing. Watched the faded jeans tight over his ass, and faded over the bulge of his genitalia. If only his mental performance was the equal of his physical, Ingrid might have considered a more permanent liaison with her father's aide. He was presentably Aryan, but he was, well, to be kind – none too bright. He approached with a reluctant beer.

'That damn thing doesn't work any more, like half of this God-forsaken country! Why did they ever decide to come here?'

Ingrid sighed. 'Because it is safe, sympathetic and there is no fear of extradition. Grow up, Franz.'

Franz sulked and sipped his warm beer with evident distaste. He had a childish taste for soft, sweet things, and didn't like beer, or whisky. She went on. 'There is something about my father. I can feel it.'

'He's scared, that's all. If Jews were taking pot-shots at me I'd be scared too. He'll get over it.'

But Ingrid wasn't listening. She had that look of distant concentration on her face. It usually meant he was going to have to do something, and maybe not get to lay her that night.

'You're going back after the Fiesta, aren't you?' Franz nodded. 'To Bad Frauburg and the Tegernsee?'

He nodded again.

She went on. 'I want you to alert all the units. Get them to a state of readiness by mid-June.'

Franz's eyes opened wide, and his mouth dropped stupidly.

She didn't like that look. 'You mean we're going to work?'

She didn't answer for a moment. 'There is still one thing I have to do. Get me a drink. Lager, anything.'

Franz moved away to the counter. Ingrid sat back on the chair and stretched herself out languidly, only to sit up quickly as a man entered the fonda and stood in the doorway for some moments surveying the scene. Talking stopped . . . the man had dignity and presence, and obvious wealth. Some even knew Don Julián Yqueras by sight. He walked to Ingrid and sat down facing her.

About the time Don Julián sat on that seat Richard Bauer was being examined by a Paraguayan doctor brought into the hotel at great expense by Garriga, who hovered and translated as the medico dressed the wound.

'I don't care what he says. Tell him it must be the smallest amount of dressing that is necessary. I have to be able to move about. My life could depend upon it.'

Garriga passed on the information to the doctor, who grunted and gesticulated and let forth a torrent of the local patois with typically Latin vehemence, but ultimately did as he was requested. Garriga beamed his golden smile, as if he had personally arranged everything.

'The doctor says you are mad, and do not deserve to be healed. He says the bone is chipped, but not broken, but the muscles are badly torn and will give much pain.'

'I don't need a doctor to tell me that . . . Jesus!'

Bauer almost hit the roof as the bandage was tightened round his leg. The doctor beamed and patted the bandage, which only made Bauer wince again, before he returned the cheesy smile and nodded his pained thanks. Garriga paid him, and ushered him from the room. When he returned he sat on the bed beside Bauer and spoke to them both earnestly.

'Is time, I think, to go underground, like they say in the movies, eh? These people very bad people. They come looking for you soon, I think. They find because the polizia help them.'

He looked from one to the other, almost apologetically.

'I think is best you come and stay in my apartada. Is not the Ritz, maybe, but there is no trace. They come to the hotel, they see no names on the books, and they look through the rooms . . . there is no one. They do not come to my private apartada. Is best.'

Mical seemed about to protest, but Bauer grabbed her hand and nodded. She acquiesced.

'Thank you, José. That is very kind of you. I agree, I think it is best. They know now that there is not just one of us. I believe that they will come looking for us.'

Garriga grinned widely, obviously pleased that his hospitable suggestion was not decried. He picked up the bags, more or less unpacked, and urged them to follow him. Mical went to Bauer, who swung his heavily bandaged leg over the bed edge, sat for a moment, then accepted the offer of her shoulder He put his arm round her and she helped steady him. For a moment their faces were close together and their eyes met. Just for a moment both wondered if something were about to move from the general to the particular, but both held back. It was better that way, at least for now.

Garriga's private quarters backed onto the courtyard and ran down one side of it. Access was from the main stairwell or from the courtyard itself – if you knew your way about. It consisted of a living-room, one bedroom, small kitchen, small bathroom, and a roof 'off' which was shown to them later. The interior was very Latin, very Spanish, and – despite protestations as to his agnosticism – very Catholic. A few cheap pieces of modern mass production rubbed shoulders with the odd inherited heirloom of dark wood and brass. Family photographs in ornate silver frames stood next to highly-coloured, and quite revolting, china ornaments of no conceivable use to anyone. The mirror over the fireplace had cut ornamentation in the corners, then was surrounded by a 'mount' of ruby and deep ultramarine glass in two-inch squares. The whole in an ornate gilt frame. One wall was draped with a huge, and tattered, piece of faded lace that Garriga swore his mother had made with her own hands. The elderly Singer sewing-machine, in black and gilt, with elaborate cast-iron stand and treadle, under the window, and the heavy lace curtains testified to a female presence at one time. Almost certainly the much-mentioned and much-adored mother, alas now deceased. Two bunches of waxed-paper flowers in fluted trumpet-flare vases completed the picture.

Garriga shoved a heavy armchair of dark material forward with his foot.

'Please, Señor Bauer, rest the leg, and the Señorita Rak and I will make some coffee. Do you like pigeons?'

Both Bauer and Mical looked askance for a moment. Under the circumstances yaks might have been equally unlikely. Garriga took their silence for vague interest, and beamed once more.

'Is my hobby. How you say? My pride and joy? Yes. The Pride and The Joy. I show you. Please . . .'

Garriga led them over to the double-doors in the wall opposite. Doors with glass panels that had waxed, printed, stained-glass patterns rendering them opaque. He opened them gently, and beckoned that they should follow him through the bead-curtain hanging across the opening. They did.

Inside the room, lit by a green corrugated-plastic roof, it was possible to make out shelves and boxes, sacks and perches. In the room sat and flapped some dozen tame, white pigeons. Garriga displayed them proudly as they fluttered to rest upon his head and shoulders, and he found a paper bag of seed and corn, which he threw by the handful into the recesses of the room. The constant soft cooing and flutter gave an air of unreality to the scene. Mical found it delightful, and clapped her hands like a child. The owner took evident pleasure in her delight, and beamed again.

'These are my children. See how they love me! Is very pleasant.'

Mical put a finger out to take one, but it would not leave its master.

'Don't they take a lot of looking after? I mean . . . you have the hotel and other things. Who feeds and waters them?'

Garriga shrugged happily, and implied that despite his great burden he could manfully cope.

'Now I make some coffee. Señorita, I show you where the things are.'

Garriga's innate male chauvinism showed as he led Mical into the tiny kitchen, and indicated the whereabouts of everything necessary for beverages and general cooking. Obviously when there was a woman in the house the man did not intend to do anything. Mical sighed, but accepted it as her lot. In the Middle East – Israel or no Israel – a woman knows exactly where she stands, and it isn't very high on the ladder.

Garriga returned to his other guest, men together in the permanent order of the world, and sat down opposite Bauer.

'I like this lady. She is very pretty, I think. You are fortunate man, Señor.' Bauer had no time to protest at his lack of proprietary rights. Garriga leant forward. 'So. This Kessel is not killed, and the others fly away like the birds. Maybe this is good for you, maybe not so good. I cannot tell.'

Bauer eyed his host curiously. 'Señor Garriga, forgive me asking, but why do you tolerate these men in your midst? Why don't you kick them out? Why didn't you do it long ago?'

José Garriga made a face and shrugged.

'What for? They do us no harm. They bring money. Is good for us. They made trade with countries in Europe, is also good for us. Why we mus' kick them out?'

Bauer sucked his teeth. 'You know they are very bad men. Some of them . . . very bad indeed?'

Garriga's eyes clouded for a moment and the look was veiled. 'Señor, what happens in Europe is no concern of ours. And what happens here is no concern of *yours*!'

'But these are wanted criminals! Men responsible for the deaths of thousands of human beings. You can't just aid them as a nation without incurring the condemnation of the world.'

Garriga made an 'it makes no difference in the long run' gesture, when Mical's voice came from the kitchen doorway.

'We can also level that argument at you, Richard. What is Germany doing about putting its own house in order?'

The sore was open in Bauer's conscience, and he felt the caustic in the open wound. He had never liked that, but it was familiar. He sighed wearily.

'Not much, I agree.'

Mical advanced with the tray of cups and coffee in her hands. She laid them down on the occasional table before them, and straightened up as she looked closely at him.

'What I have never understood is why you did nothing immediately after Nüremberg, when everything was geared for it, and before it was a crime to chase criminals? Why, Richard? Why did Germany not show itself to be what it pretends, when it was still possible to do so?'

For once the calm and controlled Bauer lost his cool. That sort of unrealistic, liberal-thinking rubbish was more than he could take amiably, and his voice was unexpectedly harsh when he spat his reply.

'Oh for God's sake, girl! Grow up! You weren't alive. You have no idea what it was like! Germany was in ruins! Ruins like you cannot imagine! What do you expect us to have done? Every mark, every pfennig, every effort went into rebuilding houses, factories, anything that would make us viable as a nation. Anything that would give us bread. You expect us to have spent valuable time, and hundreds-of-thousands of marks in chasing criminals round the world? We were more concerned with building hospitals and schools for those left *alive*. There was *nothing*! Literally nothing! Let's get our priorities straight, shall we?'

Mical was chastened and showed it. 'I'm sorry. I never thought of it quite like that.'

'You Israelis don't, understandably perhaps, but Jerusalem is not the centre of the universe! And, please understand, I don't feel guilty any longer!'

Mical could not stop herself glaring at him. She was responding to his anger with her own. It was Garriga who flashed his gold smile, and held up the slip-ware bowl.

'Sugar?'

# SEVENTEEN

Kessler was washing his hands at the cracked basin when he saw the cockroach creep out from under the bed. He stared at it, watched its curious movements, its antennae moving with a lazy, drunken motion. Kessler's pink face became suddenly infused with blood, and took on an expression of anger as he brought his foot down on the wretched insect and heard the sickening crunch of the bursting carapace. It was the implication: the dirt, decay, lack of husbandry, disorganisation, domestic filth . . . it was all too much. The whole aspect of Latin America was more than he could stomach. Always a fastidious man, Kessler could not bear the thought of the unclean. It went with decline, physical and moral decline, and there was no place for such thought in Kessler's pantheon of awareness. It was one more exemplification of the whole failure. Kessler was not merely disturbed, he was sick inside. Troubled as he had never been. He folded the towel carefully, and laid it down squarely, neatly. He turned and looked at the two beds. Rückert's and his own. Well-made, primly, crisply orderly, military.

On top of Rückert's folded towel, pillow case, and personal things there was his lighter and packet of cigarettes. Kessler bent over and took one, lit it, and blew the unaccustomed smoke into the room. He seldom smoked these days . . . hardly at all since the war . . . almost never since Madeleine died.

He was standing that way, stiffly by the bed, smoking awkwardly when Rückert entered and regarded him curiously.

'So. You're back!'

Kessler did not reply, merely puffed once again.

'A successful meeting, I trust.'

Kessler put on his prim face. 'Not particularly. I helped myself to one of your cigarettes. I hope you don't mind.'

Rückert shook his head, and crossed to the small chair, turned round, and straddled it facing Kessler as the latter went on.

'I am in agreement with rumours I have heard. The Reichleiter is no longer totally in command of himself. I will not go as far as to say that he is "ga-ga" far from it, but he is not fit to control.'

Rückert looked at him coldly, his mouth pursed slightly, and his eyes very hard. When he replied it was with wariness in his voice.

'There are others capable of doing so.'

Kessler snorted. 'Who? That butcher Mengele? Günther? Or are there spectacular schemes to rescue Hess, or capture Speer? No, Hans. You and I are the only ones capable. But exactly where are our followers? Where are our legions?'

'We have no shortage of supporters – as you well know. We have our people placed strategically throughout the world. In Germany alone we could assume control in forty-eight hours when the word is given.'

'I cannot think you really believe that. Oh, we have muscle, no one denies that. But in another five years we will have none. Our muscle will have atrophied! We have kept ourselves apart from the young for too long.'

It was Rückert's turn to become incensed. 'They are lunatics! Carpetbaggers of terrorism!'

'And what have we here, Hans? Let me SEE them. Show me! Strutting dagoes in fancy dress! My daughter is right.'

Rückert's eyes narrowed again, and his mouth became a tight slit. After a moment of controlled silence he spoke very quietly.

'But you reached agreement with Bormann? You are able to operate the account?'

Kessler drew himself up, then stubbed out the cigarette on the saucer ash-tray. He turned and looked directly at Rückert.

'Yes. *I* am. No one else can! All those billions of marks are now in MY power, Hans. Does that not worry you?'

Rückert forced himself to give his charming smile. But the birds on the trees were not convinced, not this time.

'No. It doesn't worry me. It worries Josef, but that is because he is a mean-minded man, basically a crook, and assumes all others are as he is. I know you to be an honest, and just German. One who loves his Fatherland before all things. I don't think I am wrong. You have proved it time and again. Should I worry?'

Kessler frowned. 'No. Seeing the Reichleiter has upset me and that gargoyle Mengele makes my flesh creep. There is a smell about him, Hans. The smell of death stained with mendacity. What could be worse?' He paused and did not look at Rückert. 'You have talked with Josef, then?'

'Yes. On the radio. He said that they had been forced to leave in haste due to this wretched Israeli girl turning up, apparently not alone. They are too well-informed, Kessler. Too persistent. And my senses were right, weren't they? She is not alone.'

'So it would seem.'

Rückert lifted his head and looked directly into Kessler's eyes.

'I also find it odd that you have been back for some time and did not report to me. I had to come and wheedle it out of you, and even then you would have said nothing about the Jew attack if I hadn't asked. Why? Why, Kessler?'

Kessler sighed and turned away. He walked to the window and looked through the narrow space between the shutter louvres.

'It just didn't seem to matter. As I say, I was upset and I knew Josef would be on to you screaming blue murder and demanding the whole State of Israel be immediately liquidated If they are coming after anyone, surely it has to be Mengele.'

'You know we will not permit the organisation to be threatened, even by you. If it comes to that, we would either kill you, or leave you to your fate without any possible help. The Kameraden come first. The Reich must survive.'

Kessler swung round and glowered at him. 'Aren't you forgetting something? I have sole access to the Great Fund. Without me, there is no money. None!'

Rückert returned the look unflinchingly. 'Since the war ended I have brought eighty-seven comrades to safety. Together we have built the Kameradenwerk, and linked it with all National Socialist movements still in Germany and Europe. I am able to come and go because the world knows me as a war hero, honoured even by my enemies, they neither know nor suspect my part is anything other than my outspoken right-wing sentiments.' He grinned with clenched teeth and for once his age was apparent. It was the grin of a death's head. 'I have built an organisation that could have held the world in its grasp *if it so wished*. It will do as *I* say, because they believe and trust in *me*! Whatever might be our goal, it does not matter one iota by comparison with the lives of the comrades. That is the word I have given.'

Rückert almost spat out the last two sentences, and Kessler opened his eyes wider to stare at his old friend.

'And our grand design?'

Rückert held his look for a few moments without reply, then stood up, moved his gammy leg with one hand, and picked up his stuff from the bed. He said nothing as he crossed the room and went out of the door. Kessler's face remained blank and without emotion, but his eyes had gone dull.

They were still dull two hours later when he turned his head slowly from the seat and looked at the reddish glow visible through the shutters. He stood up and walked from the room. The hacienda was, as ever, quiet, almost unoccupied. The men remained in their quarters in the stable-block unless they were on duty as guards, or called for duties by Colonel Rückert. At all other times they melted into the wallpaper.

Kessler walked slowly down the corridor towards the main room, what had once been the large reception room of the house and was now the operational centre. He hesitated outside the double-doors then pushed one open, and looked inside before entering. It was deserted, shuttered, and lit only by the roseate glow that filtered through from outside. He walked in, closing the door behind him. The court-martial format remained. Behind the tables the two Nazi military flags hung limply, in this light brown and indistinguishable, only touches of white showing amid the folds. Kessler walked to them, touched the drapery as if to make sure that it was real, then sighed and walked round the walls of the room, covered as they were with old posters and framed photographs of the old party hierarchy at war and in peace.

In one of the cupboards that he opened he found an old parade-ground eagle glinting with Roman splendour. Behind them were four Fahnen and Standarten, with standard-bearers' sashes belonging to the old Army Korps VII, and a framed photograph of General der Artillerie von Reichenau presenting them at Munich, dated 19 April 1937. Above them on the shelf were two Feldjägerkorps gorgets, and two cloth bands, Führerhauptquartier cuff-titles. The ringkragen were tarnished, and the colour had almost disappeared.

Kessler felt his throat constricted and he wanted to sob . .

He heard the voice from behind him.

'So, you are Ludwig Kessler?'

Kessler spun round in panic. He knew the soft, high-pitched voice with the slight accent. He blinked at the centre of the room. His heart pounded inside his shirt and the blood thudded against his temples.

Heinrich Himmler shook hands with the twenty-eight-year-old Kessler who stood before his opulent desk in crisply ironed shirt and arm-band, his breeches tight round his waist.

'The Fatherland is pleased with you, Kessler. You are a credit to the National Socialist Movement. I am delighted to welcome you into the SS.'

The Reichführer beamed at him over his rimless glasses, and his famous blue-chin did nothing to dispel the great moment of Kessler's young life.

But when Kessler took a step forward the desk was not there, nor was Himmler, nor was the young, eager, starry-eyed SS volunteer who felt privileged to have been born German. He touched the table as if for support, though he did not feel faint or even surprised, and sat down on the folding-chair, looking at the backs of his hands.

The sounds of the piano were perfectly clear. It was no Steinway, but the keys were gently touched, and the melodic line had great sensitivity and clarity. Schumann, always Schumann. The first piece of the *Kinderscenen – Von fremden Ländern und Menschen* – and it so suited the cottage upright piano his mother was playing. She sat well away from the keyboard as was her habit, and leant forward, lifting her hands in the coquettish manner fashionable at that time. Kessler stared at the plain, Berliner *hausfrau* face that was his mother's, and felt the sudden ache and pain of loss in his heart before he glanced at the twelve-year-old boy sitting on the wooden stool listening in awe and love to his favourite piece. Behind the group the brilliant light of a golden morning shone through the window and diffused the halo round the apparition.

Then he felt himself drawn towards the window and the sound of the piano faded, to be replaced by the steady crunching of booted feet marching in great numbers. He hastened across to the open window and looked down from the balcony into the Berlin street. The great Wehrmacht marched with order, precision, and authority symbolising the all-conquering, masterful Germany.

Suddenly he was in the street amid the watchers of those marching armies, laughing, and his breast swollen with pride. He looked up from the street to the great balcony where the leaders, the generals, the Führers were taking the salute and the balcony was empty. There was no one.

Kessler bent his head over his hands on the simple folding table in the empty, darkened room and wept. The sunset had gone. There was only darkness, and a man – old, disenchanted, sitting amid junk furniture in a backwater in Paraguay.

The guards who saw Kessler walk from the house were adamant that he was in good health. He walked with an upright bearing as always, he did not reply when greeted, but that was not unusual from the arrogant Germans who commanded the Latin ranks, but they admitted that there was a slight air of unreality about him. Especially as the wind that had come up blew the wisp of white hair across his forehead, and lent him a slightly wild aspect. He just walked out, no one thought to ask him where he was going. He was, after all, Standartenführer Kessler.

Having arranged to have dinner with her father Ingrid was not unnaturally worried when by eleven-thirty he had not arrived at the hotel, or telephoned. It was not her father's pattern. He was punctual to a fault. He always had been. It was his way. When eleven o'clock arrived she had decided something was amiss, and that he was not coming. She wasn't very hungry so contented herself with a modest salad sent up to her room, bathed, undressed and retired for the night. Franz had strict instructions to either remain in his room or find companionship elsewhere.

The knock on the door came at exactly eleven-fifty-five. She read the time on her bedside alarm clock and sat up, reached for her light robe, and crossed to the door.

'Who is it?'

She recognised her father's voice immediately, and shot the bolt on the inside of the door, aware that there was an oddness about his manner of speaking. Kessler entered and flopped into a chair. He looked dishevelled and very tired. She noted his trousers bore traces of dust and dead cactus. She looked closely at him, terribly aware that he was an old man. Gone was the sprightly, well-preserved senior citizen. She crossed to the phone and rang for service, ordered a bottle of brandy to be sent up, then returned and sat on the floor at his feet, and waited for him to tell her whatever it was had brought him to her door. At length it came in a quiet monotone.

'It is something of a shock to recognise that the men one revered, worked with as comrades in-arms, are no more than empty husks. The stuffing has gone from them . . .'

He paused, seemed unwilling to continue, then did.

'You know, Ingrid, I have admired Hans Rückert all my adult life, almost loved him as a brother. You have no idea how we looked up to him during the war. His victories were legendary. His record of missions was second to none. Mölders, Galland, they were great fighter-pilots, but Rückert had a special charm about him, perhaps because he was a bomber-pilot and not one of the glamour boys, he had a sort of mystique. He was stitched together with bits of metal, and still remained the great warrior, the handsome charmer. Every woman in Germany was in love with him.'

Kessler paused again and remained utterly silent for some moments.

'He was more responsible than any one man for saving so many of our people. The more they were wanted by the Allies, the greater was his determination that they should not have them. He worked with Bishop Hudal in the Vatican. He worked with Perón, and others, here in South America. He made it safe, economically possible. He even persuaded the Reichleiter to fork out money from his private horde to assist in the upkeep of old comrades. He built the Kameradenwerk. His was the vision and the purpose. He, more than any other, would make the Fourth Reich a living possibility. That cause that one had hoped for, lived for, planned for is nothing but a delusion. The comrades are geriatrics hoping to be left alone to die in peace. Nothing more. Nothing! That cracks my heart, Ingrid. Oh, yes, my dear, I do have one.'

Ingrid smiled gently at him. 'I know that.'

She rested her head on his knee and held his hand softly as he rested his head back against the chair, and remained silent for what seemed an age. The knock on the door broke their reverie, and Ingrid took the tray of brandy, soda-syphon, and dish of ice-cubes and glasses from the night porter. After she closed the door there was a second subdued knock. The porter whispered to her.

Kessler heard her muffled '*Entiende . . . gracias*' as she closed the door again and crossed to the tray, broke the bottle seal, and poured a large and a small brandy into two of the glasses. Kessler didn't even look at it as he sipped.

'What was he whispering?'

'Just to remind us that Asuncion Fiesta is tomorrow, and that the drumming will start at midnight and we are not to be alarmed.'

Kessler grunted and glanced at the bedside clock. It read two minutes after midnight.

'The clock is four minutes fast. I always keep it that way. It keeps me on time.'

'I don't understand that. If you know it is four minutes fast you automatically make allowances, don't you?'

She giggled, then became purposeful and serious.

'What is to happen to the money, father?'

'I am returning to Buenos Aires the day after tomorrow. Telex your leaders. They are to meet me in my hotel suite on –' he checked his watch '– on Tuesday the twenty-seventh. I am making the party fortune available to your group, *not* to the old guard.'

It had come at last! Ingrid's millennium was upon her. Her heart pounded with excitement, and she felt as if she were bursting. She flung her arms round his neck, and hugged him until it hurt.

'Father! Oh, father!'

Then she stumbled upon a thought, and turned to him.

'But what about the Reichleiter? Don't you need Bormann's help, his token, whatever it is?'

'You hear more than is good for you. I already have what I need. That, correctly disposed, and my own living handprint will activate the release.'

Ingrid looked earnestly at him, as if weighing up a difficult decision.

'You will guide us?'

Kessler smiled and nodded.

Outside the clock of the cathedral started to chime the midnight hour. Immediately upon that summons came the most eerie, awe-inspiring sound, wafting over the midnight air across and through the city. It seemed distant, yet immediate, and all-pervading. From every direction came the sound of random disorganised drumming. It came from instruments, it came from hollowed logs, it came from the walls of shanties and the rows of trash-cans.

Some long, and reverberant, some a rhythmic beating, mostly just a long roll. As it raised itself above every other sound, almost visibly above the city roof-tops it seemed to swamp everything else in existence.

# EIGHTEEN

The dawn crept over Asuncion without visible warmth. It had a lime green tinge which could have implied a rain storm from the north-east, but there was no taste of rain in the air. In any event it was hot, and had been all through the long night. The drumming still reverberated through the streets and over the roof-tops. Then it stopped.

It was the sudden silence that woke Kessler. He had dozed off in the chair after three brandies and Ingrid merely covered him with a blanket. There was no point in waking him. Old people can sleep anywhere. He did not start, or sit up, but his eyes clicked open. Another manifestation of his past military training and experience. Ingrid sensed it rather than saw it from the bed where she lay under a single sheet.

'The drums have stopped. The sudden silence woke you.'

Kessler sighed and rubbed his forehead with finger and thumb. 'Have you been asleep?'

Ingrid murmured a yes, and swung her legs out of the bed, and sat for a moment. Kessler straightened with difficulty, and felt the rigid set of his back, aggravated by sleeping on a chair, unwilling to give and let him sit up. Young people never quite understand how the aged are plagued by arthritic pains and stiffness, even in hot, dry climates. But he was, after all, nearly eighty.

'Do you think if I phoned they would send us some coffee, maybe breakfast? It's very early.'

Kessler grunted. 'Tell them it is for guests of Don Julián Yqueras, they will send it.'

He stood up, and Ingrid picked up the bedside phone while he walked stiffly to the bathroom. When he returned, wiping his hands on the pink hotel towel, he had an air of expectancy about him, even eagerness.

'After I've had some coffee and a bath I will go back to the hacienda and pick up my case and my papers. Ingrid, did you say that Franz was going back to Germany on Tuesday or Wednesday?'

'Tuesday, father.'

'Then I want him to go to Augsburg and Memmingen, then on to Garmisch-Partenkirchen. There are documents to deliver if we are to alert our people.'

Ingrid stiffened. '*My* people, father . . .you said.'

'Yes, my dear . .your people. But we will need help from certain persons I know. Organisation is everything. I am good at that. I always was.'

'Will you go to the hacienda straight away? You must be careful, father. If Colonel Rückert knows you are leaving them, and taking the money he will try to kill you. Please take care. Say nothing.'

Kessler smiled at her concern. It comforted him to know that his daughter cared for him. Only his mother, Madeleine, his wife, and Ingrid had ever cared for him. He knew he was not the most likeable of men. His manner was off-putting, but he was capable of considerable feeling for the few he cared about, and responded to affection when it was given.

'I think we may find that Hans Rückert is secretly delighted, even relieved, that all he has to consider is the welfare of his old comrades. He has lost the stomach to reshape the world. But I will take care, I promise.' He paused. 'Which reminds me, Ingrid, are any of your young friends on my tail?'

Ingrid frowned and looked at him questioningly.

'No. Why? You are being followed by someone? It must be the Israelis.'

'I don't think so. I never did. I don't accept that there is any Israeli hit-group thirsting for the blood of Ludwig Kessler, or Manfred Dorf. It does not make sense and the Israelis, in my estimation, always make absolute sense. Also the technique of tailing is one I recognise. I almost wrote the manual, you know. I just wondered.'

The porter brought their coffee and rolls, and was highly

deferential, even refusing to accept a gratuity. That, in Latin America, is the final accolade of a person's status in a community. Kessler himself poured the coffee, and went on talking.

'Now we will have something to bring us very close together, my dear. Together we will reshape Germany.' He dropped two sugar lumps into his coffee and stirred. 'Like most good Germans I have been content to obey. It had not occurred to me to take the reins, but the more I think of it, the more it appeals. I am too old to be more than a figurehead, but if I could shape it I can try to realise some of the Führer's great visions.'

Ingrid looked at him, saw the visionary gleam in his eyes and smiled happily.

'I do wish I had known him. I can see in your face what he must have meant to you.'

'He was an extraordinary man! He inspired and fired the nation in a way that you could taste on the air. Germany, as a nation, has never been united, neither politically nor racially. But he gave us one Reich.'

'*Ein Volk, Ein Reich, Ein Führer.*'

Ingrid repeated the old slogan piously, like some mantra, as her father took her hand and patted it, and beamed at her enthusiastically – just a trace of moisture in his eyes.

The morning was an early one for most inhabitants of Asuncion. Few could sleep through the drumming. Only the children, but, then, children will sleep through anything.

It was an early breakfast for Garriga, Bauer and Mical. She placed a plate of eggs and beans before the little Paraguayan who was already appreciating the aroma from the plate before Bauer. It was not often he had breakfast at all. Certainly never served to him, not since his mother died.

Mical had accepted the role of domestic slave with equanimity. Male chauvinism knows no frontiers. Once or twice she had wondered how on earth her sex had ever managed to obtain a vote anywhere, then on the one visit she had made to distant relatives in the States, she became aware that a matriarchal society was actually possible. Four weeks of it had made her doubt the wisdom of the arrangement, and she accepted the Jewish family structure as the one that suited her best anyway. The mother was, in effect, the uncrowned ruler. She merely permitted the men to think that they were.

Here it was little different from the Middle East. She had watched the women working in the fields, carrying the burdens, ageing that little bit quicker, but then men like Garriga were so helpless in a silly way, and very likeable.

Garriga beamed at her. 'Is very pleasant having such good friends in my apartada. Señorita Mical makes the good breakfast. Please to eat.'

He shovelled the beans into his gilded mouth with his knife as Mical went to the tiny kitchen to fetch her own food.

'So. What is to do? The Big Man and the very bad doctor will not be seen again for many months, I think. Why you not go back home? They will kill you, señor, you mus' understand this. Is better you go.'

Mical put her plate on the table and sat down as she spoke. 'I am not going anywhere until I have done what I came to do. What is the point?'

Garriga sucked his teeth noisily. 'Is very dangerous, I think. How are you to find this man Kessel?'

'Kessler,' Mical corrected.

'Yes, Kessel.'

'We need to find out where the Nazis have their headquarters, José. We can take it from there. It will lead us to Kessler eventually.'

'And Mengele.' The flat voice of Mical implied she had a double purpose now, and was going to maintain it.

Garriga shrugged. 'I think they leave Asuncion. Maybe Señor Yqueras finds a nice safe place for them in the Alazar, anywhere. He has much money.'

'I don't think so, José. Kessler himself may elect to stay here, remain relatively safe, but his daughter won't. You see she is actively tied up with the Neo-Nazi movement in Germany and Europe. She isn't going to leave all that.'

Mical glanced at him. From time to time she had been aware that Bauer knew things he had not told her. She sensed that it was perhaps not an intent to cheat her, merely a policeman's caution, or an intelligence man's directive to reveal nothing to anyone for whatever reason. Garriga frowned.

'There is still this sickness in Germany?'

'Not just in Germany, though my country is still the centre, the focal point, for whatever it is they propose to do. You see, José, there are still those in Germany who regret the passing of Hitler and the Nazis, still those who wish to see it all rise again. I suppose they need the stimulus of the flags, the parades, the mass hysteria to get their adrenalin moving. I find it frightening and shaming. That is why I do my best to stamp it out.'

Mical looked at him. 'How many, Richard? How many Germans still want this terrible thing back?'

Bauer avoided her eyes. 'Oh, I don't know, there is no means of knowing accurately. Five or six millions, I doubt if it is any more, but I could be wrong.'

Mical bowed her head and remained silent. Garriga looked at them both, from one to the other, then went on.

'Then why are you not looking for these people in your own country? Why bother with old men on the other side of the world?'

Mical spat out her own answer. 'Because I have a personal score to settle.'

But Bauer spoke quietly in his firm but authoritative way.

'That is not my reason. These geriatrics are the original criminals. They still control an organisation that runs through Europe's entrails like an enormous tapeworm. They are more dangerous than the others because they *have* that organisation, that experience. They *believe* in what they are doing. Never underestimate that sort of belief, my friend. It is indestructible.' Bauer paused. 'They also have access to almost unlimited funds to further their aims and somehow I feel that there is imminent danger from that fact. I think that is why Kessler is here. That is why – for me – he must be stopped. At whatever cost.'

Garriga was serious for once. He nodded sagely.

'I understand. I remember Perón.'

Mical stood up and mumbled something about doing the dishes, no doubt hoping for a volunteer to assist. She was disappointed. Garriga beamed as he watched her walk to the kitchen.

'I like this lady. She understand me, and is so pretty.'

He made a kissing gesture with his fingers, and giggled at his own extravagance before he lit a cigarillo and tipped his chair back, only to cough his guts out after the first deep inhalation.

'Excuse, please, I think I have the bad chest. Is no good this smoking. I think maybe I give it up again.'

When he had finished coughing and wheezing he looked coyly at Bauer.

'Tell me, señor. You have maybe a little money, yes?'

'Not much.' Bauer was wary, but it was also the truth. His resources had been severely strained by the air fare to South America, and he could hardly claim expenses when he was on suspension.

'Why?'

'I think is possible I find out where these Nazis have their place. Maybe this is where Kessel stays.'

'Kessler.'

'*Si*, Kessel. There is in the Polizia a man I know, who takes money from these people . . . maybe, for a little more money – not little, but not so big – maybe he give me this address.'

'We can draw some cash from the Bank.'

'Señor. Is fiesta. Banks they not open for maybe two, three days.' He considered his new friend and seemed satisfied. 'Okay. I have a little money from things I do. You pay me after the fiesta. But it is dangerous, I think.'

His face betrayed that he knew it was. A look that disappeared just as quickly as Mical came back from the kitchen. Garriga smiled his usual golden smile.

'Is very, what you say? Agreeable, yes, agreeable to have friends in my apartada.'

He watched Mical take out the rest of the dishes without even a complaint, and turned to Bauer.

'Why these Germans not like Jews? They are pretty.'

# NINETEEN

Kessler's absence was not reported. It was entered in the guardhouse log as someone leaving the compound. No one bothered to remark upon it, no one saw fit to even read the evening log. It came to light when Rückert arrived at nine. He had stayed with a friend in Rosario rather than use the hacienda bunk bed yet again, though his reason was motivated by necessity of contact, not comfort. The unreported absence filled him with fury, not because he cared where Kessler was, but because it was slack and unmilitary. These useless Latins were all the same. Thank God his aides were German! He turned to Krebs.

'See if you can make contact with either the Reichleiter, or Doctor Mengele. Try the emergency frequency. If nothing there, then frequency for Bolivia.'

Krebs left smartly, Rückert turned to his next best junior, Schaper, who was from Breslau, another exile.

'Schaper, see if you can get me some coffee. This damned climate plays hell with my hardware. Put some brandy into it, eh?'

He turned to the taller of the two heavies who hovered around waiting to be used.

'What about the Jews? Anything?' The man shook his head and made a long face.

'There was a police report that they had found the girl's address, that she was seen walking with two men. This is it.'

He handed the flimsy piece of paper to Rückert who scanned the intelligence quickly, then snapped at the heavy.

'Follow it up, now. If there is the girl at this address, finish her off. Anyone else, get rid of them, too. Don't wait for explanations.'

The heavies departed slowly and deliberately, as Krebs

returned from the wireless room, shook his head, and shot out his hand to pick up the table phone the moment it rang.

He turned to Rückert, covering the mouthpiece with his other hand. 'Inspector Naval, polizia.'

Rückert nodded and took the receiver. '*Buenos dias*, Inspector. *Como esta usted*? Mmh. When was this? I see, yes, my friend, you did right. *Gracias, hasta la vista*.'

Rückert held the receiver for a moment before replacing it on the cradle. He was thinking hard. The inspector was in their pay, and had just told him that he had been approached by a doctor of his acquaintance who informed him that he had attended a man who had been injured by a man-trap. He had thought the girl with him was possibly Israeli. Then later, he had been approached by a Paraguayan of his acquaintance who kept a small hotel – El Paradiso – who had attempted to bribe him to reveal the whereabouts of the Nazi hacienda, which he had, of course, steadfastly declined to do.

Rückert turned to Krebs. 'I am informed that a man attempted to bribe the good police inspector to reveal the location of this place.'

Krebs looked him straight in the eye. 'Which we may assume he did, sir.' Krebs was a realist.

Rückert chuckled cynically. 'Are you saying that our trusted Latin militiaman would take a bribe to reveal what he was being paid not to reveal?'

'Yes, sir. I am. Naval has done it before.'

Rückert sighed. 'And you're damn right, too! So, we must assume they now know where we are. Schaper, send out Ascoli and two men to speak with the Inspector and find the enquirer. They are to eliminate him. Krebs, I want you with me.'

He started to walk towards the door when the phone rang again. He stopped and nodded for Krebs to answer.

'*Oiga*, oh, yes, of course, fräulein. I will see if the Colonel is here.' He covered the mouthpiece again and turned to his superior. 'Fräulein Kessler.'

Rückert frowned, considered for a moment, then nodded, and took the receiver once more.

'Ingrid? My dear, how nice to hear from you. Are you

going to the fiesta this evening? Your father is not with you? I see. What? Yes, as a matter of fact we did find out the Israeli girl's whereabouts. Hotel El Paradiso, Plaha de Piedra. Er, if your father should appear ask him to contact me, will you? Of course . . . *aufwiederhören.*'

Rückert walked from the room followed by Krebs. He was thinking, puzzled and concerned. There was the possibility of an Israeli attack. He had already sent half of the men to Yqueras, as he had asked. There was the missing Kessler, and why had his daughter telephoned? Why did she want the Israeli's whereabouts? And how did she know the telephone number of the hacienda? Had Kessler been indiscreet enough to tell her? Or was he actually with her at that moment? If he was, why was she lying?

He turned to his aide as they walked the corridor.

'Is everything ready if we need to evacuate?'

'Yes, sir, but I think we ought to stay and fight them. There can't be all that many.'

'There are four Germans in this building at this moment. There are eight, possibly nine, latins who will disappear the moment shots are fired in anger. I don't mind the odds. We can whip a bunch of Jews, but it will draw attention to us at a time when we wish to avoid it. I cannot permit anything to jeopardise our organisation.'

'I have informed the duty officer that transport should be fuelled with enough reserve petrol to take us to the border. I assume it will be to the old fonda?'

Rückert nodded absently. Something was nagging at him.

'What about that Standartenführer, sir? How will he know if we have gone?'

'He will know because there will be no one here, Krebs. We abandon him because I think, in his heart, he has already abandoned *us*.'

Krebs frowned. He didn't understand what his colonel was talking about, but he knew something was bothering Rückert. He didn't know what it was, nor was he likely to find out. The ways of some officers were most odd, but Rückert was a marvellous officer, and that was all that mattered.

'If we move, Krebs, take *everything*. No, we leave the two flags in the room. Let them see that we *exist*! We won't be back, not here.'

The sound of trucks outside became louder. The engines choked to a stop, and voices were heard shouting and slapping the sides of the vehicles. The clatter of boots down the west corridor was followed moments later by muffled commands. Little by little the place was stripped, everything packed in tea chests and crates, and carried out to the trucks to await the final order to evacuate.

Bauer and Mical parked the small hire car across the street from the hotel. It was the best hotel in Asuncion and their information was that Kessler's daughter and servant were lodged there. For all they knew Kessler might be, too, but Garriga's bribed enquiries had elicited only confirmation about the first two. The chances were that Kessler was at the headquarters, if only José could find out where that was. The little man knew it was dangerous to enquire, to attempt to bribe, but he was willing to have a shot at it and take the consequences.

They sat in the cramped space of the vehicle and watched, talked intermittently and casually. Both seemed to wish to avoid subjects of great moment.

The street was one of the two main shopping and commercial thoroughfares in Asuncion. It was quiet. Two women had walked past and stared at them sitting in the car. Since then, nothing.

A truck turned into the boulevard and stopped by a street lamp. The markings on the truck and the uniforms of the three men who alighted showed that they were from some municipal department. They produced a ladder and a large cardboard box, together with a metal tool-box. One mounted the ladder they placed against the street lamp while the two attempted to unravel the paper decorations from the cardboard box.

Suddenly the drumming recommenced. In the street itself it was deafening, and for a moment disconcerting.

Bauer shuddered. 'God! That drumming again!'

Mical giggled. 'Three times José said.'

'For two hours each time. *Two hours*! I don't think I can survive it,'

The workers had stopped all activity, and could be seen standing still, heads bowed, their sombrero-like hats clutched across their chests as they crossed themselves repeatedly.

In the houses of the city, particularly in the poorer quarters, the open doors and windows permitted the drumming reverberating within to ride the hot air of the morning and spread through the maze of narrow streets. If one looked in the windows and doors one could see the solemn, intense Inca faces which looked as if they were mesmerised by their own drumming as the hands beat and cajoled whatever was to hand. All with the solemnity of ritual that only the truly simple can bring about.

Bauer suddenly sat upright from his slouched position.

'Kessler's daughter!'

Their eyes bored through the windscreen to watch Ingrid as she came from the hotel entrance, looked about her for a taxi, realised it was hopeless, and started walking away from them down the boulevard. Bauer, in the driving seat, shoved out the clutch and winced at the pain in his leg, but the car moved gently forward, following her from a distance on the opposite side of the road.

Without warning she turned up a side road. A way only for pedestrians. Instantly Mical opened her door as Bauer stood on the footbrake.

'I'll go on foot. You can't!'

There was no time to argue. She had crossed the road and was out of sight. Bauer knew she was right in any event. He could walk, but it was a hobble, and very limiting. He sighed, and switched off the engine. As he leant forward he noticed Mical's handbag on the floor where her feet had been.

A rush of concern swept through him and he fumbled around in the handbag amid her private debris. It was there in the bottom of the bag: their revolver. She had gone out unarmed.

The labyrinthine alleys would at any other time have been bustling with crowds of laughing, noisy humanity, edged off the pavement and sidewalks by a proliferation of stalls all displaying the coloured and gay produce with which their purveyors sought to entice the passerby. The gutters would normally be full of bruised merchandise, peeling, broken eggs, offal, cracked china ornaments, wooden strips from crating, wire-bands, plastic string in shrieking colours. Today there was nothing, no one. The gutters were free of all but trodden cigarette butts. There was only the sound, the constant all-pervading sound of drumming.

Mical hurried after Ingrid, watched her grey blouse disappear round a corner, to be sighted again far ahead as she moved in and out of the warren. Then it was gone.

Mical ran forward to check, then round the other way, then across to peer down the side streets. Nothing. The brown sandstone church stood before her, but the door was padlocked. She could see that. She hurried round the church and found herself facing the German girl. They both knew in a flash who the other was, what they were each trying to do, and were also simultaneously aware that they were each unarmed. They simply faced each other and stared. It seemed to hold for longer than was reasonable as face searched face, and crossed swords with the eyes. Then as quickly she was gone. It was a moment before Mical realised that Ingrid had slipped through a narrow passage between the church wall and the wooden wall of the slaughter house which abutted it. The sight of the stone paving coming under the wooden partition stopped Mical in her tracks. It was disgusting. The most awful area of natural stone she had ever seen in her life. The stones had been laid probably a hundred years previously. Crude, roughly-flattened stones to form a paving. That pavement had witnessed the massacre of thousands of cattle, sheep and goats. The stone had developed a leathery patina of dark reddish-brown where blood from those wretched creatures had flowed, been brushed, trodden and scraped. The smell that arose in the warm morning air was choking and fetid. Mical felt faint and physically sick. The thought of the German girl had left her

The desire to avenge, to kill, was a thought she could not stomach. These stones at her feet said the same thing as the altars of Cuzco and Tenochtitlan. It did not matter that the victims here were not human. It was slaughter in anyone's language, and the vomit rose in her gorge.

She turned away and did not look back.

In the car Bauer was champing at the bit as he gripped the wheel, feeling totally helpless and deeply concerned about Mical's safety.

He finally could stand it no longer, and got out of the vehicle, crossed the road, and turned into the side street, almost bumping into the Israeli girl who was hurrying back.

'I lost her, let's get back into the car.'

This time she took the driving seat herself, waited with ill-concealed impatience as he lifted his damaged leg into the car and closed the door only as she was pulling away in a very tight U-turn.

'What are you doing?' He stared at her curiously.

Mical drove for three blocks then stood on the brake. Bauer banged his head against the windscreen as he jerked forward. He turned to remonstrate with her and found her staring straight ahead over the wheel. She was crying. He kept his words to himself and let her take her own time.

'For a moment back there I was going to kill that girl. Kill her Richard! Someone who has never done anything to me. She is just his daughter! Oh God! I am so sick of all this. Rabbi Pressman, on the kibbutz, was right. Blood begets blood. The Torah says "Vengeance belongs to God." It is *His*. He can keep it!'

She turned quickly to him as he put his arm round her slender shoulders, and she wept copiously.

There were no such nice sentiments from Ingrid Dorf. She returned to her hotel, only concerned for her own safety, and telephoned Don Julián Yqueras immediately. She asked him what had been done, what his men had reported, did he know the Hotel El Paradiso, and informed him that she was going to that small hotel herself to confront the Israeli girl and kill her.

'He is my father, Julián. I am not going to stand by and let them murder him. If the Kameraden cannot protect him, I will!'

She picked her suitcase from the stand, laid it on the bed and opened it. The false bottom was well-concealed, and the slim Smith and Wesson she carried with her was ready for immediate use. She picked up her lightweight jacket, put the snub automatic into the pocket, and left her room.

Ingrid had to enquire where the Plaha de Piedra was. It was not marked on the street map she had been given by the hotel. Or perhaps it was, but half the names in the tiny point size were indistinguishable, or had merged into a grey spludge on the badly printed map. When she found it, the hotel was almost the only thing to be seen actually in the square. One side of the hotel was painted lemon yellow, and large blue lettering stated that 'El Paradiso' was a hotel of quality. A statement almost belied by the very painting of the wall.

Ingrid double-checked the street signs in order to find the entrance; a task which had seemed obvious to both Bauer and Mical was for her – used as she was to entrances being obvious and opulent — not without its problems. The small doorway hardly looked like the entrance to a hotel, nor did the hall and stairway that she found herself in. The reception desk was unoccupied, which was fortunate for her. Garriga was attending to the needs of his pigeons at the time and heard nothing. Her information was that the room facing the square on the first floor belonged to the girl. The doctor was clear about that when he reported to the police. Yqueras' information confirmed it.

She crept up the stone stairs holding on to the blue-painted iron rail. She was half-way up the squared 'spiral' when the drumming stopped. Her footfall was suddenly audible to anyone who was listening. She removed her shoes and continued up the stairs in bare feet. She found the room by simple deduction, and pushed the door into the room after listening carefully. There was a little noise in the square outside, enough to mask the sound of a black Packard drawing up.

The room was, of course, unoccupied, but Ingrid decided to find whatever clues she could by searching the drawers and cupboards. She was kneeling, examining a piece of paper left in a waste tin by the side of the sink when she was aware that someone had entered the dark room. She turned quickly, and opened her eyes wide as the two bulky heavies bore down upon her. For one instant she caught the flash of steel wire and saw the cheese-cutter in the man's hand. There was no sound.

In the hacienda radio room Rückert stood behind the young latin operator.

'See if you can make contact with them. Try the alternative frequency again and keep trying.'

He swung round to the young German who entered.

'Kurt . . . as soon as the men have returned we start the evacuation. Your driver knows the fonda in the north, Marisjetana?' The man nodded. 'Good, let him lead the convoy. There are to be no more than three vehicles, is that clear?'

The telephone brought him to the small mahogany desk and he answered sharply.

'Yes? Where are you? I don't understand. If you've killed the girl how can you have just seen her with another man? Then who was the girl in the room?'

Rückert knew before he finished the question. There was only one likelihood. It was that possibility that had been nagging at him without his being able to unravel the puzzle. It had to be Kessler's daughter. After he had given the address it had worried him, something had worried him. Rückert gritted his teeth and mentally swore. Well, damn the girl! It was her own bloody fault! He put the receiver back on the cradle without saying anything further. The men knew where to go.

He left the radio room and walked to the main room. It had been cleared of all but the two flags against the wall as he had instructed. He took his uniform from the cupboard, his precious neck-medallion and medals. There was nothing else. A quick glance round the interior, then he limped out and away from the building. His leg was playing him up. It always did when he needed to be active. Psychosomatic. Or just age.

Kessler had made his two calls, and drove the hire car to the back street fonda where he was to meet Ingrid before he journeyed out to the hacienda, and collected his gear and his documents. He wasn't concerned about getting them. He had been an SS officer for a long time. He knew all about intimidation, and he knew he intimidated better than most. No one would question him, no one would try to stop him, except upon an order from Hans Rückert. Well, that bridge would be met when he came to it. He wanted to pass the details he had picked up, together with the two lists of South American active units, on to his daughter.

He entered the fonda through the bead curtain, and glanced at the interior. There was no one there apart from the proprietor. The fiesta morning was a time for contemplation upon the significance of the Lord's Ascension. The churches were full this morning. Not the bars.

The sound of a fly buzzing about was all the interior offered in the way of life. The fat and heavy-lidded face of the proprietor looked sullenly at him. He knew the man was a German visitor. He would have money, but why did they not stay at home on a feast day?

Kessler carried his tepid coca-cola to a table, and sat watching the proprietor drying endless glasses on a dirty towel. Behind his head a cheap, tin clock implied that the morning was half-gone. Under the counter the glass-fronted cabinet displayed tired comestibles, sandwiches, tamales sleeping in a cold sauce in a metal tray.

The fat Indian wife came from the back of the bar carrying a tray of small, brown pancakes which she placed with extraordinary delicacy with metal tongs onto a heated tray, then filled the metal ladle with gravy, and poured the cold mess over the tamales to liven them up, at least visually.

Kessler stood up and crossed to the counter.

'I wish to make a phone-call. Do you have a telephone? Telefono? My daughter was supposed to meet me. *Puedo usar su telefono?*'

The proprietor looked at him without expression, giving no clue as to whether he understood the request or not, until a simple jerk of his head directed Kessler's eyes to the wall phone round the corner of the bar.

There was no answer from Ingrid's room. The concierge remembered that she had gone out and had not returned. Kessler muttered to himself and replaced the ear-piece. He returned to the table, and lit a cigarette from the container in the centre of the table. It was foul, and he stubbed it out very quickly.

A shuffling noise at the entrance prepared him for Ingrid's entrance, but it was not her. Three local peasant types – all youngish – entered. One carried a simple, cheap guitar, his companion a tin flute and the third dragged a battered harp into the fonda, getting the broken ornamentation of the head caught in the bead-curtain. Their glance at the proprietor asked, 'Why is this German here?' but their grins and empty smiles at the foreigner had just enough courtesy to stop them being belligerent.

It was the guitarist who started the music by strumming quietly, and then picking out a melody of sorts. The harpist picked it up, and hinted at simple harmony devoid of any rhythmic impulse until the tin flute gave shape to what they performed.

The fat wife returned with a pile of home-made torn-paper decorations on string, set them on the nearest table while giving a solemn glance of disapproval at the musicians, and one of open hostility to Kessler. After she left Kessler tried the phone once more without success, then stormed out of the fonda throwing a coin onto the counter as he passed. The proprietor glanced down at it, saw that it was a Deutschmark, and muttered under his breath.

As he stepped outside into the hot morning sunshine Kessler heard the music come to life, followed by and interpolated by the harsh deep voice of the Indian wife. He got into the car and drove away

In the hotel room the phone was ringing again, and again. But the man waiting at the other end of the line was Don Julián Yqueras. As he replaced the ornate phone he heard the sound of car tyres on his gravel drive, and the challenge of his guard, followed by a respectful muttering. He peered through the curtained window. It was Kessler.

# TWENTY

At the same time Mical's small hire-car drew up in the courtyard of the Hotel El Paradiso. She got out, then helped Bauer to get his heavily-bandaged leg over the ridge, and between the seat and door-jamb, without making him scream too much.

When they reached the door of Garriga's private apartment they found the door locked.

'José, it's Richard and Mical.'

There was no reply. When they repeated the call it seemed obvious that there was no one in. Bauer looked at Mical and frowned. José had only been going to the police station to see the man who might be bribed into revealing the location of the Nazi headquarters.

'Look, I don't like this. I'm going to break in.'

Mical looked at Bauer and saw that he was serious. Something about the 'feel' of the place made her, too, apprehensive. She nodded, then watched as Bauer showed his expertise. The piece of plastic inserted so professionally took, perhaps, eight seconds to open the lock. Bauer muttered about having to tell José to change his lock, it was too easy The door swung open silently.

The moment they entered they realised something had happened. The place was a mess. It had been turned over and partially wrecked in the process. There was not a drawer, not a cupboard, whose contents were not strewn about the floor and furniture.

'They certainly turned this place over. I wonder if he was here at the time.'

'Perhaps they took him away.'

'I didn't want to involve him,' Bauer was already blaming himself. 'It was US they came looking for. Not him.'

The fluttering sound of the pigeons came from the annexe. Mical frowned and looked tearful.

'He was harmless. Why couldn't they leave him alone?'

The sound of fluttering persisted, and then, as if by telepathy, both thought the same thought. They exchanged looks, and Bauer limped quickly over to the annexe door. He opened the aviary, and peered through the beading. The door did not open properly. José's foot was in the way. Bauer looked down, sick in his stomach at what he might find. Garriga lay there, quite dead. His throat bore the mark of a cutting wire, and his eyes protruded from their sockets. Half-a-dozen pigeons stood on his body and head, already disfigured with droppings.

Mical had peered in after his silence and took a sharp intake of breath followed by a stifled sob before she stepped back into the room and covered her face with her hands.

Bauer came back in and looked at her. She stepped back again and obviously didn't want anyone to touch her.

'Please don't leave him in there, please.'

Bauer didn't reply, but he dragged the little Paraguayan from the aviary as gently as he could, shooing away the pigeons who seemed to want to rest upon their keeper. He picked an ornamental cover from the back of the elderly settee and laid it over José. It was when he tried to tuck one arm inside that he noticed the hand was clutching a small piece of paper. Rigor mortis had not yet stiffened his fingers so it was easy enough to extract.

After he read it he turned to Mical. 'It's the address of the headquarters. He got it for us. Where's the map?'

'In the car. Is that all you want to say? Does that concern you more than José?'

'No. But there is nothing I can do about him now. And time is running out . . . or had you forgotten?'

Mical didn't reply for a moment, then, when she did, she had obviously pulled herself together.

'You think Kessler will be making for that place?'

'I don't know. It's the only lead we have.'

'We should phone the police. Someone must look after José's body.'

'Not until we get back. Kessler is on the run, we have an advantage. Let's keep it that way. Where did we put the spare box of ammo?'

'It was in a cardboard box?' He nodded. 'I left it under the bed, in my room. Shall I get it?'

'My leg's none too good on stairs, would you mind?'

She hurried out, glad to get out of the room if only for a few moments. Bauer crossed to Garriga's body and knelt down, uncovered the face for a few moments, assessed the dark, bloody ring round the neck that had almost severed the neck from the torso, a particularly disgusting job of garrotting, the old Nazi way. He was going to search José's pockets when he heard a cry from upstairs. He stood up and limped towards the door as Mical burst into the room sobbing hysterically. In her hand was the small cardboard box, but she was shaking uncontrollably.

He hugged her tight to him, and waited before he asked her anything. When it came out it was in sobbed snatches of words.

'In the room, Kessler's daughter. She's been garrotted. Oh God! These people! I don't understand. Richard, why would they kill his daughter?'

'I can only guess that they mistook her for you. They probably had little idea what she looked like. Kessler kept her away from them, I think. This whole thing is becoming *vile!*'

Bauer found a bottle of brandy in one of Garriga's cupboards, and poured them both a very stiff drink. He sipped his in silence for a moment before he spoke reflectively.

'You know, with this wretched leg I was beginning to feel vulnerable. I think I was ready to call it off. But not now. Not after what they've done to José, and not after what I think I know inside my gut.' He paused, then looked at her. 'Kessler is the key, Mical. He is the fountain-head of their finance. Somehow I've got to stop him, or this sort of thing will go on, and on.'

'I'm scared, Richard. Very scared, and very sick. I thought it was easy to kill. I've done it on the Golan Heights, but they were just distant blobs. I'm not sure I can do it face-to-face. When I was shooting at Kessler before – out in the Alazar – I think I wanted to miss him. D'you understand?' She looked at Bauer appealingly, then glanced at the covered body of Garriga and thought about the girl upstairs. 'Oh Richard, this is an *awful* game! I want to go back to Tel Aviv.'

Bauer nodded. 'Soon. It is almost over. But not quite yet.'

He held up the piece of paper taken from Garriga. 'José gave his life for this. Shall we give it a try?'

Mical swallowed hard, refused to look at the corpse, and nodded quickly, tightly. She took the hand that was offered to her, and they left the apartment, closing the door quietly.

This time he made no attempt to get into the driving seat. There was no point in pretending. He was, to all intents and purposes, lame. Mical started the engine as he unfolded the map and checked the address once again. The car slid out into the deserted square. Soon the third and last drumming would start, then the Christ would have ascended into Heaven and the fiesta would start with a bang. Bauer took the cardboard box from his pocket and extracted the last of the revolver clips, fitted it, and slapped the weapon shut.

In the very beautiful and well-appointed hacienda the guards patrolling the perimeter could just hear the piano being played inside the house. It was a common enough sound. Don Julián played every day, sometimes several times during the day. If they had listened properly, or had any real ear for music, they would have known it was not Don

Julián playing. It was not bad, not clumsy. But it was not professional playing of the high order that Yqueras showed. Kessler was very much an amateur with a very limited repertoire. It was the Schumann *Kinderscenen* piece, the one he always started with.

Yqueras smiled at his guest. 'Schumann, always Schumann. You are an unashamed romantic, Kessler.'

'It reminds me of the Germany I knew as a child. I love it very much.'

'It is not the same any more, my friend. Prosperous though it may be, it is becoming flaccid.'

Kessler finished his piece with a sentimental rubato that brought the tiniest of smiles to Yqueras' lips. He didn't launch into the second piece but dropped his hands to his knees. Something was unsaid in the air, but could not remain so.

Yqueras broke the silence. 'Ludwig, do not make the transfer as planned.'

Kessler looked at him, unstartled, but the pained look was unmistakable.

'You, too, eh? Why, Julián? What is *your* equivocation for breaking my oath and deflecting my loyalty? Why does it concern you?'

'The same reason it always did.' Yqueras lit the second cigar calmly, blew out the match. 'I became a supporter of your Führer in 1936 because he was the only one capable of stopping the Comintern. Nothing has changed. I do not want to see the dirty fingernails of Castro at my table. Cuba, Chile, Panama, El Salvador – who is next?'

'And the Kameraden?'

'They are too old to be even war criminals. Chasing them is obscene. So I ask you, what will you do? What *can* you do?'

Yqueras' question was a veiled challenge. He half-knew or at least suspected what had transpired at the meeting he had arranged. He half-knew what needed to be known anyway.

Kessler held up his hands, and examined the backs.

'I can do as I decide. The Reichleiter gave me the token. What is required to draw upon the account is *my* handprint wearing the Reichleiter's ring on a certain finger. This ring.'

He drew it from his jacket pocket and held it up for Yqueras to see. Not an easy man to impress there was nevertheless the slightest gleam for a moment as he beheld the key to so much wealth.

The ring was a large, flat, round, red stone set on a simple gold band.

'I wear it so,' Kessler twisted the ring so that it was palm down. 'My palm print, and the electronic pattern contained within the stone placed on the correct finger will activate the identification plate. Without that signatures mean nothing.'

'And without *your* hand there is no fortune. Your own idea, I presume.'

Kessler smiled quietly. 'That part of it was. I am not a complete fool, Julián, which is why I had the circuit constructed so that it would respond only to my living hand. Without the pulse of life it is nothing. I am indispensable!'

Yqueras chuckled. 'Bravo!' Kessler started to play the Schumann *Arabesque* – the most taxing piece that he knew. After some moments Yqueras laid one hand across the keyboard, preventing him from continuing.

'Then do as I say. Leave them to their fate Fight with whatever active means are available. I mean it, Ludwig. The sands are running out, very fast.'

'You did understand what I said about my *living* hand, didn't you? No *Duchess of Malfi* here. I tell you because you have been plotting with my daughter, Don Julián Yqueras. I understand your reasons. They are sound. Ingrid loves me, I am quite sure, and you are my dear and valued friend but, were it not for my precaution I *would* be expendable. I have lived too long not to understand that. If you have not spoken with her today you will not know that I have agreed. I am with you. You can draw off your hounds, Julian.'

Yqueras was genuinely pleased, and showed it. 'I am so pleased. I had no wish to harm you.'

He poured two large brandies for them, and they enjoyed them in silence for some moments before Kessler looked up at the aristocratic Yqueras.

'Where *is* Ingrid, Julián?'

'I tried to reach her earlier. I presume she was making her bid to save your neck. She said she was going to settle with this Israeli girl and her associates, for your sake, my friend.'

Kessler looked at Yqueras, concerned, and bit his lip.

'Then I think I had better enlist some aid from the comrades. She could be in danger.'

# TWENTY-ONE

It was late morning on Ascension Day, near Asuncion, in Paraguay, as two cars made their way independently towards the out-of-the-way hacienda that neither party knew had already been evacuated. Kessler knew the way. He also had a better car. He was, in any case, eight kilometres nearer, so that when he turned off the main highway and bumped over the dirt track to top the rise that concealed the hacienda from the sight of travellers, Bauer and Mical in their small, grey, rented, 1200cc saloon still had twenty minutes, or thereabouts, to make up. *If* there was to be any contact.

The latter had been meandering trying to follow the map, which must have been years out of date. It didn't even show the main highway route, and there was no one about to ask. Not until they found an old man working at the edge of his field. Mical stopped the car, got out, and tried in halting Spanish to make herself understood. All she got was a cold, uncomprehending, or unforthcoming look of the obstinate peasant. She shrugged and returned to the car.

Kessler drove his vehicle between the rows of cacti and the Joshua trees that led to the hacienda. The more he thought about it the more he realised that his Ingrid was walking into danger. If there were more than one person in this Israeli group she could find herself overpowered and even killed. It did not bear thinking about. She was not only his much-loved daughter, she was his contact and guide with the

Neo-Nazis she fronted, the group he was now committed to help.

His eyes narrowed as he rounded the entrance into the courtyard and area. He scanned the roofs, the out-buildings, the trees, the rises of ground. There were no guards. There were no vehicles, nor even a suggestion of there having been any. Even the ground had been raked and brushed. He got out of his car and walked quickly across to enter the building.

'Guard! Anyone!'

There was no answer, no movement. Nothing. The dry wind from the open door blew the white hair across his forehead, and he realised he was perspiring.

'Guard! Damn you! Where is everyone?'

Only silence. The outside door slammed gently in the draught.

He stormed down the corridor and made for the room allotted to him. He knew inside himself what had happened. The clues were everywhere – to him, who knew the place – to no one else. Gone were the pictures, the posters, the framed photographs. Gone was the radio equipment, the lockers, the sparse furniture, everything. He kicked open his room door. Again nothing, not even his small case and overnight-bag. Picked clean.

'Abandoned! *Me*!'

The fury was choking him as he stormed out again, and made for the main room that was a sort of atrium to the surrounding smaller rooms. When he stepped inside he found it laid out as before. The court-martial layout of tables and chairs was untouched. Only the furnishings and pictures had gone. The two flags leant against the wall as before. Somewhat reassured Kessler crossed to the cupboard. He swung it open and found his case and bag placed there. The wire hanger that had held Rückert's prized uniform tinkled weakly as it moved, bereft of its splendour.

Kessler knew they had gone. There could be no doubt of it.

Mical stopped the car and Bauer peered once again at the map.

'It has to be about here . . . Look. That one. There isn't

another track. D'you want to chance it?'

'Why not?' Mical reached for the gears and let out the clutch.

'Hang on a minute. This is the lion's den, girl. I have not got the faith of your Daniel.'

Bauer fished out the last clip he had for the rifle, and inserted it, double-checked both weapons, then sighed. 'Not much to storm a fortress, is it?'

They smiled at each other, and the car moved forward, turned into the track, and bounded over its lumpy, dirt humps. Bauer looked keenly about him as Mical concentrated on the track itself and keeping out of potholes. There was not much to see but rows of cacti, a few Joshua trees. There might be something over the rise. At least they would see if it led anywhere.

It obviously did. The last hundred-and-fifty metres had the aspect of a 'drive' not a dirt track. Bauer signalled to her to stop.

'We'll go on foot from here.'

They left the car, carefully turned round for a getaway if it was needed, and moved towards the rise of ground that displayed trees, or some greenery on the other side. As they neared Bauer signalled to her to keep down. She smiled to herself. Despite her Army training he still treated her as a child to be protected. She liked him for that. They flattened their bodies to the ground and crept to the ridge. From the top they could see the silent, buff-and-white hacienda on the flat depression beyond, hidden from all sides. A near-perfect situation, Bauer admitted.

They remained hidden for several minutes while Bauer cast a careful eye over the surrounding terrain and Mical gave her attention to the hacienda itself. After a few minutes Bauer turned to her.

'Do you get the feeling that maybe no one is about? There is the one car, but no sign of human beings. I'm going to show myself. That should bring a reaction . . . somewhere.'

He stood up, and walked forward several paces. Anyone watching, even casually, would have seen him. Still no reaction. Together they moved forward, each with a weapon ready, and approached the house entrance. Bauer indicated that they should halt, and crossed to the car. The radiator was hot to the touch. Not just from the sun. It had been recently used.

Slowly they advanced to the doorway. Bauer pushed it open and waited. Nothing. They stepped inside the dark interior. A moment to get used to the lighting, or lack of it, then the keen searching of eyes and ears. Still nothing. Together they walked warily down the corridor, opening each room door as they passed. All were empty of anything.

Mical whispered to him. 'If this *was* the place, they've gone. They've abandoned it.'

Bauer was trying to fight against that conclusion himself. If it was the answer then they had failed. It was unlikely they would find Kessler again. He was warned. He was nobody's fool. He looked at Mical's face, her disappointment was tempered with a sense of relief, and he understood that feeling, but it was not his. Not any more. He wanted Kessler. He wanted him dead. The tables had turned completely. The Israeli girl, initially motivated by personal hate and vengeance into the desire to kill the offending person, had slowly come to realise that she was incapable of killing. He, the man of law and order, wishing only to bring a criminal to justice and lay the ghosts of yesteryear, had come to realise the enormity of the possibility he had uncovered. The representative of responsible government had come to realise that such government was rendered powerless in the terms available to it, and that he, the lawman, was moved to dispense the summary execution he knew was the only thing to halt the evil he sought to quell.

He put his arm round her shoulders, and they walked back down the corridor, round the other side, and glanced down the parallel corridor. She looked at him again, and he sighed his acquiescence. They turned to make for the door, and had almost reached it when they heard the sound.

It was nothing much. Possibly a chair-leg moved on wooden floorboards. It might have been the cupboard door shutting. It could have been anything, but it had been made and there was no doubt that it was not activated by temperature or weather. It had been caused by human, or animal, agency, and the betting was on the former. Mical took the lead as they walked silently up the corridor towards the double-doors behind which the noise had originated. Bauer limped into position by the side of the door itself.

The door was very slightly ajar. Again the sound of movement within. Mical crossed the corridor silently and looked through the opening. A man stood with his back to her, across the other side of the room. He seemed to be putting papers into a briefcase. She knew the back, the suit, the head.

She turned to Bauer, and their eyes met. She mouthed the single word, 'Kessler.'

Kessler sensed rather than heard the door opening behind him. He stiffened, aware that it was not Rückert, nor was it any of the Kameraden. His tongue made the smallest of circling movements inside his dry mouth, and he turned to face the door.

He saw the Israeli girl at the same time as her eyes lifted to regard him. A momentary hold, then his glance clicked to her side, where a man with a heavily-bandaged leg stood pointing a sniper's rifle at him. A French F1, as near as he could judge.

'So. We meet at last. I congratulate you.'

Bauer limped forward, and quickly frisked the older man before Kessler coldly and quietly informed him that he was unarmed. As indeed he was.

'That won't save you, Kessler,' muttered Bauer.

'Save me? From what? Am I to be ignominiously killed, here and now, or is there some spectacular glass booth awaiting me in Jerusalem?' He turned to face Mical. 'You *are* Israeli, I take it?'

Mical did not answer. Bauer looked curiously at the old man's face before him.

'No, Kessler. No spectacle. You aren't important enough for that. At least, not in the eyes of the world. Outside of Belgium they haven't really heard of you.'

'Good. I abhor publicity. A trial with Hebrew commercials in the breaks would be more than I could stomach.'

Mical stepped forward and lashed out viciously. The slap

must have hurt Kessler, as well as dislodged his glasses, but he glared at her, recovered his composure, and took a clean handkerchief from his top pocket to wipe the place she had slapped.

Bauer curled his lip slightly. 'You aren't bleeding.'

'It wasn't blood I was wiping away. It was the touch of Jew.'

Bauer grabbed the girl as she hurled herself at the old SS man, and shoved her to one side, anxious not to lose his advantage in covering Kessler with the rifle against his chest.

'He is only trying to provoke. Leave it, girl!'

Mical knew Bauer was speaking the truth, and she bit her teeth together as she controlled her anger. Kessler watched them for some moments, then looked curiously from one to the other.

'Is this the entire strike force? I see it is.' He chuckled quietly. 'I was right after all. Tell me, *why* have you tracked me so persistently? Why *you*, and why *me*? I want to know.'

It was the old Standartenführer who demanded the last remark. There was no mistaking the authority. Mical, was, of course, only too happy to tell him. It had burned inside her for so long.

'Because of my family, who were killed through you, humiliated through you, and tortured through you. Because of my friend, Ruth, who was not even involved, because of a little Paraguayan man I came to like very much. They are the personal things. But also because of thousands who you sent to their deaths, because of world Jewry, and the victims of the Holocaust.'

Kessler stiffened and looked curiously prudish.

'I was not involved in that lunacy.'

But Mical rounded on him shouting. 'You did not stop it!'

Kessler stared her out, and then calmly sat down on the chair against the wall. He spoke quietly, dismissively.

'The end justifies the means.'

It was Bauer who picked that one up with his own quiet intensity.

'No. Kessler, it does *not!* The end *is* the means, and the sooner mankind learns that the sooner we may have a chance of survival.'

'Indeed! And what is your part in this witchhunt? I do not detect the odour of the Hebrew.'

'Oh, I am here for the best reason of all. I'm here because I am German, and would like to be proud to be so. I need your death to wash my German soul, Kessler.'

The burning light in Bauer's eyes inspired fear because of its intensity; his quiet zeal was intimidating in its own particular way. It made Kessler push his chair further back against the wall and the flag that hung so limply from its standing pole. He held himself against the cloth in such a way that it was as if he was almost seeking protection from it. But, like a cornered animal, his eyes glared at Bauer, and hurled defiance.

'You call yourself German! The true Germans are *here*, and dispersed throughout the world, waiting to reassert themselves in a great new Reich.'

'To end in ignominy like the last?'

Kessler sat upright once more, and spoke with all the conviction of a man convinced. 'The Third Reich was the bastion of the West against Communism. The only one! The Allies were too blind and self-righteous and self-interested to see it. The Führer saw it and knew–as he saw everything. Today, *can you say he was wrong*? If Germany had defeated Russia in 1943 the world would be spared its present and future wars. Half of Europe and Asia would not be writhing under a detested Communist yoke. There would *be* no threat to the West, to civilisation as we understand it.'

Bauer breathed hard and tried to think of an answer. There were few. Mical, however–always personally motivated, like all women–sprang back with her accusation.

'And what of the Jews, and the minorities you exterminated?'

But Kessler was ready and rounded on her. His own conviction again carrying all before it.

'Without the Final Solution there would *be* no Israel. Never forget that! It was the guilt of the Allies that gave you your Promised Land, not the Balfour Agreement. You have no more right to it than present-day Normans have to Britain!'

'That does not exonerate the genocide!'

'Perhaps not, but I would remind you that the so-called Nazi scourge liquidated some nine million people. The Communists have accounted for one-hundred-and-thirty-seven-million at the last count. Their *own* figures! They make our "crimes against humanity" look like musical chairs! Where is your direction? Where is your pride, your purpose? I see none, anywhere.'

Mical shrank back from him, frightened that his arguments could convince her of something, anything . . . they must not. She could not bear that.

'I will not listen to this. You are an evil man. Your whole life has been evil and dedicated to false Gods. It is because it is so plausible that we must fight you with everything in our power.'

Kessler snorted contemptuously. 'Plausibility is the stock-in-trade of political creeds, religions, and all other opiates. There is nothing more plausible than Communism or Christianity and nothing has done so much villainy. Show me the balance in the Great Book of the World, if you can stomach it.'

Bauer shook his head to dispel whatever was forming, or trying to form. 'Words, just words. The world is sick and tired of words. Your deeds speak for you, Kessler. They speak for the Third Reich, and all you stand for, and you are not going to survive. Your friends have abandoned you, Standartenführer. We try to exterminate our vermin, those that we miss can die in their holes.'

'The new Reich will rise again, you will see.'

'If you mean your daughter and her friends you can forget it. They are slowly being rounded up. Nations will not stand for their brand of terrorism because it has no creed, no "words" to create plausibility that attracts the unthinking. Your daughter is dead. She was killed by your own people.'

Kessler reacted to this last in a way that Bauer had not calculated. He had hoped to throw him completely, and use that disconcertment to his own ends. But Kessler just accepted it. As if he had already known it to be true, and the weak protestation he gave was no more than an involuntary reaction.

'I refuse to believe such disgusting rubbish.'

'She was strangled with piano wire. Probably a cheese-cutter.' Bauer spat it at him cruelly. 'Ye-es, you recognise that, don't you? Your lot haven't changed in fifty years. Still the same barbarous methods.'

It was the confirmation. Kessler recognised the method only too well. He bowed his head slightly, the balding, white head of an old man. For a moment Mical felt a sudden, sharp pang of compassion for a man who had lost his child, but she steeled herself quickly, and lifted her head accusingly.

'I imagine it was meant for me. They just killed the wrong one.'

Kessler did not speak for some moments. Bauer looked at Mical, who returned the look with a questioning one of her own. A look which said helplessly, 'What do we do now?'

'Then if you intend to kill me I would prefer you to do it before I have time to dwell upon anything.' He looked from one to the other. Slowly the dawn of realisation crept into those experienced, cunning eyes, and a sneer formed on his mouth.

'If you have the guts.'

Bauer stood up stiff and straight. 'It isn't guts, Kessler. It is a revulsion from taking life, anybody's, even yours and your kind. But you wouldn't understand that.'

The old man held the look and intoned solemnly.

'No, I wouldn't. It is the fate of the strong, the determined, to be the instrument for doing what the weak know is necessary, then be chastised for doing it while the hypocrites hide behind the cloak of humanitarianism.'

'Just words, Kessler. More words . . . always words. Mankind is perishing because of them, because of ideologies. Let me tell *you* something. There is *no* faith, *no* cause, *no* belief worthy of the taking of one single human life! There has to be another way. There *has* to be.'

Mical once again turned to Bauer, and the look exchanged was one that said, 'We'd better get it over with', but Mical's eyes said unequivocally that she was unable to do it. Bauer swallowed, and felt his mouth go dry. Felt the tightening of his stomach, and heard the pounding of his own blood in his head and ears. Kessler, watching them, tightened his mouth, and his eyes further increased his look of contempt.

'When it comes to the crunch, you just haven't got the iron, have you? God help Germany!'

It was the basic contempt for life that was inherent in that statement from Kessler that overcame their objections. Kessler and all his kind used human beings to an end. There was nothing particularly unusual in that, every faction throughout time had done just that. It was the absence of any realisation of the enormity of that attitude which stuck in Bauer's gullet. To die or kill for a belief is one thing, provided that the killers are aware of their crime, have the essential humanity to find a conscience fighting it. To not even consider that human life has *any* function, *any* right of its own, but must be merely unthinkingly, unconcernedly, swept out of the way is quite different. It is the action of swatting a fly, crushing a beetle, not avoiding the hedgehog in the road. It shows a basic contempt for life. That could not be permitted to continue, and Bauer had the honesty to acknowledge that he was bordering the same territory by considering executing the offender himself. An underlying, inherent Catch-22.

He felt his face had gone pale. He avoided Kessler's gaze. He refused to look at Mical. Time was standing still for the moment of indecision, suspended in limbo. He felt his own eyes blink in the slowest of slow-motion moves. There was one last hope. One vague possibility that would keep him off the hook of his own conscience.

He removed all but one round from the magazine of the revolver, snapped it shut. He took up the rifle again, and pointed it at Kessler, pushed the revolver across the table towards him.

'Do it your own way. If it's not finished in five minutes I shall find the courage and the conviction, Kessler. Make no mistake about that.'

Bauer nodded to Mical, and together they backed from the room. At least they backed the first few metres, and then both, as if by unspoken consent, turned their backs upon him and walked from the room. It was a gesture of contempt for *him*, the old man of an old Germany that was gone, and would not be permitted to re-emerge. It was lost on him. He did not even see them go. His head had sunk onto his chest. They had ceased to exist for him.

Kessler had waited his moment, then shut out the unessential and concentrated, as was his lifetime habit, upon what really mattered to him. The pang he felt at the news of Ingrid's death he had prepared for. It broke his heart, but it was not a shock that knocked him sideways. The end of his purpose, his life, his beliefs was another thing he had mentally prepared for. The small upsurge of hope and direction that the pact with his daughter had given him was, he knew, a chimera. It had no substance. Financing terrorists, being treated as the 'old man of the new regime' was not for him. Germany had abondoned *him*, just as, symbolically the old guard – the Kameraden – had too. They had no stomach for a new Reich. They would follow their Pied Piper to the grave. Just for a fleeting moment Kessler's mind smiled at the analogy. Rückert, he remembered, hailed from Brunswick.

In the corridor outside the room Mical turned to Bauer, and looked up into his pale visage.

'What did you mean, Richard? If he doesn't do it, you will. Can you?'

Bauer nodded slowly. 'Oh yes. I don't find it comes easy, which was the principal reason I ceased to be a field operator. I don't kill easily. But in this man's case I will do it. It is too important *not* to.'

Mical lowered her face. 'I'm sorry. I'm a fraud. I just can't. Not face-to-face, not like that. Not even remembering. Can't we take him back to Europe? Let the courts settle it?'

'No . . . not this time. They would, at best, give him a short sentence. It is not *him*, Mical. It is the whole thing. It has to be stopped *here* for *good*! Kessler is the signatory to that account. Without him there *is* no money. So he has to die. You must see that.'

She nodded. Then quickly looked up again. 'Shouldn't I go round to the window side, in case he tries to escape?'

'The shutters are bolted on the outside. I noticed as we came in. It's my job to notice such things. He's not going anywhere.'

Bauer leant back against the wall and tried to imagine what his sworn enemy was doing at that moment.

Kessler was, in fact, doing nothing. He still sat shrunken on the chair, against the flag, against the wall. The thought of escape had not occurred to him. It was unimportant. Then, with a typical Kessler frown, he stood up, crossed to the table and his briefcase, and began to extract those documents he considered important enough to destroy.

One by one he tore them into pieces, and placed them in the fireplace, took a match from his pocket, and lit them. As the flames rose up into the large chimneypiece he continued adding whatever he considered needed destroying. He added his pocket-book, his address-book and then, taking it from his pocket with a certain reverence, the Bormann ring. He bent down and crushed the stone with the end of the iron poker before he threw it into the flames, then stood up, looking down at the burning, flaring pyre.

'It is finished.'

Just a muttered phrase, without histrionics, or implied dramatic allusion.

Then he turned on his heel. Quite a creditable military turn. He stared at the revolver on the table, picked it up, then laid it down again and crossed to the flags standing against the wall. With infinite care and love he laid them out, open on the floor in the centre of the open space before the tables where he had sat to be interrogated.

Bauer glanced at his watch and then at Mical. She knew he was looking at her and refused to return the look.

Suddenly there was a single shot, which echoed and reverberated inside the closed room. It was then she looked up at Bauer, after almost ducking her head, and frowning to dispel the thought of yet another death . . . even his.

Bauer stood up and walked towards the room. Mical followed behind him.

Kessler lay in the centre of the room, lying on top of one flag, the other wrapped round his body. Blood was slowly seeping through, staining only where the white cross was showing . . . the black merely became darker, the red only more so. Bauer knelt down over him. Kessler was still breathing, and his eyes stared upwards into space. He did not see Bauer, nor hear anything but what was in his mind's eye.

For Ludwig Kessler, one-time Standartenführer of Hitler's Third Reich, one-time Höherer SS-und Polizeiführer of Belgium and the Low Countries, honoured Alte Kämpfer was no longer in Paraguay, South America, nor was he in their time.

Kessler was in Berlin, in Nuremberg, in Munich, and the year was 1936. About him the flags and the banners, the eagles, and the standards shone and glittered as the red, white and black cloth unfurled in the breeze that blew across Germany and tasted of the Schwarzwald, of Garmisch and the Zugspitze, and was heady like champagne. Hundreds-of-thousands of Germans stood round him, tall and blond, blue-eyed and proud, they all stared with excited devotion towards the distant stone promontory where a small, dark figure was just visible. Every hand and arm shot forward as the trumpets blared and the kettle-drums rolled. A hundred thousand voices echoed and re-echoed round the stadium.

'*Sieg-heil! Sieg-heil! Sieg-heil!*'

The sound was awesome in its sheer immensity, and Kessler's lips smiled slightly as they froze on his face. He was dead.

Both Mical and Bauer were silent as they looked down at him. They, too, had heard the echoes of the *Sieg-Heils* in Kessler's death rattle, and their hearts – unlike his – had chilled at the sound. Bauer fitted another bullet into the revolver and carefully fired the shot into Kessler's right palm. Then they left.

Outside, the warm, morning light seemed a different world. One that understood about flowers and trees, one that smelled of the maquis and the red earth, and one in which living creatures moved and existed in their own environments. The world inside the hacienda, the whole Wagnerian charade that stank of gunpowder, and the incense of Oberammergau was unreal. It was not true! Never again could it be true!

Bauer and Mical sat on the doorway step feeling the sun beating down on them hot through their shirts. He bent forward and picked up a twig, played with it in silence for minutes.

'Why did you fire that bullet into Kessler's hand?'

Mical's question was one of sheer curiosity. It was not accusing him of unnatural practice or implying distaste for his action.

'Let's just say, "insurance".'

She looked sideways at him for a moment.

'You haven't been very honest with me, Richard. I think you know things that you've never told me.'

Bauer sighed, and continued fiddling with the twig. He didn't look at her.

'Not a lot. Fragments. Police information, Bank information. A lot of people in Germany don't want the Nazis back. Don't forget that, Mical. Tell your friends back home.'

She sighed again, and looked away as Bauer tilted up his face to stare at the sun through crinkled eyes.

'What happens now?'

'I was hoping you'd tell *me*.'

There was a silence before he continued hesitantly.

'You, er, you'll be going back to Israel, I imagine.'

'I have to. My life has to start again. This has been so unreal.'

'You aren't going to pursue the Mengeles of this world, then?'

Mical shook her head. 'I've realised it is not for me, and people like me. I have lost the taste.' She turned full face to him. 'Oh Richard. I am so sick inside. I hate it all . . . all!'

He put his arm round her and tried by gentle pressure to offer comfort and understanding.

'Life is so easy, you know, if you haven't got a conscience. Don't you think?'

They sat there for at least an hour. About them the insects hummed, and the cactus plants sucked the warmth from the white-hot orb in the sky. Life went on.